Winter at the Light

by

Stephen B. King

This is a work of fiction. Names, characters, places, and incidents are either the product of the author's imagination or are used fictitiously, and any resemblance to actual persons living or dead, business establishments, events, or locales, is entirely coincidental.

Winter at the Light

Contact Information: info@thewildrosepress.com

Cover Art by *Kim Mendoza*

The Wild Rose Press, Inc.
PO Box 708
Adams Basin, NY 14410-0708
Visit us at www.thewildrosepress.com

Publishing History
First Mainstream Historical Edition, 2020
Trade Paperback ISBN 978-1-5092-3176-8
Digital ISBN 978-1-5092-3177-5

Published in the United States of America

Molly sat up in bed cringing, with the bedclothes wrapped around her as the thunder cracked furiously across the sky. She remembered her earlier promise to Derek and agreed; there was no way she was going outside the building with a storm directly overhead.

It's just a storm, calm down and grow up, Molly. She knew the lighthouse was sturdily built and wasn't going anywhere; it had stood for nearly eighty years and she was safe while inside. Just as her heart slowed back to normal, she heard the wailing noise for the first time.

She snapped her head up and listened to the sad, soulful sound which ebbed and flowed with the wind. *Someone is out there and needs my help*, she thought. Then she assured herself it wasn't; it couldn't be that. *It's just my imagination after that horrible story Derek told me of the skeleton in the cave. No one is outside, making that noise, it's the wind under the eaves, or howling through the lean-to.*

She had to check; she knew she had to. Her logical internal voice did not convince the more dominant panic-stricken side of her brain which assured her it was a ghost, or a shipwrecked sailor washed up on the reef, perhaps injured.

Molly thought it had been all well and good promising not to leave the safety of the building, but what if someone who needed medical assistance washed up on the island? It certainly sounded like that, or did it? Was it just the wind after all?

Praise for Stephen B. King

"I found the book so involving, it felt like I was watching a film whilst I was reading. Plenty of atmosphere and mystery with only a few characters. To me this is a similar genre to some of my favorite adventure books from my childhood, only written for adults—though suitable for all ages. As well as the great story-line, I also loved learning about life on a lighthouse before electricity/automation, that made this book extra special. So five stars from me for this wonderful, easy to read, novel."

~Emma B Books

Dedication

This story is dedicated to all the lighthouse keepers
of the vast Australian coastline,
who over the years led lonely lives in order that
shipping could pass through dangerous waters safely.

Chapter 1

One Slip

Forbes Rock; Forbes Reef
Nineteen nautical miles Southwest of Augusta, Western Australia
August 1952

Forty-eight-year-old Malcolm Dougal McLaren knew he could die that day and would if he didn't possess the courage to crawl across the rocks back to the lighthouse with a broken leg in fifty-plus knot winds and driving rain. The distance was close to a half a mile across jagged slippery stones, from where he lost his footing and slipped, snapping his lower left leg as if it were a twig.

A sudden gale-force gust picked him up like a rag doll just as he crested a hill. It tossed him aside with disdain while his ankle was in a crevice, to show his insignificance in the face of Mother Nature. He fell heavily and passed out from sudden blinding pain and shock. When Malcolm regained consciousness, he knew he'd broken his tibia and fibula, though he had no idea how much time passed while he'd been oblivious. Malcolm was a qualified doctor though he didn't need his training to tell him the worst. He realized he was in a world of trouble.

It had been sometime after a solitary lunch of corned beef with homegrown boiled potatoes, served with bread he'd baked, he decided to check out the ropes on the boat mooring. The storm came raging from the north during the night, and from his experience of weather patterns, he knew this one would last two to three days. What he would do if the boat had torn free of its mooring he didn't know, other than radio in the loss, but he was restless and decided to make the trek anyway.

Malcolm's home was on Forbes Rock surrounded by Forbes Reef, two and a half hours away from the mainland by supply boat. The tiny island was part of a large shoal of interconnecting reefs which covered several square miles. It was named after a nineteenth-century appointed Governor of the State, William Forbes, who didn't get a chance to set foot on Western Australian soil. The ship carrying him from New Zealand ran aground on the reef at midnight of the thirteenth day of June, in the year 1867, with all lives lost. The shoal became known as Forbes Reef out of respect, and his death showed the necessity of placing a lighthouse there to warn other seafarers of the dangerous waters. Plans for Forbes Light were commissioned and drawn up by a prominent architect, but building it was not a simple matter due to the difficulty of getting there, and it took six months to complete. It was then a further year for the light and prisms to be shipped from England, constructed, and installed. By then the jetty had been built which provided somewhere to dock to unload the fragile cargo.

Malcolm set out on his mission to check the boat

earlier on that fateful day dressed in his oilskin cape and hat, so it kept the worst of the cold and teeming rain out. When he woke up sometime after the fall, the cloak had blown up around him, so his lower half was soaking wet, and he felt so cold his teeth chattered uncontrollably. He knew he could not stay where he was and wait for help; the next supply ship, carrying the kerosene fuel, and food, was at best three days away, or if the storm hung around, it would be more likely a week. Everything was dependent on the weather because Forbes Reef created treacherous waters and was challenging for an experienced skipper to get to on a good day. He could radio for urgent help, but the radio was in the lighthouse, so he had to get there first. There was nothing for it, he had to crawl and drag the useless leg behind him across the rocky terrain. He had to get back; lives depended on him to light the lamp, and he took that responsibility very seriously.

Malcolm had gone down to the jetty, situated on the leeward side of the tiny island to check on the mooring ropes for the small boat he used for fishing and catching crayfish. The twelve-foot dinghy was supposed to be used only in dire emergencies, more as an escape lifeboat than for his fishing pleasure. Not that he would ever put to sea in the dangerous waters around him on anything less than perfect seas in such a small boat. Waves had a habit of appearing out of nowhere, and hidden currents below the surface could drive an unsuspecting craft up onto the rocks and dash its hull to pieces within seconds. It was one of those stupid government rules. A solo lighthouse keeper had to have the means of escape from a remote island, even if he couldn't use it because of inclement weather. It made no sense to him, so he used it for his own purposes.

He took a few minutes to assess his situation, calmly, despite the shooting pains. He was a doctor and knew his leg was broken, but so far as he could tell without the benefit of an x-ray, it appeared to be a clean break. Clambering over a rocky terrain would be terrible for it, and agonizing, but he had no alternative. His main concern was to ensure he did not suffer an internal hemorrhage and bleed to death, and he wondered what he could do to improve his chances of success and complete the journey before dark.

The bloody vegetable patch, of course, ya dumb bastard, he admonished himself in his best Scottish accent. It wasn't too far away and with only a slight detour, it was still on the way back. There he had wooden stakes for his tomato, green pea, cucumber, and other climbing plants. There was good quality twine too so he could make a splint, at least a temporary one, and he knew that would help enormously. From the vegetable patch, he could use the constructed path they used to carry the drums of kerosene unloaded from the boat to the lighthouse. That would be a lot easier than crawling one-legged over the rocks. Possibly, he could jury-rig a walking stick or crutch with some spare stakes, so the more he thought about the detour, the more it made sense.

The lighthouse was on the highest point of the island, considerably loftier than sea level where the dock lay. The twisting path had been cut and filled with gravel and concrete so it wasn't too steep. The drums of fuel and supplies were transported with a trolley, and it was no easy task, being uphill all the way. That was why when he went on foot to the jetty, he cut across the rocks to save time; a trip he had made safely many times before.

He crawled at a snail's pace and passed out on two occasions, but for how long each time he had no way of knowing. Eventually, he made it to the small gully in the rocks, panting and sweating from exertion. It was located sufficiently out of the wind which tore across the island and provided shelter enough to help his plants grow, fed by his loving hand. The sun was low on the horizon, a faint glow through the gray clouds, and he knew he daren't waste time; nighttime was approaching, and he had a way to go. He dragged some stout wooden stakes with him and crawled to the large boulder he often sat on to admire his crop and smoke his pipe. It was alongside the wooden box which housed his gardening tools, secateurs, and balls of heavy-duty string. He allowed himself a few moments to calm his beating heart and pluck up the courage for the task of splinting. He wondered what his daughter Molly was doing at that precise moment.

He adjusted his position on the soaking wet rocks, groaning and swearing, his back pressed against the boulder. Screaming in agony, Malcolm used his hands to position his leg. His foot was at an unnatural angle, and he knew he had to attend to that. Malcolm realized the pain that would bring and took a deep breath. He remembered back three years prior when he read an article in *The Lancet Medical Journal*, which he thought at first was rubbish. Great strides had been made in pain management, he read, and there had been studies performed to try to harness the power of the mind as a panacea, or placebo. He was in enough trouble to try anything and strained to remember some of the tests performed. It was a form of self-hypnosis, he recalled, and with nothing to lose and everything to gain, he decided to try.

He bowed his head to his chest, closed his eyes, and focused on the sound of the raindrops beating rhythmically on his oilskin covered shoulders and head. He regulated his breathing and imagined his heart beating in time with the rain. He tried to find some serenity among the swirling agony and waves of pain radiating up from his lower leg. He imagined he was back at the light in the warmth in his bedroom. He opened the cupboard where he kept his medical bag and took it out, then lifted the clasp and prized it open. There, on the top tray in a clear pouch were his glass ampules of morphine. He lovingly took one out and held it up to the light to admire the clear liquid. From the lower section of the bag, he took out a syringe and a fresh hermetically sealed needle. With long-practiced ease, he imagined breaking the seal and fitting the needle. Then he snapped the top of the glass container and drew the morphine out. In an instant, he saw himself injecting it, and even imagined he felt the prick of the needle going in. He dropped the now empty syringe onto the top of the cupboard, and miracle upon miracle, the throbbing in his lower leg eased.

Malcolm opened his eyes back at the vegetable patch and looked down at his twisted leg. Before he lost his nerve, he used his hands to lift his foot up against a convenient rock into what looked to be as normal a position as he could. It hurt badly, yet somehow not as much as before; the agony now more muted. Tears trickled down his face to mingle with the still falling rain. He didn't pass out as he thought he might, and that was a bonus. *Mebee there's something to this mind over matter stuff, after all*, he thought, not wanting to dwell on it for too long in case it broke the spell. Malcolm grabbed two stakes, drew his pant leg up to expose his boot and forced the ends down into it, one on the instep, and the other on the outer.

As quickly as his trembling hands would work, he used the string to bind the stakes tightly as far below the knee as he could reach. He cut it off with his penknife, and then did a second binding higher, wrapping around half a dozen times. He realized when he started moving, the tendency would be a lever-action from his thigh, and the twine alone may not be strong enough. He reached inside his oilskin coat and undid the knot in his woolen scarf. The red and green tartan plaid dated back to his ancestor's clan, and he never needed it more than then. He wrapped it tightly, and tied a new knot at his lower thigh, above the knee.

It was good, he grinned, damned good if he was honest; his medical skills were wasted with him being on Forbes. He cut another length of twine, doubled it over and made a loop which he lassoed over his foot and then tied the ends as securely as he could to the scarf, again one inside, the other out to try to keep the foot in the right position. That was to ease the pain and minimize the risk of tearing something internally and bleeding to death. The last job was to bind three stakes together, which he hoped would give sufficient strength to use as a walking stick. He needed to put a lot of weight on it if he was to have any hope of limping back. He could see the tower of the lighthouse in the distance as a beam of sunlight broke through the cloud cover. He thought of it as his guiding light, and that gave him comfort.

Malcolm used his hands to lever himself up, so his backside sat on the boulder, from that position, he placed one hand on the cold, wet rock, and the other on his makeshift walking aid. "One, two, three," he counted aloud and pushed himself up, screaming with pain which eddied around him like fog trying to drag him inside. Suddenly, much to his surprise, he realized he made it. He stood, tottering yes, but with his weight on his undamaged leg, and injured side supported by the stick, he was upright. *Now, laddie, shake your ass and get back to the warmth*, he thought with a lot more confidence than he believed he possessed.

Taking the strain on his good leg, he slid the stick forward, and using it as a prop, swung the broken one to rest on the ground. Then, using both hands on the stick, he bunny-hopped his right leg jerkily, expelling the air from his lungs in a half gasp, half scream. He had done it; he'd taken his first step to safety. *Only a few hundred to go, ya bastard*, he congratulated himself and moved the stick again.

He made it. How long it took, he had no idea, but he didn't fall as he thought he would. In the early evening, under the dying embers of light, he leaned against the wooden door of the lighthouse, his forehead resting against the painted surface, feeling glad to be alive. But, Malcolm realized what he achieved could be the simple part; he still needed to climb the spiral staircase to get to the first level of the living quarters. *Can I hop up, with one hand on the railing, and the other using the damned stick?* He thought he could; he had to, there was nothing else for it. He had come that far; he would not give up. He was exhausted, weak and in agony, but the real dose of morphine was so close he could taste it. There was also his bed where he wanted to lie down, and he still had to light the wicks, which was his whole purpose of being at Forbes.

The design of Forbes Lighthouse was unusual for the time it was built. It was much bigger than others with the only outhouse being for storage of the drums of fuel, firewood, tools, and such. There was also a lean-to construction, with an iron roof, used to collect rain and to provide shade for the tanks underneath. Often, at other stations there were residences, but when Forbes was in the planning stages, the designers believed at certain tides, with a storm behind them, there was a substantial risk waves could reach the base of the lighthouse. The conclusion was if they built a house, it could be dangerous for the inhabitants. For that reason, the lighthouse had a bigger diameter, with two floors reserved for living quarters, including a kitchen and bathroom and the watch room which housed the light and prism.

Malcolm had never seen the sea come anywhere near the building, and with a broken leg, he hated the thought of climbing the stairs. But he knew once he was up on the residential floor, he wouldn't have far to go to keep the light burning while waiting for evacuation.

He waddled across the threshold and slammed the door behind him, then leaned against the wall, grateful to be out of the howling wind, and rain. He shrugged off the oilskins and hat, leaving them where they fell. Malcolm's pants were soaked and stuck to him, but there was nothing he could do about that. He knew precisely how many iron steps he had to climb but was determined not to bring the number to the front of his consciousness. He was in for a world of pain, not just from the broken leg, but the good one too having taken his weight thus far and would get worse as he hopped his way up.

"You have to ask yerself a question, laddie," Malcom asked in a weary voice. "Do ya want to live, or do ya want to die, ya bastard? What would Molly do if ya dinna survive, aye?" He grinned despite the pain. Malcolm loved to lay his Scottish brogue on thick when he talked to himself. Somehow it gave him comfort to use the voice of his father. His own accent had mellowed considerably over the years, when he spoke to others, especially since arriving in Australia, but when alone, he let his heritage run riot. On some occasions, just for fun, he would conduct entire conversations with himself doing two different voices, one Scottish, and one British. The Scot swore and blasphemed during those chats, but of course, the Brit didn't know any decent cuss words; he was far too cultured. He lurched up the first step, grimaced, and hopped up the next.

After twelve steps, he had to stop; his good leg was on fire, and the pain rivaled that which was radiating outward from the broken one. Before it gave out completely, he maneuvered around and sat, giving himself a much-needed breather. When Malcolm decided to try again, he stayed sitting and used his hands behind him and his uninjured leg to lever him up. As the splinted leg cleared the step though, it connected with the next riser and made Malcolm scream in agony.

Malcolm wiped the sweat from his dripping forehead with his thick checked flannelette-covered right arm and took stock of the situation. He was in trouble, with a capital T. "That's for bloody sure, ya bastard." But could he make it? If he wanted to see Molly marry and walk her down the aisle—even with a pronounced limp, and become a grandfather, then he had no choice in the matter. He must press on. "And, what about the book, ya bastard? Ya wanna finish it, or let it rot?" The book he was writing was why he took the job of keeper in the first place.

He'd found some motivation, so before he got so tired he wouldn't be able to move, he stood, and fidgeted his way around, and once again began the agonizing climb.

"The question ya need to ask yerself more than any other, ya bastard, is this…" he said, after another five steps to distract his mind from the white-hot shooting agony from his leg. "If Molly's firstborn is a son, would ya like it to be named Malcolm, or Donald?"

Donald had been his father's name and his before that. He worked on the Clyde as a welder building ships, and Malcolm remembered him as a mountain of a man, with a long ginger beard, a quick temper and a love of beer. "Aye, either would be nice," he continued his monologue as he worked ever slowly upward, "but what if she's a bonnie wee lass?"

His mother's name was Gertrude, and there was no way he would permit that to be handed down, but her middle name had been Mae, and that was pretty. "Aye, Mae will do nicely, Mae McLaren; that's a good name." But then it dawned on him, for her to have a baby, she would be married so would no longer be a McLaren, He shrugged, and winced as he took another step upward. "No doubt, her husband will have something to say about naming rights too." But still, he hoped for Mae if it was a girl.

He was weakening severely, he dismally realized. The sweat was running in rivulets down his skin, and he felt clammy all over. Periodically, Malcolm cleared it from his eyes as they stung and burned, and his sleeve was soaked through from wiping. He took another break and sat down; fearful he may not possess the strength to rise again for what must surely be the last hurrah. The imagined injection had long since worn off, and Malcolm lacked the willpower to go through the exercise a second time, while the real stuff was so close. The thought of his father's beer-drinking habits made him realize just how thirsty he was.

He was not, nor ever had been, a big drinker. Growing up, he had seen his father become violent when drunk and he got that way often. Sure, Malcolm liked an occasional shot of rum, especially when it was cold; it was his naval history he had to thank for that. A bottle of beer went down nicely on a hot day, too, but in general, he didn't drink much at all. He licked his lips because he thought a beer would go down very well about then. "Aye well, there's no a barmaid serving wench ta bring ya one, yer bastard, so get off your bum and go and get one. First, you survive, and then you drink."

But Malcolm sat there, with neither the will nor the strength to carry on. His broken leg was on fire, while his good one felt like it had been boiled in hot oil. His back was killing him, and if he could go to sleep, maybe, he thought, he could continue when he woke.

The next thing Malcolm was aware of was his head jerking up as his body pitched forward. Suddenly, he was afraid. Malcolm knew he had fallen asleep and could have tumbled down the long winding spiral staircase to the bottom and died, had he not woken when he did. *Aye, but would that be so bloody bad*? All he wanted, the only thing that mattered, was to drift off again, and slowly he felt himself ebbing back to oblivion.

Molly appeared, ghostlike, in front of him. "Dad," she said, and he felt her hand on his shoulder, shaking him urgently. "Dad, wake up. You have to climb. Do it for me, please. Do it for me. It's only another eighteen steps to go. You can do this."

"Molly, my lass," he mumbled, "I'm so bloody tired, can yer no get that? Leave me in peace."

That was when she slapped his face, hard. His head snapped to the right, and his cheek stung. He shook himself like a dog that had been in the ocean, angry at Molly for hitting him. But when he opened his eyes, she was gone, and he was alone on the steel stairs. He rubbed his cheek, softly, wondering what happened, because while he knew it could not have been Molly, his face bloody well hurt. "For Molly, yer bastard, get off your fat ass and get up those stairs. There's only eighteen to go, she says."

Malcolm knew he must make it, not only for Molly, but he had his job to do to help seafarers stay safe. He was, after all, the keeper of the light. Malcolm knew in his bones if he didn't light the wicks and ships came to grief because he hadn't, Molly would be ashamed of him, and he could not bear that thought.

Mumbling and groaning that she, Molly, was the root of all evil, but he loved her to the moon and back anyway, he gripped the handrail, turned around, and climbed once more.

****

When he finally reached his medical bag, Malcolm still heard Molly's words ringing in his ears, and he knew were it not for her, he could not have made it. He injected the morphine into his arm with shaking hands and felt the rush of sudden pain relief and euphoria course through his body. Once the drug took effect, Malcolm climbed to the floor above and performed his duty by starting the clockwork and lighting the wicks. Coming down the stairs was much more comfortable, and he rewarded himself with a measure of rum.

He hobbled to the radio room which doubled as his study and made the call he knew he had to make. For the first time, Mr. Harpington came to the radio to talk to him about the seriousness of his predicament. He was the manager of all lighthouse staff in Western Australia, and they discussed how early the boat could come to get him. Malcolm told him there was no point until the seas dropped, that he doubted he could withstand being on board a heaving boat in mountainous seas and would rather wait it out for the weather to ease. A helicopter wouldn't be able to land either because the wind was too strong; there was no flat spot for it to set down so he'd have to be winched, and the wind was too strong. Malcolm assured Mr. Harpington he would be fine for two or three days. He was after all a doctor, with extensive experience in emergency trauma, so who better to treat the problem?

Malcolm asked if the department had a replacement keeper available who could mind Forbes while his leg repaired, which he thought could be two to three months. After a stony silence, Mr. Harpington replied they did not. They continued to discuss whether he would be able to resume his job at Forbes when his leg recovered for the next twenty minutes, with Malcolm becoming more agitated. Suddenly, just before his temper burst, Malcolm had an idea that he thought could work.

****

Malcolm never wore a wristwatch, or pocket watch, as there was little point in knowing the difference between eleven a.m. and three p.m. on any given day. Each was much like another. He had his chores to carry out, which he did with monotonous regularity, such as carry drums of kerosene up the spiral staircase from which he topped up the tanks every other day. He cleaned the prism every few days and washed the windows more often during inclement weather so the beam of light wasn't diminished. He would trim the wicks, and every other month replace them when they became too short. But most importantly, every evening, before dark lowered its cloak, he would light the wicks and start the mechanism which rotated the beam. He was the keeper of the light and being an ex-mariner, he took his responsibility of keeping boats from crashing into the reef very seriously.

When his work cycle was complete, he'd start all over again, then the next day, and the next, ad infinitum. Occasionally, he would apply a coat of whitewash to the tower, or re-paint the doors and window frames, check the rainwater tank, and other maintenance jobs which cropped up from time to time. He carried firewood up the stairs for the wood-fired kitchen stove every day and regularly topped up the kerosene reservoir for the large refrigerator and the Tilley lamps, used for lighting the interior of the living quarters. He often thought it was little wonder some lighthouse keepers went mad with the tedium, not that he believed he ever would.

Malcolm would never get overly bored because he loved the lifestyle. He spent his days when he wasn't doing his chores, amusing himself by fishing, or collecting mussels or oysters off the rocks when the weather and tide permitted. That supplemented his meat rations which were brought over from the mainland on the *Morning Dawn.* He grew some vegetables in the little copse among the stones he'd made with the soil brought in by the supply boat and Malcolm proudly looked after himself and his circular home. He had ten chickens which provided fresh eggs; sometimes far more than he could eat. The birds roamed free on the island, but he fed them under the lean-to building, which also housed their nesting boxes. Without any predators, they thrived and clucked their happiness to be with him on Forbes every day they saw him. They also provided the fertilizer for his vegetables.

His passion, which he got to enjoy most, was writing, which had been his life-long dream. He was penning a considerable volume of a book, based on his life in the British Navy during the war, when he was Chief Convoy Medical Officer in Great Britain, though by birth he was Scottish. He served on three warships; two frigates and one destroyer, which had all been sunk by German U-boats. He'd been lucky to survive one, let alone three extended swims in the freezing waters of the North Atlantic, but survive he had. His mantra, while he was in the ocean was, *first you survive, and then you drink.* Malcolm recited it endlessly when he thought about his rum ration, and wishing he had a flask in his pocket to sip from as he bobbed up and down on the waves; his life jacket the only thing keeping him alive in the cavernous yaw of the seas.

Malcolm replaced Wilfred Stoats; the previous keeper that had served for twelve years and reached his retirement age. Derek, the skipper of the supply boat, the *Morning Dawn*, waited at the dock for four hours while Wilfred showed Malcolm his duties before taking him away, leaving a very satisfied new keeper. Malcolm could at long last start his memoirs, which he'd wanted to write ever since the war ended.

Life was good for Malcolm; better than he could ever imagine. He soon found a schedule that worked for him, and he enjoyed the solitude the position brought. His daughter Molly visited once and stayed for three weeks, though by the end of her vacation, she was more than ready to return to the hustle and bustle of her life as a nurse in the busy city hospital. Malcolm went back to his writing with contentment he had never known. He was satisfied Molly was happy and managing well without him in Perth, and the words flowed freely for his writing endeavors.

****

Malcolm lay propped up in bed, tired from his earlier exertions and the concoction of morphine and rum. His doctor's training told him he shouldn't have mixed the two, but he promised himself during his ordeal if he survived, he deserved a drink, and Malcolm had survived. The empty tumbler sat forlornly on the bedside cabinet, and Malcolm could still smell the dregs of the rum ration he'd drunk. The light was turning above him; shipping would be safe for another night, and he could relax as best as the broken leg would allow.

Malcolm had forced down some cold meat in a sandwich, then as best as he could he re-splinted his leg after removing his wet trousers, which brought the pain which had been simmering in the background to boiling point once more. He used scissors to cut his pants off, and the pain returned from where it had receded under the influence of the morphine. With nothing more to do, except have a loaded syringe ready for when he needed it later, Malcolm went to bed, hoping he would be able to rest.

His leg burned with an ache that wouldn't permit sleep straight away, and Malcolm felt as if no matter what he did, he would never be able to get into a comfortable enough position, but he so wanted to drift off. Earlier, sitting on the stairs he almost fell asleep and tumbled all the way down. Now he was in bed, and he couldn't find sleep's welcoming arms. With nothing else to occupy him, Malcolm let his mind wander back to the events which brought him to Forbes.

****

Two days before his final rescue from the *HMS Warwick*, which was sunk by a German submarine in the North Atlantic, his wife Brigitte was killed in an air raid. They lived in the port city of Southampton where a fifty-pound bomb scored a direct hit on their terraced home, and left Malcolm to bring up their daughter Molly, alone.

Luckily, like many children in cities which were targeted by the *Luftwaffe*, Molly was evacuated to the countryside, or she would have perished with her mother. She was eleven years old and had been boarding with a family on a farm in Worcester.

Malcolm traveled by train to tell her the tragic news once he recovered from the dose of hypothermia, courtesy of four hours in the frigid ocean awaiting rescue. He broke the news to Molly that her mother had been killed because God wanted her with him. That was the explanation he gave her, and they had been inseparable right up to taking the post at Forbes.

For the remainder of the war, they lived in a small apartment in Portsmouth, and he worked at the Naval Hospital. Malcolm wore his tragedy on his sleeve and never sought to replace the only love of his life. For him, the memory was better than any second wife he believed he could find, and he was happy being alone with Molly. He shared her school achievements, sporting prowess, and loved her with every bone in his body.

After the war ended, Great Britain was a miserable place to live, so with his naval pension assured, he applied for migrant status to relocate to either Australia or Canada. At forty years old, and with his medical training, the Australian Consulate agreed on almost the same day. The brochures they showed him of hot days and white sandy beaches provided an overpowering lure, and he left the gray, bleak weather and pebble-coated muddy shores of Portsmouth behind, promising Molly a better life on the other side of the world. Malcolm worked hard to keep his word and make sure she was happy.

He was readily accepted in the emergency department of the Royal Perth Hospital shortly after arrival and it was his job while he brought up Molly. She did well in her lessons and made friends quickly at school. Malcolm noticed her focus seemed always to make him proud of everything she did, which naturally, he was.

They lived in a small, but comfortable, cottage near the river in East Perth and had a part-time nanny to help out when Malcolm worked late. Molly bloomed and time flew by as she crossed the threshold of childhood into womanhood. She reminded Malcolm so much of his late wife in looks and mannerisms, and they never had a cross word between them. Molly always waited up for him to come home from work and listened in wide-eyed wonder as he told her of the patients he had helped. Sometimes an hour disappeared before they knew it while chatting, such was her love of medicine, and neither of them wanted to miss that special father and daughter bonding time.

When Molly was old enough to leave school, he used his influence and helped enroll her into a nursing career at his hospital, because she wanted to follow in his footsteps into medicine. Molly moved into the nurse's quarters at age eighteen, as was the custom, although it broke her heart to leave her father. They made a point of sharing their lunch or dinner breaks at every opportunity when their work shifts permitted—a date neither wanted to miss.

Malcolm yearned to write the memoir he'd been planning for many years, but he knew he had to stop being a doctor to do so. Time was his biggest enemy while he toiled in the ER. He worked twelve-hour shifts, which frequently turned into fourteen or sixteen hours when emergencies arrived, as they often did just before he was due to finish. His work schedule changed every three days to night shifts which left him too tired to sit at his desk with a pen in hand. He had all the best intentions in the world, but often found he fell asleep after barely completing half a page of scribbled lines.

One evening, six years after they arrived in Australia, he read an advertisement in the newspaper for a job for a married couple to be a lighthouse keeper, and he thought that could be his version of utopia. He applied immediately to the Department of Marine and Harbors, and again, his medical credentials held him in good stead. They wanted someone intelligent, reliable, and stable, and who would be better than a doctor? He was familiar with working long and stressful hours and his interviewers thought it would be situations of physician heal thyself if something untoward should happen while alone, with no hope of immediate assistance.

The decision was reached almost immediately. Within a week, he passed his physical and signed a contract to work for one year. All he had left to do was resign from the hospital and tell Molly he was going to tend a lighthouse over two hundred miles away. Molly was, and always would be the apple of his eye, and naturally, she was upset she could no longer have him close to guide and protect her. At the same time, she understood his dream to write the book he'd been talking about for years and would not stand in the way of him seeking happiness.

Ever since she was a child, he'd told her stories of his time at sea, while her wide eyes bored into his. He talked about silent running to evade the U-boats, and the bitter cold suffered when keeping watch at night. Of hoping they could cross the channel and into port with a full load in the holds of the freighters his fleet was protecting. He spoke of watching an unfortunate ship in convoy destroyed, the gout of flame from a torpedo, the smell of burning oil mixing with the ozone in the air, and the screams of people trapped, or diving into the cold, black sea. He told her solemnly there was no sound on earth like that of a sinking ship. Molly would listen to him for hours, and she told him repeatedly she wanted him to write the book, even if ultimately it meant him moving away from her.

During his interview, he asked permission for Molly to be able to visit a few months into his tenure. Malcolm was told that would be permitted. He could book her passage on the supply ship which visited the island every three weeks, depending on weather, and take her back on its return, his interviewer informed him. The trip was around two and a half hours from Augusta where the *Morning Dawn* was moored. He knew this information helped her put on a brave face, knowing she could visit and stay with him, and she assisted by packing up his things to get ready for the move.

She was also permitted to visit the Port of Fremantle Harbor Masters offices once a week so she could speak with her father by radio. She never missed a Sunday talk with him, and he regaled her with his enthusiasm for the book, which was, "Coming along, Molly, my girl," he would say. Then he would recite a few new paragraphs he had written that week.

His new island home sat atop the cliffs of Forbes Rock, nineteen nautical miles southwest of Augusta, Western Australia. Augusta was home to an unusual phenomenon. It was where the Indian and Southern Oceans met and created a fierce water-based line of turbulence. Someone standing on the cape, by the land-based lighthouse, could look Norwest and see the line across the ocean which disappeared into the horizon. The phenomenon was caused by the waves coming from two different directions at once crashing against each other.

Just as he drifted off into an uneasy sleep, he hoped Molly would agree to help him keep his job. He didn't think she would say no, but he also knew it was a lot to ask a twenty-year-old woman to do.

Chapter 2

Molly McLaren

Molly McLaren was generally regarded by her friends as *"the quiet one."* At least she was until she lost her temper, then they thought of her as *"the hot-headed one."* She had inherited her mother's fiery red hair, which she kept in a bun, or ponytail generally tied with a black ribbon, which fought to hold back the unruly strands from her face. There always seemed to be one or two which annoyingly worked their way loose. Her cheeks contained more than her fair share of freckles, her nose was dainty, her teeth straight, and she was pretty, without the accolades of being beautiful. When anyone annoyed her beyond that which her placid nature could take, they got the full force of her Scottish heritage, complete with swear words picked up from her father and grandfather. Everyone who knew her regarded Molly as someone who was a dear friend but would make a dreadful enemy when riled.

She mostly kept to herself, only associating with a handful of fellow colleagues. Molly occasionally went out with nursing friends, but she was generally not interested in attracting men. She did have three boyfriends in her last years at school, though none of them had been too serious. At the time, her father encouraged her to see young men, but was always quick to warn her, and them, what would happen to them if they got too friendly. Generally, Molly found that warning frightened them into not coming back for a further date. She lovingly thought of her dad as a smiling assassin; his Scottish persona scared her suitors, especially when he exaggerated his accent, which made him sound violent, yet she knew he was no fiercer than a teddy bear.

Molly harbored dreams of being a doctor like her father, whom she had always adored. But medical school was not easy to get into, especially for females following the war. The medical fraternity was controlled by a male-dominated hierarchy, which was reluctant to accept that women could be trusted to hold down a career in the field of medicine. The Directors of the Hospital, it seemed, feared that after years of expensive training, most women would ultimately leave to have children. Therefore, she found doors were often closed to her, while held open welcomingly for men. Molly became a nurse instead but was always hopeful she could work her way up from inside, rather than complain from outside.

Her biggest personal asset, other than her smile, which could, it was said by more than a few people, light up any room she entered, was her ability to not only care for others but empathize strongly, and Molly's patients thought of her as a born nurturer.

She was the one whose friends could turn to for a caring shoulder, down to earth advice, sewing and mending of clothes, and she would always help others with their exams. In short, she was everyone's best friend.

Molly missed her father terribly since he took the

job at the lighthouse. After her mother perished in the bombing raid, it had been the two of them against the world. They traveled halfway around the world together to find and build a new life, and she loved that he cared enough for her to do that. In her quieter moments, she appreciated his willingness to uproot his life so she could have a brighter future. She idolized him for many things, but for that more than anything else.

He had never dated another woman since her mother died, and she hadn't been too bothered with boys as a teenager. She was content to wait for one to come along with her father's qualities, but she had to admit they were hard to find. It had been just the two of them, and deep down, she was happy with that, though since he moved to an island over two hundred miles away, she found she did get lonely.

During the war, she, like many children who lived in dangerous areas, was evacuated for her safety, and went to live with a lovely farming couple named Sulwich, in the Worcester countryside. They'd never had children of their own due to a horse riding accident when Margaret Sulwich was seventeen. Living on a farm had endowed Molly with a love of animals and increased the depth of her caring nature.

Southampton was a regular target of the Luftwaffe because of its docks, so raids were almost nightly and caused widespread destruction to the city. Those who weren't killed by explosions were often burned to death by incendiaries, which caused flames to jump from house to house in growing infernos. Though Molly missed being with her mother, while her father was at sea, she was delighted to escape to the country and be with so many animals. Molly loved her adopted family right up to the day she was given the news by her father that changed everything when he came to Worcester and told her that her mother had died. Their terrace home in Cotswold Street destroyed by a fifty-pound bomb. Tearfully, he explained that her mother had not made it out to get to a shelter in time. They cried in each other's arms, and he did not go back to sea, and she loved him even more for staying with her. In the early days, she recognized he needed her every bit as much as she needed him, and they became inseparable—right up to that time many years later when he dropped his own fifty-pound bombshell of going to live on a tiny island as the keeper of the light to write a book.

Since she was a little girl, sitting on his lap, he had enthralled her with tales of his seafaring days. He had the knack of taking a mundane story and turning it into a heart-stopping thrill-a-minute fight for survival. She knew, if he could ever get his book finished, it would be a best-seller, and possibly a film, so she understood his desire for solitude. He needed to find time to write, but she still didn't like him being so far away. By anyone's definition two hundred miles by road and a further twenty by sea was far away.

****

It was around three p.m. when Molly was summoned from the surgical ward, where she worked, and told to attend Mrs. Frost's office, immediately. Mrs. Frost was the head of nursing, and the staff had an assortment of cruel nicknames for her which they used behind her back. Most favored was *the head bitch*, but others which did the rounds were *Mrs. Dreadful*, or *old frosty knickers* depending on who was doing the complaining. She ruled her nurses with an iron fist, and to be called to her lair was never good news. In the past, some nurses had been ordered off the premises for a misdemeanor, and while they may have deserved it, the undercurrent was they had been mistreated at worst, and brusquely at best.

Molly fretted all the way there; her sensible shoes clacking on the terrazzo floors as she walked briskly. She was positive she had done nothing to warrant being summoned, but if *the head bitch* wanted a fight, she was in the mood to give her one. Molly tucked an errant wisp of hair behind her ear, knocked on the door, and heard the single word, "Enter" from inside. She turned the cold brass knob, took a deep breath, and walked in.

A man sat on a chair in front of the desk, and Mrs. Frost waited with fingers tented. "Come in, Molly, please take a seat," Mrs. Frost said softly and smiled, but to Molly, it looked like a shark grinning. She was in her fifties with silver, gray curly hair and wore a yellow shirt buttoned to the neck with a ribbon tied in a bow at the collar. "This is Mr. Darcy Harpington, from the Department of Marine and Harbors; he has some news for you about your father."

The man stood up and held out his hand to shake. He was short, balding, with spectacles which sat halfway down his nose and wore a gray pinstriped suit. Molly barely noticed as her heart leaped inside her mouth. "What about Dad, what's wrong, is he hurt?" She struggled to retain tears of fear from pouring forth. She knew it would be terrible news; it had to be, *why else is he here?*

The man smiled and raised a placating hand. "No need to panic; your father is a remarkable man, Miss

McLaren. He broke his leg out on the rocks while checking the moorings for the boat during a severe storm. He made it back to the light basically by crawling. It was quite a journey, he tells us. Being a doctor, he has splinted his leg and been in constant radio contact since. We are sending a boat out to pick him up tomorrow; the weather forecast is for the storm to ease enough to go and evacuate him. We need to get him into hospital for X-rays, set the leg properly, and make sure he's done no permanent damage from crawling over the rocky ground."

Molly looked from one to the other, unable to understand what they were saying. *Dad broke his leg,* she thought. She realized she was in shock. Molly sat down, hard, on the straight-backed chair, as the man sat back down too. Just for a moment, she had a mental image of her father dying, and her world went black.

She knew he could be stubborn and obstinate when he had a bee in his bonnet, and how typical of him not to lie down without a fight. *Crawled back to the lighthouse with a broken leg in a severe storm?* She was incredulous. Molly had spent three weeks there and knew the terrain well from her frequent exploratory walks. He'd achieved a miraculous result if the accident happened anywhere near the dock. Tears welled in her eyes, never did she realize just how much she loved him and needed him in her life until then. "He's going to be all right?" she asked in a quivering voice.

"Yes, Miss McLaren, we believe he will be fine after a lengthy hospital stay. It's possible, I'm told, the doctors may need to reset the fracture, and put him in a cast, possibly stretch the leg back into place. Either way, he is going to be bedridden for quite some time while the bones knit. You must understand, by the time we get him back on the mainland, the first break will be three days old and may have reset in the wrong position." He nodded slightly and stared pointedly at her; the implication of the seriousness unsaid.

She understood there could be all sorts of complications. Infection, even gangrene could have set in, and if the bones started to knit in the wrong position… She shuddered at the thought of re-breaking it all over again. One thing was for sure; her father would be out of action for some time. She exhaled when she realized she had been holding her breath. "I'd like to thank you, Mr. Harpington, for coming to tell me personally. That was very kind of you."

"Oh, think nothing of it, Miss McLaren. Your father has done a sterling job for getting on toward two years for us, and he is a valued member of our lighthouse staff. Um, that brings me to another matter, which he asked me to discuss with you."

She had been staring down at her hands as they gripped and clasped each other but looked up sharply at his words. She didn't like the sudden change in his tone. "And, just what is that?" She recognized the defensive aggression in her tone of voice, and it shocked her. *Calm down, Molly girl, you've had a shock, be careful,* she told herself sternly.

He made a performance of taking his spectacles off, then removing a handkerchief from his jacket pocket and wiping them. "Miss McLaren, your father understands, we cannot leave the light unattended, and if we replace him with another employee, then…"

"You won't let him go back?" She saw the predicament immediately and was suddenly angry, enough to slap the officious looking man. Molly stood up, furious and almost shouted, "Dad donates a leg to the cause, and he loses his job, is that what you are telling me, Mr. Harpington?"

"Mind your tone, Molly," Mrs. Frost interjected. "Sit down; there could be an alternative which Mr. Harpington and I have discussed. Mr. Harpington has sought a special arrangement with his Department, and this hospital, at your father's behest, to find a solution to the problem. I would suggest you hold on to that temper of yours until you've heard what he has to say."

Molly was past caring about being nice. It was her father they were discussing who was losing his perfect job; didn't they understand that? Molly would fight to the death for him. She glanced from one to the other, wondering just what special arrangement they had discussed before she arrived.

Molly took a deep calming breath and sat down. "Go on; I'm listening," Molly murmured. She was bristling for a fight; Molly could feel her rage simmering like a pot of milk on the stove just before it boiled over. They would not discard her father, not if she had anything to do with it.

"Miss McLaren," he began, slowly, "you must understand, the department responsible for the lighthouses in Western Australia has limited funding granted to it, and we do not have on our staff someone we can send there just for a month or two. Without a viable alternative, we have no option but to replace him with a full-time employee, whom we cannot very well get rid of when your father's leg heals. It may be possible when he is well enough to resume duties, we can find another posting for him, but that would depend on what is available at that time, and where, if indeed anything. If we don't have a suitable posting, we cannot create a job out of thin air, so he would need to wait until one became available, and then he would be given priority due to his previous experience. The alternative, of course, is if your father has a friend or relative, who is acceptable to the department that could step into his role and be willing to relinquish it when he is well enough to return."

He stared at her pointedly, and Molly's heart fluttered as she saw what was coming. "He has asked me to discuss this with you and see if you could do that for him. Before coming to speak with you, I sought permission from my superiors. Despite your young age, because you have spent three weeks on the island and know the responsibilities, and your excellent character reference from Mrs. Frost, I gained permission to appoint you if you choose. Mrs. Frost has agreed to grant you a leave of absence if you decide to accept the position. We know you are aware of what is required of you in the position. Your father impressed upon me during your stay on Forbes he trained you on all facets of taking care of the light. We would like you to accept the role, just until your father is fit enough to return when his leg heals. Mrs. Frost has offered to support you in this noblest of endeavors, by granting you leave for up to three months, and holding your position open until you return."

She sat, open-mouthed. *Me, run the lighthouse for two to three months? I'd go mad with boredom. They can't be serious, can they?*

"Molly," Mrs. Frost said in an unusually soft tone. "I can tell you that you are highly regarded in this hospital. You are well-liked, dedicated to your patients and their care, and we have never received a single complaint against you. I know how close you are to your father, and if you need this time away to support him, I am very understanding of that, and would welcome you back upon your return."

Molly sighed. She was shocked but knew she couldn't refuse. When she had visited the island, she saw how happy and content her father was, more relaxed than she had ever known him to be. He let her read some of the passages he had written, and she knew it was good. She could not possibly refuse to help him; the very idea was unthinkable. But to counterbalance that, Molly also knew she would go mad all alone for that long. It wasn't as if she had a book to write, so what would she do with her time?

As if she could read Molly's mind, Mrs. Frost interrupted her thoughts. "Molly, you've never made any secret of the fact you wished to follow your father's footsteps into medicine. I could loan you some excellent volumes for you to study while away. It is possible on your return you could sit the entrance exam for our medical school. There are some exceptional circumstances where the hospital grants scholarships for those whom they think deserve it, even women. You would need to study hard, but I think you have the right aptitude, and I would be happy to give my recommendation to the board, which would carry some weight, for them to accept your nomination."

Molly was dumbstruck but knew she had to reply. "Mrs. Frost, I will be eternally in your debt. Thank you for such a wonderful offer. I would love to take you up on the loan of some books to study. Mr. Harpington, thank you too for your generosity. Of course I will support my father, and mind the light until he can take up his station again. I'm sorry if I appeared hot-tempered before. I didn't give myself time to take in the full story, and all its implications. My first thought was for my dad's wellbeing, and I was in shock."

Mrs. Frost nodded, a satisfied smile on her face, while Mr. Harpington wriggled on his seat, seemingly embarrassed. "Oh, we do what we can, when we can, Miss McLaren. Now, can you be at my offices, packed and ready to go for seven a.m. tomorrow? I have a vehicle going down to Augusta then, with all the supplies you will require. Bring along what you think you might need for an extended stay. Dave will brief you on the way and make sure you are up to speed on the lighthouse keeper's responsibilities. Its winter, so warm clothing is a must along with any food supplies you think you might like in addition to what we provide."

Molly nodded earnestly as she made a mental note to stop at the store and buy several boxes of red licorice; that was her favorite and would help pass the hours on the lonely nights. The thought flitted across her mind maybe she should keep a diary, and almost burst out laughing. *A diary to make a note of what*? Perhaps she could count the seabirds that visited or the number of revolutions of the light; she had no doubt it would be a tedious two to three months' vacation.

****

Once she finished work and ate dinner at the nurse's canteen, she went to the small general store which was within walking distance. The woman who served her gave the most questioning look when she placed her purchases on the counter: twenty, one-pound bars of chocolate and three boxes of red licorice. Molly would have bought five but three exhausted the store's supply. She also purchased numerous bags of boiled sweets. "I've got a sweet tooth," she said by way of explanation to the shocked assistant.

Once back in her room, she packed her clothes and debated what to take. One thing she knew she wouldn't need was a bathing suit; it would be far too cold being winter for that. Molly realized with a touch of dismay; she didn't own too many clothes to worry about it, once she excluded her going out dresses. But, Molly reasoned, there would be nowhere to go, and nothing to do, no visitors she would need to impress, save for the three-weekly supply boat. Other than an outfit for traveling there and the return, slacks and jumpers were all that would be required. But then again, she did own two pretty frocks, one of which she could take, just in case. In case of what she had no idea, *but it couldn't hurt to have something beautiful to wear, just in case*, she repeated.

She packed her toiletries bag and debated whether to take perfume. Would she need it on an island? *There's always the supply boat, and who knows, Mr. Harpington or one of his minions might come calling to check on me,* she wondered. Molly decided to take her bottle of Lily of the Valley—*it couldn't hurt*, she told herself in a serious tone of voice.

She intended to draw the line at stockings and garter, after much soul-searching. She wanted to take some, but her logical mind told her there would not be any opportunity to dress up for anyone to that extent. It wasn't as if she was going to a dance at the local ballroom, but she tucked a pair down the side in her suitcase, just in case.

By nine, she was done, but not tired enough to go to bed, even though she knew she had an early start. She walked to the recreation room, where on the wall just outside was a coin-operated telephone. She booked a taxi for six a.m., and then went in to see the girls, and say her farewells.

Molly had never been one for making close friendships; hers was more of a scatter-gun approach whereby she had numerous acquaintances, but very few who she would call close. She sometimes wondered if that was due to the upheavals she'd experienced in her life—first the evacuation during the war, then living with her father in a rented apartment in Portsmouth. Next came the move halfway around the world to Australia and a brand new school. It seemed to her, though she acknowledged it was a somewhat feeble excuse, she hadn't ever had a chance to feel settled. This relocation to Forbes Rock was a good case in point. She thought she had just got her life on an even keel after two years in the nursing home, and now she was leaving it for two or three months. Yes, the cause was just, but still, it perpetuated the belief she held deep down, that for her, nothing stayed the same for long.

A group of young women were playing gin rummy at one of the tables and called her over. "What's this about you deciding to leave us, Molly?" Cynthia Shrewsbury asked, looking up from the fanned-out cards in her hand.

"Yeah," Dorothy Masters chimed in. "It's all over the hospital, that you cracked the shits with the head bitch and told her to shove the job where the sun doesn't shine."

Molly gave a short little laugh; her friends were always so crude. For a moment she wondered whether she should perpetuate the rumor mill by agreeing with the story but decided against it. "You know what Oscar Wilde once said, don't you?" she asked, smiling at them each in turn.

"Shut the bloody door; there's a draft blowing up the crack of my bum?" Dorothy asked, and the others giggled at her profanity.

"No, dummy, he said there 'was only one thing worse than being talked about, and that was not being talked about.' So, it's nice you've been talking about me, but it is all nonsense of course. I'm taking a leave of absence to help my dad out, and Mrs. Frost was not only supportive by granting it, but she's holding my job for me. Not only that, but she is loaning me some books to study while away so I can sit the exam for a scholarship entry to medical school when I get back."

"So, let me get this straight; you're going on holiday, and she's giving you work to do, yet she's been supportive. Explain to me how that works. Gin, by the way." Dorothy laid her cards down.

Molly dragged a chair over and spent the next fifteen minutes telling them the whole story. "So, you see girls, Mrs. Frost has been very kind to me."

Everyone nodded, while the next hand was dealt. "Molly, Molly, Molly," Cynthia said with a grin. "Just because she throws you a bone, doesn't mean she's Mrs. Wonderful. She's still set you a ton of homework to do when you are going on a working holiday. She's still our very own head bitch, and Mrs. I'm so fahbulous dahling, but let me ruin your vacation,

Frost."

Molly realized she was going to miss her workmates. They were all similar in age and could always be relied on to lighten her mind when things troubled her. They had an easy way with each other, and all used a sarcastic kind of wit, though each of them also possessed a venomous tongue when angered. They had a bond, one not easily broken, and when one of them became upset with the decline or death of a favored patient, the others would be there to rally around.

Cheryl, who had been strangely silent through Molly's narrative, suddenly spoke in a quiet, reflective voice. "I'm going to miss you, Molly. Not just while you're away, but if you do get into medical school, you won't want to socialize with us mere nurses anymore, you'll have doctor friends."

Molly felt shocked. Firstly, that her friends would miss her, but also that they thought she wouldn't want to associate with them if she did get into med school. She was about to protest until she realized as much as she might not want it to be true, it probably was. Then another idea hit her; none of the nurses liked the doctors they had to work with very much. Most of the doctors looked down their noses at them, as if they were employed just to make their lives easier, rather than to help in the health and wellbeing of the patients. Most doctors, except for her father, though she never had the pleasure of working with him directly, were arrogant men. They were in the habit of bossing nurses around, unless they were trying to get inside their knickers, of course. Then they were sickly sweet, especially the older married ones—they tended to make Molly's skin crawl with their syrupy sexual innuendos disguising their chat-up lines.

Molly felt compelled to refute the assertion. “Cheryl, I am who I am, and whether I follow my father’s footsteps into medicine, or stay nursing will not affect who I am, merely what I do for a career. My personality won’t change, and yes if I’m studying hard, I may not see you girls as much, but I promise you I’m not going to be treating you any differently than I do now.” She said, softly and gently.

“That’s what they all say,” Dorothy said, but she was smiling, so Molly knew she was kidding. She had made her point and hopefully eased her friends’ minds.

“When you say all, Dorothy, are you talking about all the women who have gone from nursing to medical school, because I think I’m the only one so far? And there are no guarantees it’s going to happen at all, yet.”

Cynthia held up her hand as if stopping traffic. “Shush, did you girls hear that? Sounded like a bloody doctor whining to me.”

They all laughed and, shortly after, Molly took her leave as she had an early start and knew she needed to get some sleep. She hugged each one, in turn, blinking back tears, and assured them she would be back as soon as her father could take up his station again.

****

The taxi was on time, thankfully. Molly had been up for what felt like several hours, showered and washed her hair then waited nervously chewing her thumbnail. The driver helped her with her bags, and the wooden box full of anatomy and medical science books Mrs. Frost had loaned her, into the cavernous Chevrolet’s trunk. She turned and gave one last look at the building which had been her home for over two years and suddenly felt a pang of worry. Molly experienced a deep sense of dread as if she was never going to return. She shook her head, told herself she was being dramatic and climbed into the back seat which swallowed her whole, like the whale that swallowed Jonah.

The weather was gray and was drizzling a light rain, which only made her feel even more depressed. It was still dark, but edging ever brighter in the east, when they pulled away from the car park. She wasn't going on a vacation; she was embarking on a new vocation. *A damned lighthouse keeper, me?* She almost cried with misery, and probably would have but for the one saving grace; she was doing it to help her father. That was the least she could do after all he had done for her.

The early morning traffic was building up, but the cab made it in plenty of time for her seven a.m. appointment. It was six forty-six when the driver helped put her things in the foyer of the Department of Marine and Harbors, and she paid him off. Just for a moment, she considered going back with him and running away, but she shook her head and gave the man a small wave of dismissal.

She sat on a chair next to a coffee table with a pile of magazines on it as instructed and waited for her ride to Augusta and a new chapter in her life. At seven on the dot, Mr. Harpington appeared with a much younger looking man, who wore brown dungarees and a red checked shirt visible underneath. "Hello, Molly, all ready to go? Meet David; he will be driving the supply van. Good news, the forecast is holding, the seas have dropped after the storm, and it shouldn't be too bad a trip out to Forbes."

She stood and politely held out a hand to shake, and noted his smile appeared genuine, and his grip was firm without being overbearing. He seemed to be in his thirties, with straggly brown unkempt hair, and large brown eyes. "Nice to meet you, miss, is this your stuff? We better get it loaded and get on our way; it's a long drive, and we have to get there in time to catch the tide."

She nodded in agreement. While she was in no hurry to get to Forbes to begin her lonely life, she was keen to see her father and make sure he was okay. Between them, they picked up her bags and the box of books and walked in single file through the open doorway, down a long passage with offices to either side. Eventually, they came to a kitchen and through there to the rear entrance. In the car park, by the back door, sat a white Ford van, and they put her things in the rear with the other boxes of food and supplies.

Once done Molly shook hands with Mr. Harpington. "Thank you for what you've done for my father."

"Think nothing of it, my dear, you keep good care of our lighthouse. Oh, and don't forget your radio check-ins, once a day, but I'd like you to do it twice, ten, and again at four. I want to make sure you are coping all right and will be here if you feel you need to talk about anything."

"I'll be fine, Mr. Harpington, but yes I will radio in as you've asked."

He opened the passenger door for her as David started the engine and she climbed in, still unable to shake her feeling of impending doom. She gave a wave through the window as they drove away, and watched him acknowledge her, then turn to go back inside just as the drizzle picked up and turned into rain.

Chapter 3

The Keeper of the Light

When they arrived at the harbor after the long and tedious drive from Perth, the drums of kerosene were already aboard, lashed securely, and everyone pitched in to transfer the food, firewood, and other items from the van to the boat. The skipper of the forty-plus-foot cray fishing boat, Derek Johns, seemed to be a kindly soul. Derek did, however, appear shocked when told he was taking a woman to be the keeper of the light. He sported a grizzled gray beard and a slightly dirty cap upon his mop of gray hair.

During the drive, Dave told Molly the crew worked well together. Like a well-oiled machine, they were well-rehearsed and knew each other's roles, so they were usually on and off the island within two hours. That included taking the new drums up to the lighthouse, setting up, and bringing back the empty containers using handcarts. The food and supplies would also be carried up, usually by her father, but this time it would be Molly who assisted.

After they loaded everything, no time wasted on pleasantries, the boat got underway as the sun shone bright through gaps in the decreasing cloud cover. Molly was pleased she didn't become seasick during the trip, as two hours later she watched the lighthouse on top of Forbes Rock, appear ever closer through the front windows of the *Morning Dawn*. The boat plowed through the gray, green waves, holding a steady course as they drew nearer to the reef complex. Derek glanced at her, tutted, and shook his head. "'Taint no place for a woman, least of all an unmarried one," he grunted, barely above a whisper Those were the first words he spoke to her other than hello when Dave introduced them. "We skippers rely on the light to guide us to safety, 'taint no place for a young thing like you. No disrespect, lass."

"None, taken," she replied, her chin set in a steely manner. "I'm a nurse, Mr. Johns, would you trust me to stitch your wounds, lower your fever, and clean up your mess if you were ill in bed? If so, I think you can trust me to tend the light, my father's been doing it for two years."

He reacted as if slapped. "You're Malcolm's lass? Well, why didn't you say so? Last time I brought you out here, you didn't say boo to a goose, so I didn't know you were his kin. Every now and again, I pop in to see your dad, spend the night, share a couple of rums with him, and play cribbage. He's a good man, a man of the sea, and if you're anything like him, I think you'll do nicely. Your dad can tell a good story, that's for bloody sure." He grinned and showed the gap where a front tooth was missing, and Molly felt herself become more comfortable with him as her temper eased.

"Yes, he can spin a good yarn about his days at sea, Mr. Johns. Don't worry, I'm only temporary, as soon as his broken leg heals, he will be back, then I can go back to the big smoke, where I belong, and he can get back to finishing his book."

"Aye, he's let me read the odd page or two, should be a corker of a read when he's done. Call me Derek, please, by all means. Now don't worry about your dad; we've brought the stretcher and Mikey, and I will lash him to it and carry him down those bloody stairs, and then tie him to the bunk when we're back on board in case the sea comes up. When we're close to docking at Augusta, we'll radio for the ambulance to come and take him to the hospital in Busselton."

Mikey was the young deckhand, whom she had been introduced to when they climbed on the boat. He was standing at the stern, smoking and talking with Dave while she stood with Derek in the cabin. Molly thought he was quite handsome, and he seemed close to her age, but he barely spoke and seemed shy. As Molly understood it from Dave during the drive, the Department of Marine and Harbors contracted Derek's boat to resupply the island with fuel and supplies. They would take a day off from pulling their cray pots when required. *Obviously,* she thought, *a day's charter for the government gives them a better return than pulling pots for crayfish.*

"Well, Derek, if ever you're passing, and feel like dropping in, I make a decent cup of tea, and I dare say I'd enjoy the company," she said, smiling, not wanting to let on how nervous she felt about the prospect of being alone.

"Aye, and wouldn't the missus love me visiting a young beautiful single girl at the light." He exaggerated a shudder as if he were terrified of his wife, and then broke into an evil-looking grin. "Mind you, if I bring young Mikey with me she'd be all right about it. I saw the way you looked at him earlier, lass." He shook a finger at her comically.

She gasped loudly and her face blushed a deep shade of red. “I did no such thing, Derek. Don’t you dare tell my father that; he’d be hobbling after him with a shotgun.”

They both laughed. “Well, I tell you what, I’ll write down my radio call sign and frequency for you, and if the weather is good, we fish every day between seven a.m. and two, weather permitting. So, if you need anything, you can give me a holler. On Fridays, again so long as the weather is amenable, Mikey and I will come and visit in the afternoon, for an hour or two, just to make sure you’re coping with the solitude, how’s that?” he asked, and Molly noticed he seemed to be blushing.

“That would be fantastic if you could do that, thank you so much. I’m not sure how I’m going to cope being alone for two or three months, other than when you make your resupply visits. Thank you for being so kind, Derek. That’s thoughtful of you. Oh, and by the way, I play a mean game of cribbage myself; I had a good teacher,”

He shook his head dismissively, plainly embarrassed to be thanked, and peered out of the front window. “I like your dad and consider him to be a friend, so I’m happy to help keep an eye on his girl. Maybe we can teach young Mikey to play cards. Talking of the lad, will you go tell him for me we’re coming up on Forbes, so he’s to step lively? I want him up on the bow to keep watch for rocks when we go through the passage.”

She nodded then turned and stepped over to the door to the rear deck. Mikey looked up as she approached, and for a moment, he turned red, fidgeted, and looked down at his feet, which Molly thought looked cute. “Derek would like you up on the bow,” she said, and he walked around her with a nod, before sidling around the side of the cabin, sure-footed, like he’d done it a thousand times before.

Molly glanced at the approaching island, which looked cold, gray, and uninviting. Waves crashed on the rocky shoreline as the cliffs stretched upward as if trying to escape the unrelenting inherent violence. She gave a shiver and hugged herself. From this direction, she could see why the seas were so notoriously dangerous, as she watched the turbulent water break over reef outcroppings. The white lighthouse stood out proudly against the mottled gray sky, and a sunbeam flashed from an opening in the clouds on the glass prism as if it were winking at her. Her sense of foreboding returned.

“There’s your home for a little while,” Dave murmured. “It’s beautiful, isn’t it?”

She had to admit, if you liked craggy islands with nothing but rocks and cliff faces, other than the stark white lighthouse, surrounded by turbulent reef laden waters, then yes, it was beautiful. “It’s certainly remote, and quiet, Dave,” she replied, thoughtfully.

She felt the boat lurch when the speed dropped, as Derek steered the hull through the narrow opening in the reef channel to get to the protected jetty on the other side. Small waves hit from both sides, sometimes together, causing the boat to bob, dip, and weave. Molly had to hang onto the side rail to keep from stumbling.

At the slower speed, the smell of burned diesel

fumes became stronger when the breeze caught a cloud of it and threw it back in her direction. For a moment, she wondered why people like her father and Derek romanticized the sea and sailing upon it. To her, she found it unenjoyable, cold, and dangerous; therefore, far from romantic. The deep water held all manner of terrifying perils, not least of which were sharks, including the fearsome great white which inhabited the local waters. Her imagination wandered, as she thought of the boat sinking after hitting the reef, and then trying to swim to shore with an unseen monster of the deep closing in. *Stop that thinking right this minute,* her inner voice said sternly. *Derek is a great skipper, who's made this trip hundreds of times. He's not going to sink, and you're not going to get eaten by a shark.*

Eventually, with the sound of cawing seagulls wheeling overhead, the boat made it through the twisting passage to the inside of the reef. They turned right and picked up speed making for the cove with the jetty on the leeward side. Molly's nerves jangled as she realized they were now close to her being able to see her father so she could make sure he was okay. She headed back into the cabin to speak with the skipper, now he'd completed the hardest part of the journey which she knew would have taken all his concentration.

"Derek, would you mind if as soon as we dock I race off to check how Dad is? I'm not trying to get out of carrying bags and such, but I am very keen to see him."

"Sure, you can, lass. Don't you worry; we will bring your things up for you."

****

She bounded up the spiral staircase, gasping and

panting from her exertion after the run from the dock. Molly pushed open the oak door to the living quarters and dashed to the right where his room lay. "Dad," she yelled, "we're here."

Molly stopped in her tracks. He lay on his bed, a shadow of the man she spent time with some months before—pale, drawn, and sweating. He lifted a hand to give a small wave. "You're a sight for sore eyes, Molly, girl. Come and give your old man a hug."

She dashed over and flung her arms around him, careful not to touch his leg. "Oh, Dad, what the hell have you been doing to yourself?" She moaned, fighting back the tears.

"Aye, I'm a wee bit of a mess. One slip was all it took. That's all it ever takes for an accident. I suppose that's why they call them accidents. Don't fret now, I had the morphine to help with the pain, but they going to have to re-set the leg, and it's picked up a bit of infection too, but once I'm back on the mainland and get some penicillin into me, I will be as right as rain." He stroked her back softly. "If I donna look my best, it's just because I've no taken anything for the pain today, I was saving it for when they carry me down that bloody staircase."

"Are you sure that's all, Dad?" She stood back up. "Do you want me to look at it for you, redress the splints?"

"Nay, lass, leave it well enough alone. Four or five hours from now I'll be in a ward bed, and it can wait that long. I want to thank you for giving up your time and watching after the light for me. I promise as soon as I'm able I will come back, I just love it here, and would hate to lose my post."

Molly didn't want to let on how much she was dreading being alone, she figured he had enough on his plate without worrying about her. She dragged an upright chair over and sat down, smiling as she did so. "It's fine, Dad, don't you worry about that. You just get better. Mrs. Frost was ever so nice about it, even loaned me some books to read, she says she is going to propose a scholarship for me to go to med school when I get back if I study hard."

"Well, good on her." He beamed. "I will have to write her a letter of thanks. You'd make a damn fine doctor, Molly, that's for bloody sure, a lot better than some of the male ones I've worked with over the years. I've got some money put aside so if you get in, I can help out with your fees and such."

She nodded gratefully and found her eyes brimming with tears. Could there ever be a better father in the world? She didn't think so. "Thanks, Dad, you're the best. How about I make us a cup of tea while the men are unloading?"

"Only if you tip a measure of rum in it, purely for the fortitude you understand." He smiled and winked, and she smiled back, knowing she could never refuse him anything.

****

The stores were put away, and the drums of kerosene were stowed. All that remained was to get Malcolm down the stairs, and onto the boat. Molly gave him an injection, and they transferred him from bed to stretcher. Derek passed two ropes around and tied them securely. "That's to hold you in tight. With the angle we've got to hold you at going down those damn stairs, it's going to be tricky," he mumbled.

"Trust me, Derek; it won't be anywhere near as bad as when I had to climb up them. Don't you dare drop me just because I beat you all the time at cribbage." He burst into a fit of the giggles.

That's probably an effect of the morphine, Molly thought.

Derek took charge. "Right, Dave and Mikey, you're at the front, try to hold him high, and keep him level with my end, I will bring up the rear. Molly, you go ahead of us to open the doors. Are we ready?" They all nodded, Molly stood by the door, and the three men took the weight.

"Maybe I should sing you all a sea shanty, you know, just trying to do my bit to help," her father said, a little too happily.

"Don't you bloody dare," Derek replied, and off they went.

****

It took a little under an hour, but they made it to the boat without any mishaps. The men all cussed and groaned under the load going down the spiral staircase, but Molly thought it was good-natured stuff. On the gravel path, they stopped twice to take a rest, and each time she asked her father how he was coping, as she wiped the sweat from his brow. She knew the pain he would be feeling must be unbearable with the movement, but he didn't complain.

Derek said she should ask how they were doing, carrying his weight, but she saw he was kidding. It seemed to her this was one of those unwritten rules of the sea, to help a fellow seaman, and she thought the men were wonderful. Every now and again, she grinned as her father yelled out, "Mush, mush, mush." As if whipping a team of dogs on a sled, which gave a surreal atmosphere as if it was all a joke, instead of taking a severely injured man to the hospital. Molly wondered if the camaraderie between women was the same as with these men. Sure, she liked the nurses she worked with, but would they be this giving? After a few minutes, she decided they would, but then another question snuck up on her: *Was that because they were nurses?* Then she wasn't so sure.

"Do you have any rum on this bloody barge?" Malcolm asked as the men laid the stretcher down on the bunk, and that was when Molly knew just how bad the leg must be hurting him. Her father, to her knowledge, hardly ever drank alcohol. "A bloody waste of money," he had been fond of saying as she grew up. Her father would know he could not have any more morphine for several hours, and further, alcohol would be the last thing he should have, yet he wanted some. The jostling journey down the staircase and along the hand-hewn path, complete with rest stops, must have been agony for him.

Molly knelt by his side. "I've got a question for you, Dad. If one of your patients, back when you were practicing, wanted to drink rum on top of a large dose of morphine, what would your reaction have been?"

She wiped the sweat beads from his brow, tenderly. "I'd have told them no more than one large glass an hour," he said, trying to look deadpan.

"Really, honestly, that's what you'd have said?"

"Half a glass?"

She stared back, not speaking, the furrows on her brow showed her stern side.

"How about one huge sip?"

"What if I get you some water?"

He stared at her for a few seconds, before speaking in a broken voice. "You know, Molly, sometimes you are so much like your mother it hurts. You win no rum." He smiled, and her heart melted.

She bent down and hugged him tightly. "I love you, Dad," she whispered.

He squeezed her back, and in a voice barely above a whisper replied, "I thought I was blessed to be loved by one woman in my life, but two? Molly, my girl, I'm not sure if I told you anywhere near enough, but I am so God damned proud of you."

"Molly," Derek broke in. "It's time you went ashore, we need to get off, so we beat the tide and get this pirate to hospital."

She nodded; suddenly wracked with a fear she'd never known and recognized it as impending loneliness. "Derek, will you radio me with updates on his progress please?"

"Of course, I will. Don't you worry. I'll drop in and see your dad and radio you the next day, let's say around ten in the morning?"

She kissed her father's forehead, and then stood up. "Okay, I'm out of here. Thanks for taking such good care of him, thank you too, Dave, and Mikey. I will keep the home fires burning and guide you seafarers to safety. It's a heavy burden, but one I shall rise to."

She stood on the dock, watching the boat effortlessly glide through the water on its way out of the lagoon. She felt it coming and couldn't stop a wave of depressing sadness hit her, and she burst into tears. *I'm in prison*, was the thought that bounced around several times in her mind, each time seemingly louder. Then she thought of her father, and that only made her sadness worse. As the *Morning Dawn* rounded the headland, she noticed a thick, dense cloud, hanging low in the sky approaching from the horizon, she hoped the boat would be safely back at Augusta before the next storm hit.

Molly wiped her tears away, told herself to *buck up my girl*, turned on her heel, and began the long walk back to the light, hands thrust deep in her coat pockets, eyes cast downward watching her steps, not wanting to stumble. Molly decided during the walk, that what she needed was a routine. Rather than have some days where she had absolutely nothing to do, she would spread the chores out so there were two or three things she must do on any given day. Molly nodded. *That makes sense*. There was the vegetable patch to tend, and her father had shown her some of the land-based fishing spots that were safe. He thought it vital not to live on canned meals and salted meat, and Molly, like her father, enjoyed fresh fish.

She determined she would have a bath every day. As it was winter, the rainwater tanks, which were fed from the roof of the outhouse, and lean-to, were full to overflowing. In summer water had to be used more circumspectly, but that season was months away. The water was pumped by hand to the tank above the living quarters in the lighthouse, a job her father did weekly, but Molly thought she might need to do it more regularly if she was to have more baths than her father would have bothered with. The bathroom housed a small tub, though plenty big enough for her, and she imagined lazing in the warm water, which would be a joy because at the hospital, there were only showers.

The water was heated by a copper coil running through the firebox of the wood-burning stove, which doubled as a room heater as well as a cook station, so usually ran all day and night.

By the time she reached the lighthouse, she had her days mapped out, plus her father had left a list of dos and don'ts so she wouldn't forget anything. Then there were the radio schedules she had to make, and Derek would be available to talk to. Suddenly, a thought flitted through her mind unbidden: *Maybe Mikey will want to talk to me on the radio. Possibly, he will lose his shyness with a microphone in his hand.* She grinned. She knew she had some sort of effect on him, but then living in a small coastal town like Augusta, as he did, just how many girls would there be his age to be attracted to? *Not many, I bet.*

An evil idea snuck into her mind to tease him mercilessly, which shocked her. She was not used to feeling any form of attraction to boys, but then working twelve-hour shifts, six days a week, she was often too tired to even think about meeting and dating members of the opposite sex. Her only day off each week was spent doing her washing and cleaning her one-roomed accommodation at the hospital and then making the trek to Fremantle to speak with her dad on the radio. So, she knew she was reasonably ignorant of the byplay and nuances between men and women.

The radio in the lighthouse was powered by a treadle that charged the standby battery, which meant a slow, steady foot action on the pedals to keep it at full capacity. The capacitors retained enough charge so she could hear a call for her without powering up. It could be tuned to the ABC so she could, if she chose, listen to radio plays and music at night, but the thought of endlessly pumping her feet to keep the power to the set made the whole idea very unattractive. *It's only three months, girl.* Molly was shocked at the stern tone she used in a one-sided conversation. *It will fly by, just you wait and see.*

As she climbed the staircase, Molly realized how tired she was, and looked forward to an undisturbed night's sleep. She would clean up a bit, make sure her bed was made with clean sheets, make herself some dinner, read a few chapters of a romance novel she was reading and hit the sack. Of course, she had to light the wicks before dark, once she checked the kerosene levels in the holding tank. The lamp itself sat in a tub of mercury, so once she attended to the clockwork apparatus, her night's work would be done, and she could relax.

****

Around three a.m. Molly was awakened suddenly by a loud thudding noise, and she struggled to decide where it came from. Eventually, she reluctantly realized it came from above her; the watch-room, where the light was housed. She knew she had to investigate but was petrified at what she might find.

Molly spoke to herself sternly. *I am the keeper of the light, charged with making sure the lifesaving beam radiates out across the ocean. Without it, seafarers could run aground on the reef and possibly die.* Her job, for three months anyway, was to save lives, and she had always taken that task very seriously. Molly got up, wrapped her dressing gown around her tightly, and tied the bow securely. She picked up the Tilley Lamp from her bedside cabinet and turned the knob to brighten it from a dull glow, then went to investigate.

Holding the lamp at eye level, she climbed the stairs, slowly and methodically, while her heart pounded in her chest. Halfway up, she heard a shuffling, scratching noise, and she very nearly turned and ran back down to hide under the sheets. Common sense told her it couldn't be a person, and she didn't believe in ghosts; therefore, there was a perfectly logical reason for the noise. A rat? she wondered, then discounted it. Her father had never mentioned them, and when she stayed here before, she didn't see any evidence of rodents. She steeled her nerves and continued.

"I'm coming up," she shouted, "and you'd better have a good excuse for being up there." Molly tried to sound a lot braver than she felt, and just for a moment, wondered what she would do or say if she did find someone in there. Not that it was even remotely possible. But, at three in the morning, everything, no matter how ridiculous, seemed like it could be real. It dawned on her, more than at any other time, she was alone on a tiny island in the middle of an ocean...*or am I alone?*

Leading with the lantern outstretched ahead of her, she opened the door and stepped into the watch room. Her eyes furtively glancing from left to right then back again, searching for what or who could have made the noise. The light was working as it should, turning in its bed of mercury, the harsh glare making her lamp useless as it revolved creating alternate light and shadow. Everything was as it had been earlier. The drums of kerosene stacked neatly; enough to fuel the light for a week should she become ill and too weak to carry them up the staircase. Molly could see nothing else until she noticed, when the beam struck it and splinted into a rainbow of color, a shadow, or splat of something on the outside of the window.

It was frustrating because it was only illuminated for a second, then the light went by, so she had to wait for it again to be sure she hadn't imagined it. *No, there's something there, but what?* She had performed her inspection before bed when she trimmed the wicks, checked the fuel tank, and ensured the windows were clean. Molly was positive the noise she heard was a result of something that hit the outside of the pane and had left the mark. It wasn't raining; she couldn't see raindrops in the powerful beam or spatter on the glass. She crossed to the outside door, turned the handle, and opened it.

The glass door was almost wrenched from her hand in a sudden strong gust of wind, but she held on, then closed it behind her as she stepped through. Molly shivered and wished she had donned something warmer, but she had no idea she would be stepping outside when she left her warm bed.

She took a few paces and stopped in her tracks, looking down. "Oh, you poor thing," she exclaimed. There was a large seagull, on its side twitching in obvious distress. *He must have been dazzled by the light or caught in a sudden gust and flew into the window.* Without a second thought, she put the lantern down and picked up the bird in her cupped hands. She snuggled it to her breast, cradling in her right hand so she could pick up the lamp in her left, then went back inside, out of the howling wind. "Come on, little feller, let's get you down to the kitchen and get you warm."

With all thoughts of an intruder gone, she walked briskly down the stairs, and into the small kitchenette. Using her foot, she dragged a chair over close to the Meters stove, put the lantern on the bench, deftly opened the firebox door and tossed a piece of wood in. Then she sat down and softly stroked the bird's neck and back with her fingers and cooed to it softly. Molly could tell it hadn't broken its neck. She hoped it was just stunned. But on the balcony at the top of the lighthouse, was no place for a wounded bird. If the wind blew him over the edge, he would have died in the fall, and Molly was determined this wasn't going to be the night Sammy the Seagull was going to die, not if she could help it.

When he regained his senses, it was with a start and panic as he tried to flap his wings to take off. Molly held her hand underneath his body, with his legs between first and second fingers, and while she didn't want to squash him, her grip was enough that he couldn't take off. "Shush, shush, shush," she whispered softly, as she put her other hand over his back to fold his wings. "You're okay, you're safe," she said, smiling that he was alive and apparently healthy.

For just a moment, he calmed and tilted his head on one side, eying her warily. Molly thought he looked perplexed as if trying to understand what had happened and who the giant was that held him in her clutches. "It's all right, little one. Let's set you free, and this time, stay away from the light."

She stood up and held him securely in both hands, then shuffled slowly so as not to startle him. She went down the stairs to the front door, murmuring all the way. She felt elated, she had saved a life on her first night, and even though it was a bird, a life was a life in her opinion. She awkwardly opened the door and shouldered her way out once more into the cold wind.

Outside in the night air beneath a carpet of twinkling stars she shuddered, chilled to her bones. "Now, Sammy, are you going to be okay to fly?" His only answer was to crane his neck from side to side and struggle to get free of her hold.

Molly squatted down and gently placed him on the ground, but as she took her hands away, he pecked her on the wrist, drawing blood. "Well, that's not very nice, Sammy," she cried, but the bird turned his back on her, and took off into the wind. Molly watched it wheel to its left, and then it was gone. Absentmindedly, she raised her hand to her mouth and sucked the speck of blood. She grinned. The bird was only following its instincts, she could hardly blame it for pecking her, though it did show a distinct lack of appreciation. A sudden gust made her remember she was freezing cold, so she turned and raced back inside.

Chapter 4

The Routine of Making Routines

Molly awoke to the shrill cry of the alarm clock, and the sun streaming through the small window which faced east. She turned the noise off with a slap of her hand and just for a moment watched the dancing motes of dust swirling and playing in the beam of light. It was quite beautiful, and she idly wondered if a poet or songwriter at some point in time ever tried to describe the sight in words far more descriptive than she could.

Molly could have drifted back to sleep, watching the specks floating in their carefree world, but she shook her head, got up, and put her slippers on. It was time to greet the morning. She wrapped the thick dressing gown over her nightdress and tied the tie in a big bow. Molly had to attend to the first of her chores and remembered the line from a poem she studied at school; 'by dawn's early light,' but she couldn't remember it talking of dust particles trapped in a shaft of the morning sun. "Molly, my girl," she said out loud, and felt somehow comforted by the sound of her voice echoing back. "Today is the first day of the rest of your life; better make it a good one eh?"

While it was far from bright inside the tower, there were sufficient windows to illuminate her way up the staircase, and she found it fun to climb through each dagger of brilliance that shone through as she rose higher. Once back in the watch room, she stood before the imposing sight of the turning light and remembered how she felt comforted by speaking aloud earlier. She also recalled her father telling her he frequently did the same thing, often having two voices, one of his father, and one of himself, and held conversations by speaking, rather than thinking. Molly decided if it were good enough for him, it would be good enough for her to do the same; anything that eased the boredom of a life spent alone she would grab with both hands.

"Good morning, light, and how was your night? Did you keep the seafarers safe from the rocks?" she asked, gaily. The light swung silently by, mocking her with its refusal to answer. "Well, if that's how you feel about it…" She switched off the clockwork and watched it slowly lose momentum and come to a juddering halt. "And, let that be a lesson to you, ignore me at your peril." She grinned at her humor.

Next, she took the douser, as her father called it, lifted the cap above the flames, and extinguished them one at a time. "Die, damn you," she said theatrically, as if she were repeating a line from a melodramatic Shakespearean play. A wisp of black smoke spiraled up, just for a second, and the odor caught in her nose and she sneezed, once, twice, then a third time. "Well, Molly, there's a lesson for you, don't breathe through your nose when you're turning off the beacon."

She grabbed the powerful Zeiss binoculars from the hook and stepped through the door out onto the balcony. The weather was beautiful and bright with a chill to it but not overly cold. It was typical of a winter's morning now the icy wind had petered out from the night before, and the sun was shining. She was required to check there hadn't been a boat that had run aground on the reef that would require her to radio for rescue.

It was a great day, one to write home about, as her dad used to say frequently when they had been new migrants to a country whose weather was far superior to old Blighty from whence they hailed. The sea beyond the reef seemed calm, like a caged tiger, waiting to be set free and pounce. Occasionally, she could see a line of swell rear up, and then drop back down to hide beneath the surface again, but there were no wind-driven whitecaps to spoil the azure blue color.

"Molly, today's the day to explore every inch of your new home." She nodded in complete agreement as she flipped the lanyard over her head, just in case she dropped the costly glasses. "Accidents happen, you know, that's why they call them accidents." That was one of her father's favorite sayings which she too used frequently in hospital. She was about to bring the glasses up, when she remembered a cartoon from years before, which made her wary. It showed a practical joke about boot polish smeared over the eyepieces, so the unaware user looked like he had black eyes when he lowered them. Her common sense told her that could not possibly be the case, but still, she held them up to the sun and checked carefully.

Satisfied her imagination had run riot, she spent the next ten minutes searching the ocean. Firstly, she scanned in close on the rocky shoal and was pleased not to find anyone stranded by running aground or holing the hull of their boat. She performed a full circuit of the balcony and found nothing amiss. Next Molly scanned the ocean, where she did find the occasional fishing boat making the best of the excellent weather, but nothing that seemed out of place or in trouble. On the horizon, a large container ship was steaming on its way to or from God knew where, and that was it. Her second job of the day could be ticked off her list.

She decided to be decadent and have breakfast in her bedclothes and dressing gown, then draw up her to-do list while eating it. Eggs, she had fresh eggs in abundance, and she thought an omelet was called for.

Thirty minutes later, having bounded down the stairs, stoked the dying embers of the fire in the stove, and added fresh wood to get it going; she dashed out to check the nesting boxes and collected eight golden brown eggs. Their hopper of grain was empty, not surprisingly with all that had happened, so she filled it from a sack in the outhouse while the birds clucked and pecked around her feet. She watched for a while, smiling, wondering at God's marvels, not that she had ever been overly religious. "You see, Molly," she said, quietly, "You give the chickens food, and they give you food in return. Isn't life wonderful? You know, maybe, this little holiday won't be so bad after all."

Molly grabbed the basket and went back inside, feeling the best she had since she knew she was coming to Forbes. Maybe it was because the weather was fine, perhaps it was saving the life of the gull, or just she was getting used to the idea of a couple of months of her own company.

****

Molly breakfasted on an omelet she thought fit for a king, and her jobs to-do list was completed by nine, so she thought it a good idea to do some washing, especially her father's bedclothes. There was no rush to do that, Molly knew he wouldn't be back for at least two months and probably nearer to three, but she felt if the bedclothes were washed and made, it was more welcoming. Being a nurse, she was used to looking at freshly made beds, and the habit was hard to break. Of course, there wasn't one of the modern electric washing machines she was familiar with that she used at the hospital. For the lighthouse, it was an ancient kerosene-fueled, and heated copper tub with a mangle mounted on the rim. That was another reason she decided to do the job immediately. The longer she left it, the more she would dread it; therefore, she told herself sternly to *get your bum in gear, Molly, and get it done so it's one job out of the way.* She realized she had said it in the voice of Mrs. Frost, the head bitch, which made her laugh.

She had everything organized, with the sheets soaking in the hot soapy water, when she noticed her watch showing it was close to ten am. *Radio time*, she realized. She'd left the kettle warming on the stove, so made a pot of tea to drink, then went to the tiny room her father used as an office and place to write his book. The light through the window was enough, and she didn't need to light the lantern. She put her tea on the desk, wriggled the chair in so she sat in the right position, and started working the pedals.

"Slow and steady wins the race, Molly, my girl, no need to bust a gut." Her father had shown Molly when she spent time with him previously, along with all the other chores and safety regulations as was required of a visitor to the island. Once she had her rhythm, she switched on the set and watched the dial, which showed her she had built up more than enough charge. The usual wheezing, whining, and popping noises began emanating from the speaker when she switched it on, which she always found so amusing. She checked the set was on the correct frequency for checking in. She glanced at the chalkboard over the desk to confirm the call sign and remembered how her father performed his schedules. "Whiskey Delta Oscar one zero, this is Forbes Light, are you receiving, over?" she said with the transmit button firmly pressed and using a voice which sounded more confident than she felt.

"Receiving, Forbes, loud and clear. What's your status, over?"

The female voice sounded quite young but competent, a good voice for radio, Molly thought. "A quiet night here, everything working and in order, nothing to report, over," she responded. Then things took a less officious turn.

"Molly, my name is Rachel, and I will be here this time of day most days. I'm to report back to Mr. Harpington on your wellbeing. How are you coping after your first night alone, over?"

Molly stopped to think for a moment; she felt fine, remarkably so. She was in good spirits, and she wondered if she should report the incident with the gull but decided against it. There was a written log; she would write it in there but didn't see the need to bring it up over the radio. "Thanks for asking, Rachel. I'm doing really well thanks. I had a great night's sleep, the weather is fine here for my first day, I've had fresh eggs for breakfast, and within myself, I feel wonderful, over."

"You certainly sound bright and bubbly, and I will report that to Mr. Harpington. I think he likes you, over."

Likes me? Molly grinned. *Now what on earth does she mean by that? He's old enough to be my dad, scratch that, grandad.* She decided to let it slide, Rachel couldn't possibly mean anything untoward; she was just being friendly. But thinking of him as a father figure reminded her that her own had been in hospital overnight. "Please pass on that I am grateful for the chance to help and thank him for his concern. Rachel, is there any news about my father, over?"

"Yes, Molly. Mr. Harpington has been on the telephone this morning. He arrived too late for them to do anything last night, and he was in a lot of pain, so they sedated him. Your father had a good night's sleep, the doctors have him on intravenous drip, and this morning they will perform x-rays. I will have more information for you tomorrow, but he is comfortable for now. Mr. Harpington did mention that if you would like to call back at four p.m., he will be here and will have an update for you, over."

That was pretty much what Molly thought would have happened yesterday, so there were no real surprises there. "Four o'clock, yes I will call back then. Thank you again, Rachel, Forbes Light signing off, out."

Molly twisted the dial for the frequency designated for fishing boat call ups, and once again pressed the transmit button. "*Morning Dawn*, *Morning Dawn* this is Forbes Light calling, do you read, over?" Only crackling and an electronic wheezing noise returned, and after two minutes, she felt alone again. She forced herself to remain calm and counted to sixty. *Derek is on a cray fishing boat so could be busy.* When she reached sixty-one, she tried again, "*Morning Dawn, Morning Dawn*, this is Forbes Light, are you there Derek, over?"

This time she counted to one hundred and twenty, but then fearing she had gone too quickly, recited, out loud, a further sixty, this time going slowly. She repeated the call sign, and held her breath, feeling the panic rising inside her like a volcano about to erupt.

"Forbes, this is Jim Baxter on *Rickadonna*, we're about half a mile away from *Morning Dawn*, and I can see Derek looking over the stern, and his deckhand is in the water. I'd say they've fouled a rope around the prop by the looks of things. I'd leave him half an hour or so and try again, over."

Her irrational fear left her, and she felt silly. *Why were you worried, Molly?* She wondered. "Thank you, *Rickadonna*; I will do as you say. Forbes out." She shook her head at her silliness, got up, and went back to the washing.

She'd finished pegging the sheets on the makeshift washing line under the lean-to, then carried a replacement drum of fuel up to the watch room, and used it to top up the tank by the time the half-hour was up. The wicks looked fine so didn't require trimming, but she thought she would stay a while longer and clean the windows, especially where the seagull had hit during the night, before trying the radio again. Molly decided the prism could wait one more day before it needed cleaning, which would permit a few hours free to go for a walk to explore the island and try to catch a fish for her dinner. She couldn't remember the last time she ate fresh fish. Though it did occasionally appear on the canteen menu at the hospital, the one time Molly tried it, it was awful, and she never bothered again.

Molly thought it couldn't have been *that* fresh.

Derek answered her call immediately after she warmed up the capacitors with the pedals and called the boat again. "Aye, Forbes, this is the *Dawn*, how are you, Molly? Did you sleep well, over?"

Molly felt at ease again. Derek had such a kindly voice; she couldn't help but feel comfortable talking to him. "I slept fine thank you, well, right up till I had an early morning visitor; a gull flew into the light and frightened me half to death, but it was all fine in the end. How was my dad when they got him to the hospital, over?"

"Listen, Molly, your dad, is a tough old sea-dog. I could tell he was in a lot of pain by the time we got him there, but he just kept making stupid jokes, and putting that daft Scottish accent on when he cussed, as he does, over."

She smiled with pride, yes that sounded just like him. Molly could tell by the tone of voice Derek used, he liked and admired him too. "You can't keep a good man down, and there's none too much better than him," she replied and felt a teardrop of love form in the corner of her right eye. "I tried to call you earlier, but you didn't respond, is everything all right out there, over?"

"Aye, I heard you but couldn't get to you straight away, then by the time I did you didn't reply, so I'm glad you called back. Out here in crayfish alley, which is what we call the stretch where we usually set our pots, it's oh, about twenty nautical miles from where you are; the recent storm tore someone's ropes free. I must be getting blind as well as stupid in my old age because I ran right over the top and it fouled the prop. Your new boyfriend Mikey got in the water with a sharp knife, and I had to spot for him, make sure he didn't get bitten by a shark, over."

She bristled with him joking that Mikey was her new boyfriend but knew Derek was the kind of man whose sense of humor meant that if she admitted to being annoyed, he would only do it all the more, so she let it ride. She also didn't want him to think she couldn't take a little ribbing without getting upset like a little girl. Molly was the keeper and should act like one. She recalled her earlier thoughts about sharks, and with his comments realized she hadn't been imagining the genuine risk of being attacked while in the water. "Are sharks a real threat, Derek? You hear about them often enough, but I didn't know it was that big a problem, over?"

"Aye, well, not so much this time of year. The salmon are running so they have lots of natural food to eat. They're around, make no mistake, we see them often enough, it's more about being prudent with me spotting. There are a lot more of the big bitey ones around in summer than winter. There's nothing to worry about Molly; I will keep him safe for you, over."

"I hope poor Mikey isn't within earshot with you talking all this nonsense, about him and me, over."

"Of course, he is; he's standing right here, hanging on to every word you say, and blushing his head off, that's why I'm teasing him, over."

Now it was her turn to feel her face turning red, and she was pleased she hadn't said anything which would increase Derek's sarcasm. Now she knew he was listening; she had to acknowledge him or be seen to be rude. Ignoring him could only make it seem like she did have the hots for the poor lad too, either way, she suspected Derek would continue to make sport of them. "Hi, Mikey, I bet it was cold in the water, wasn't it, over?"

Derek must have passed the microphone to him, as the next voice was Mikey's and Molly realized she might have exacerbated his embarrassment. "Hello, Molly, I'm fine, it wasn't too bad." But he held on to the send button too long, and she heard Derek guffaw in the background and yell out, "Don't you believe him; he came out looking like a blue icicle. He's gorgeous in his underwear, Molly."

Molly wasn't sure how she should respond. This whole conversation, while fun and helped with alleviating her boredom, made her uncomfortable with it going in the direction Derek had steered it. The last thing she wanted to think about was Mikey cold and shivering in only his underpants; that was a mental image she could live without.

"It's not true, Molly," Mikey continued, "I was all right, I've done it a few times before. Sometimes I think the skipper does it on purpose so he can see me get wet. How are you coping on your own on Forbes, Molly? Not getting too bored, I hope, over?"

"Well, it's only been one night, ask me in a week or so, but so far, so good thank you. Derek, will you be visiting Dad tonight, over?"

It took a few seconds to answer as he took the transmitter back from Mikey. "Aye, lass, I will do that for you and chat with you in the morning to report back. Will you be all right till then, over?"

"I'll be peachy, thanks. I'm going to explore the island, check Dad's vegetable patch, and try to catch a fish for dinner. I must be back at four to radio into

Marine and Harbors as they are going to check Dad's progress for me too. Thanks for the chat, and I will talk to you tomorrow, over and out."

She heard them both say goodbye as she stopped pedaling the treadle, and the capacitors wound down, leaving the needle in the green for receiving. She was smiling again as she went to the kitchenette to make a sandwich. She had a loaf of bread, freshly baked the day before from the Augusta Bakery, courtesy of Derek. Molly took two slices and buttered them with practiced ease. She had corned beef, a block of cheddar cheese in the fridge, and a jar of homemade pickles in the pantry. Once Molly made her lunch, she ate it with a fresh cup of tea and licked the drips of mustard juice from her fingers which leaked from the sides. "Molly, that was one fine sandwich. Give my compliments to the chef, will you?" She grinned.

Molly cut some pieces of the beef to use for bait; her father had told her the fish around the island would willingly gorge themselves on pretty much anything on a hook. She didn't feel like going to too much trouble, so herring from the jetty would be the order of the day. Molly had fished there with her father before, so she was well versed. "Burley, Molly, don't forget the burley," she mimicked in her father's voice, so she cut another slice of bread.

From the outhouse, she took one of the small rods with a reel attached. Her father, always prepared, had traces made up hanging from a board on the back wall. With practiced fingers, she tied one on and hooked it to the bottom eyelet to make it easier to carry. She had her jacket to keep the breeze out, a bucket to put fish in, and to hold her bait. "So, what are we waiting for, let's go catch dinner." She giggled, and off she went.

She took the path and stopped off at the vegetable patch. She smiled at the pieces of wood sticking out of the ground stating in her father's neat writing what vegetables lay beneath the foliage growing profusely from the soil. Potatoes, carrots, Brussels sprouts, cabbages, and a few others abounded in the boarded off area. Only her father would be mad enough to grow things to eat on a lighthouse island in the middle of a complex reef system in the middle of an ocean. She hoped she could dig up one or two potatoes; if she caught fish, it would be wonderful to have chips with it.

With a spring in her step, she headed off once more to the small jetty. She saw the dingy first, looking forlorn with the outboard motor wrapped in canvas to keep it safe from the elements. One of her jobs was to start the engine once a week to make sure it fired. If required for evacuation, the keeper needed a fully operational boat. She didn't want to do that today, and she certainly didn't want to go out on the ocean in it alone. *No siree thank you. It's far too small for this little brown duck.*

She tucked the fishing gear inside the boat under its awning, then stood and considered the weather and debated if she should wear the jacket on her expedition. While it wasn't cold, neither was it hot, and the breeze was gentle, so clambering over the rocks she wanted both hands free, therefore didn't want to have to carry it if she got too warm wearing it. She wore slacks, tennis shoes and socks, and a long-sleeved flannel shirt in a rather fetching purple check, Molly thought, *Okay, a purple check isn't fetching, but who am I going to meet here? No one, that's who!* She removed her jacket, folded it neatly, and tucked it under the bench seat, so if the wind did come up, it wouldn't blow it away.

Molly turned left, deciding to travel in a clockwise direction around the island. She had no good reason, other than she was right-handed, which seemed to be as good a reason as any. What Molly expected to find, she hadn't given a thought to. If she had, she probably wouldn't have bothered, because there wasn't much to see. Forbes Rock was primarily a section of reef that due to some subterranean upheaval had been thrust upward millennia ago to now sit above sea level at high tide. Some spots had loose shale and rocks on it of varying sizes, no doubt blasted ashore by storms over the centuries, and one small area did have some hardy gorse type bushes clinging for dear life to the rocky crags and crannies. There, she knew, sea birds nested. Her father once joked if ever he was starving he could probably find some Seagull, Osprey, and Mutton Bird eggs to eat. She shuddered at the idea and hoped she never got *that* hungry.

About ten minutes into her walk, she was distracted by movement out to sea, and she turned to see what it was. Something like half a mile away she watched in breathless excitement as a whale came out of the water, breached and crashed back down again on its side. "Oh my God, isn't it wonderful?" she exclaimed, giddy as a schoolgirl. Next moment a second beast did the same to the right and slightly behind the first. It was as if she were the only audience member at a circus as, for the next ten minutes, she watched them frolic in the waves, while they slowly swam away from her. "Well, Molly, if you see nothing else this trip, that was worth the price of admission." She began her trek again.

Molly was approaching what she thought of as the pointy end, which was where the island worked its way upward, creating thirty-foot high cliffs when she thought she saw something worth exploring. If she hadn't been close to the water's edge at the time, she would not have noticed, as from the sides, or above it would have been invisible. It was what looked like a cave.

When she got there and peered in, it was more of a depression, perhaps only twenty feet in diameter, with nothing remarkable about it. She ducked her head and entered, then sat for a while, on a rock slab near the back wall. Molly looked out over the ocean so that the opening framed it. The view was spectacular, and Molly imagined being an artist who could capture the vista on canvas. It would be the sort of painting she would like to buy. She had neglected to bring her Box-Brownie camera with her this trip, but she decided if and when she ever returned, to come here and take the picture for posterity. Molly had heard of people who could enlarge snapshots and frame them like artwork, and the idea held a lot of appeal.

Molly imagined being a seafarer from years before the lighthouse was built, who became shipwrecked and perhaps lived in the cave, awaiting rescue with nothing but raw birds' eggs to eat. That was a more morbid scenario, and it made her shudder as she imagined someone waiting for help that never arrived. In that era, with nothing to burn, how could someone signal for help? She shrugged; her breather was over. It was time to move on.

She circumnavigated the cliff face but enjoyed the view from on top, though the breeze felt stronger and colder, so she didn't stay too long to admire it. It was a lot easier going down the gradient on the far side, than trekking up the near. She couldn't describe it as having been hazardous, but it had undoubtedly been tiring.

Down the slope, she hurried, keen to get back to the jetty. The sun was well past its zenith, and she was mindful she had to catch her dinner. Not that she didn't have plenty of food at the light; she did, but it seemed since she had the idea to catch something to eat, it had become an irresistible urge.

The only thing of note she saw on her return was way out at sea. What seemed like ten thousand seabirds diving into the boiling ocean, and she realized there must be larger fish, feeding on baitfish, which attracted the birds for a free meal. It was beautiful, and Molly's appreciation for the ocean increased.

Later, sitting on the jetty, waiting for a fish to take her bait, she began to get an inkling of what the attraction was for people like her father and Derek. She had heard men describe the sea like a wife, or a mistress trying to lure a man away from his wife, and she thought she got it.

She took small pieces of bread, and rolled it in her hands until it crumbed, then threw it out as far as she could, and watched it drift toward where her float bobbed and turned in the small ripples. She had it working so well, as the bread swelled up and began to sink it was around where her baited hook lay, waiting to tempt what she thought of as that night's dinner. She felt so relaxed after her exertions, she let her mind wander, and she recalled being back at school, studying a poem by the English Poet Coleridge called *The Rhyme of the Ancient Mariner*.

Molly had always loved that poem, though she had not thought of it in years. Two verses emerged from her memory, and she repeated them a few times with her new love of the sea foremost in her mind.

Day after day, day after day,
We stuck, nor breath nor motion;
As idle as a painted ship
Upon a painted ocean.

~

Water, water, everywhere,
And all the boards did shrink;
Water, water, everywhere,
Nor any drop to drink.

When the brightly painted cork float disappeared for the first time, she was so shocked she nearly dropped her fishing rod. She jerked it upward and felt the tip dip and bend as a furious fish, no doubt angry at a sudden pain in its jaw from the sharpened hook, tried to escape.

No, no, no, my beauty; you will fill my dinner plate tonight, Molly thought. She remembered her father's tutelage from her childhood, and it was as if he was with her, whispering in her ear his advice. "Hold the rod high, Molly, let the rod tip do the work for you. No, don't reel too quickly; else you might pull the hook from its mouth. Slowly, steady, gently but firmly, let him tire himself out, and you shall dine on him tonight."

"Okay, Dad, I got this, don't nag me." She grinned, knowing she was talking out loud to herself, but felt so thrilled she didn't care. Slowly, she worked the fish, who was not going to the frypan without a good fight. As she got it close to the jetty, she saw its gleaming green and silver hue flash through the water to the left and right, desperate to escape. It was a good pan-size fish, fighting as if he were a giant, even leaping clear of the water before trying to dart seaward again. But she was equal to the task, and within seconds had it out and wriggling frantically in her hand. She patiently waited for the worst of its struggles to die down, then she removed the hook, and dropped it into the bucket, half full of seawater to keep it fresh.

"Yipppeeeee," she screamed. She had done it. Sure, she had caught fish before, but only with her dad there helping and guiding her. This was her effort, and hers alone, and she felt terrific for the achievement. The herring was around nine inches long, fat and healthy, with beautiful coloring; the epitome of a healthy fish, and would be fantastic to eat later, she just knew it.

Within a minute, she had baited up again, and excitedly tossed the float, split shot weights, and baited hook back out in the ocean. She reached over to her dwindling supply of bread burley, but the cork shot under the surface before she could grab some. "Woohoooo," she shouted as she lifted the rod to do battle again.

She stopped when she had four herring. Even four was more than she could eat that night, but perhaps any leftovers would be lovely on toast in the morning for breakfast. She was shocked that she wanted to keep going. *The hunter's lure*, she thought of it as, and she had to use logic that she could come to this spot any time she wanted and catch a feed of fresh fish. Therefore, why keep going? She acknowledged some part of her did want to, and that didn't sit well with her.

She packed up her rod and reel and stood up. The

leftover bait and bread she broke up and threw in the water to feed those fish she didn't catch. They could have a free meal, she decided, then smiled at the idea it may bring them back to the same spot again, and then she would catch them too. Walking back, she stopped when a sudden thought hit her. How could she sit up during the night to aid a wounded seagull, and if she was honest, what useless birds they were, yet kill fish? "Because I'm going to eat the bloody fish, and I'd never want to eat a seagull," she told herself in a giggly voice. Satisfied with the answer, she walked on.

****

By four o'clock, she was amazed at her achievements. The fish were scaled and filleted sitting in the fridge, and two good-sized potatoes harvested, peeled and cut up for chips sitting in the water near the stove. Her hands washed, and her bathtub slowly filling up with hot water after she had topped up the firewood, so could have the promised bath when the radio call to Mr. Harpington was over. The capacitors were warmed up, she was treadling smoothly, and a fresh pot of tea made with a full cup sitting in front of her.

"Whiskey delta Oscar one zero, this is Forbes Light, are you receiving, over?" she said into the transmitter, then took a sip of tea.

A man's voice she immediately recognized returned straight away. "Receiving Forbes. Hello, Molly, this is Mr. Harpington, how are you coping, over?"

She pressed transmit, feeling very proud with her first day under her belt. "Hello, Mr. Harpington, I'm doing very nicely, thank you. All jobs completed, the light is fully operational. There is nothing untoward to report, over."

"That's good to hear, Molly. From the first moment we met, I knew you had some steel in you, and you would be a good keeper. You'd like to know about your father, I'm sure. I phoned the hospital a while ago to get a report. Can you hear me all right, Molly, over?"

"Receiving you loud and clear, what is the news, sir, over?"

"The tibia and fibula suffered clean breaks, but they had started to knit in the wrong position. They don't know how your father made it back to the light with the pain he must have suffered; he must be one tough old bird, they said. They operated today, and re-broke then set again. Currently, he is in plaster, leg raised, and weighted to hold it in the right position. You're a nurse I know, is all this making sense Molly, over?"

She imagined her dad, on his back, with weights stretching the leg through pulleys in traction. He would hate being helpless, she knew, and she was proud he had survived his ordeal. Earlier she marveled at the trip he had made from the vegetable patch with only garden stakes and twine as splints. Many would not have survived, let alone get back up the spiral staircase. But not only that, he had kept the light going to keep others safe while he waited for evacuation for two nights; he deserved a medal and she felt justifiably proud of her father.

"Mr. Harpington, words can't describe how proud I am of my dad. Were there any complications at all, and how has he responded, over?"

"His doctor said his spirits are good, and he is already asking how quickly he can get back on his feet.

He picked up what they think is a low-grade infection, but so far he is responding well to penicillin; they will advise me if he has any setbacks. He said he regretted not taking his writing book; it was the perfect opportunity to get some work done on his great unfinished novel. I've told the nursing staff I would get it picked up on the next supply drop, over."

"No need, sir. Derek on the *Morning Dawn* is dropping in on Friday, weather permitting, and he is keeping in touch with Dad through hospital visits; they have become good friends over the years. I will ask him to pass it along, over."

"All right then, that's that taken care of. I don't have any other news for you but will have Rachel pass along anything else on the morning schedules. You're doing a grand job there, Molly, but you will let us know if you feel you cannot handle the solitude won't you, over?"

She looked inwardly for a moment and realized she felt remarkably carefree. Truth be told better than she had for a long time, though of course, it was early days. But, *knock on wood*, so far so good. "I'll be sure to do that, Mr. Harpington, but honestly, I don't think there will be any problems for you to worry about on Forbes. Thank you for the report. I appreciate it, sir. Over and out."

****

She enjoyed her bath. The warm soapy water eased the minor aches and pains caused by her trek around the island, and she very nearly fell asleep. She finished her cup of tea, drained the water, and stood to dry off. She caught sight of her body in the large mirror that broke up the monotony of the whitewashed walls, and without making any conscious decision to do so, wondered what Mikey would think if he saw her right then. She blushed a bright shade of pink.

Molly knew she wasn't one of the beautiful ones, like some of her friends at school, or the nurses she worked with at the hospital. She knew she was one of the plain ones, and that didn't bother her in the slightest. Molly hadn't chased boys, and indeed there hadn't been too many throwing themselves at her. She removed the towel from in front of her and gazed at her reflection. Molly wasn't an ounce overweight; being a nurse kept her far too busy to be obese, and her eating habits were generally healthy. Her skin was flawless, other than a few handfuls of freckles, or sun-kisses, as her mother had called them before she died in the air raid. Molly possessed a good enough body; she had childbearing hips, which one day she hoped would hold her in good stead. Molly wanted to have three; one boy and two girls would be ideal. From her chin down, without being too overly critical, she thought she compared favorably with other women in the communal shower block at the hospital. Would Mikey like her? She wondered again.

She shook herself from her reverie. "This is no time for thoughts of passion with Mikey, Molly, my girl. You don't fancy him, do you?"

She had to admit, she didn't, not really. It was more that Mikey seemed smitten with her, and she was not used to that attention; it was flattering. His blond curly hair was unkempt, and he had pimples on his forehead. True he was tall and fit, but she supposed, like her, he was.... unremarkable. And, on some nights, her dreams were of remarkable men. A dark, handsome, ruthless, someone who could take her away, ride into the sunset, and make wild passionate love to her repeatedly at night. *Stop it right this minute girl, settle down, it's dinner time,* said the voice of reason in her mind.

****

She lit the wicks just before sundown, checked to make sure the apparatus was working and watched the life-saving beam of light stretch outward to the horizon for a few minutes. *Keep away, keep away, keep away*, she imagined the light saying to ships' captains. She shrugged. "Time for that fish, Molly," and her mouth watered at the thought.

Half an hour later, she sat down to a meal that smelled as wonderful as it looked. The herring tasted divine, white flakey, golden brown on the outside, soft and delicious on the inside. The chips made from potatoes from the garden were full of flavor which she was unused to at the hospital canteen. There everything tasted like different shades of bland cardboard, but this meal was incredibly tasty. Molly greedily ate all eight small fillets, which was double what she thought she would eat.

After Molly cleaned up, washed, dried, and put away all the dishes, she sat on a couch with a book she found on the bookshelf in the tiny study that housed the radio. She wore her nightdress, the room was warm from the stove, and the light from the Tilley lamps was cozy. Molly again realized she felt remarkably calm and at ease. *Maybe I could get used to this lifestyle, after all*, she mused as she opened the cover to a book so typical of her father's tastes: *Moby Dick.* She had heard of it, naturally, but had never felt the inkling to read it. Perhaps with today's glimpse of a life surrounded by the ocean, and the sight of the whales putting on a circus act just for her now was the time. She turned to the first chapter.

Call me Ishmael. Some years ago—never mind how long precisely—having little or no money in my purse, and nothing particular to interest me on shore, I thought I would sail about a little and see the watery part of the world. It is a way I have of driving off the spleen and regulating the circulation. Whenever I find myself growing grim about the mouth; whenever it is a damp, drizzly November in my soul; whenever I find myself involuntarily pausing before coffin warehouses, and bringing up the rear of every funeral I meet; and especially whenever my hypos get such an upper hand of me, that it requires a strong moral principle to prevent me from deliberately stepping into the street, and methodically knocking people's hats off—then, I account it high time to get to sea as soon as I can. This is my substitute for pistol and ball. With a philosophical flourish Cato throws himself upon his sword; I quietly take to the ship.

She sat up straight. "Oh, my goodness," she exclaimed, loudly. Was this not like her thoughts earlier about the lure of the sea? While she never understood it before, except through her father's eyes, that very day she experienced it to a small degree. Was it not some sort of destiny she had picked up this book that started in such a way?

The language was hard to read, but the beauty in the lyrical way of speaking made her realize how easy it was to understand the context. One paragraph and she was hooked. She held in her hands a work of art, a classic of literature, and she told herself this must not be rushed, it should be relished. Perhaps a ration of four pages a night, rather than hurtle through it in three or four sittings. Decision made, she turned to the next paragraph and for a short while, transported herself to another time, another land, and the quest for a Great White Whale.

Chapter 5

A week on Paradise Island

Molly soon set herself a routine and found happiness in her work to an extent she never thought possible. The weather stayed calm and fine, the herring kept biting, the vegetable patch kept growing, and Ishmael and Captain Ahab enthralled her at night.

On Tuesday, she spent two hours cleaning the prism so it sparkled, along with the windows, and was thrilled with the result. On Wednesday, she trimmed the wicks, as her father had shown her, and oiled the clockwork mechanism. She got used to topping up the fuel in the Tilley lamps and refrigerator as well as replenishing the spare drums in the watch room. There was no maintenance required on the building, and she spent her non-working hours going for a daily walk around the island, fishing, and reading both *Moby Dick* and an anatomy book loaned her by Mrs. Frost. Almost every day, Molly saw whales, and the coincidence of reading about the hunt for Moby Dick and seeing them frolic and play off the reef was a wondrous experience.

On some days she made a picnic lunch and hiked to the cave, where she would sit and watch the ocean through the frame of the jagged opening while she ate. She had never been an artistic person, but she wanted to be able to capture the contrast between reddish-brown rocks and the crashing white-tipped waves. Sure, she could sit and watch the ocean from any vantage point on the island, she was after all surrounded by it, but there was something about the view from the cave that kept drawing her back.

In her routine, to Molly's surprise, she found contentment, as she cast off the hustle and bustle of hectic nursing in the hospital, for the relaxed lifestyle on Forbes Rock. Each day she spoke with Derek, and Rachel, though there was nothing to report from her father. He was recovering, and it would be a lengthy process, which did not suit his temperament. Like most doctors, he made a terrible patient.

As Friday drew nearer, she worried what she would prepare as a meal for Derek and Mikey when they came for a visit. They were only staying an hour or two, and she was looking forward to having some company so it would be only fit and proper she fed them. But what? That was the question. She searched the kitchen cupboards and drawers and found an old cookbook covered in a film of dust. With a cup of tea by her side, she scanned the pages looking for inspiration.

On page forty-nine, in the seafood section, she found a dish she thought her meager cooking skills could manage and at the same time summed up her stay at Forbes. She had everything on hand to prepare it, except the fish; those she would need to catch. On Thursday morning, she set herself a task of catching eight of her new favorite fish, which she managed by just after eleven. Back at the lighthouse, she cleaned and prepared them and left them soaking in a brine mixture. She dug out the fish smoker from the outhouse, which her dad had pointed out once on her last trip but didn't use it. She was a little nervous about getting his instructions all wrong and ruining the fish but was determined to try.

By two, she was sitting on a fold-up chair, avidly watching the smoker do its job, drinking her tea, and feeling very excited. As the fillets were reasonably small, she decided to check them at an hour and a half. Earlier, Molly had painstakingly chopped up some of the Jarrah firewood into chips and large flakes and soaked them thoroughly. As she watched, the aroma coming from the box was making her mouth water. Molly had to fight the urge to go and check them every few minutes, knowing if she did the smoke would escape and so slow the process down. *I hope Mikey likes my fish pie,* came an unbidden thought to her mind, then she immediately admonished herself. *I am cooking for Derek and Mikey.*

She sat back in the chair, sipped from her mug, and for the first time, consciously thought about whether she liked Mikey enough to try to form a friendship. *Friendship? You're not fooling me, Molly; you want more than that.*

Did she, though? The first hurdle to overcome was of logistics; she was on a lighthouse, and he was on the mainland. He didn't have his own means of visiting her, only with the man he worked for, so it could hardly be romantic. Then, when her vacation was up, and she returned to the hospital in Perth, she would be working hard, and possibly, studying even harder if she got the scholarship. Mikey lived two hundred miles away, and he probably didn't have his own car, and a long-distance romance by bus didn't hold a lot of appeal. On the other hand, he was cute, and the way he acted around her was alluring, in its own way.

Mmm, that fish smells divine, I might do this more often, she thought as she sipped her tea. The big problem with Mikey, in any romantic sense, was when she thought about men and a boyfriend in the past, Mikey wasn't how her fantasies usually ran. She pictured herself meeting someone tall and handsome, like a doctor, older than her, who would automatically know what she wanted and provide it. Molly didn't want to be dominated, in any sense of the word, but neither did she want a boyfriend who was so shy he blushed every time she looked at him. She sighed and sipped again from her mug of tea. *Now is not the time to harbor thoughts like that, Molly, my girl, it's not the time.*

When she judged the hour and a half was up, and she could wait no longer, she took the lid off the smoker, and reveled in what she saw, and smelled. The fillets were cooked to perfection, and it took all her willpower not to pick one up and eat it. She imagined the lovely smoky flavor, and how it would be too hot in her mouth, but the taste, she believed, would be divine. "Be strong, Molly; this is for the fish pie, not taste tests."

She placed each fillet lovingly on the plate she had brought down, and gingerly carried it back up the stairs, conscious of the risk of tripping and losing what had taken up half a day to get to that point. Once the fillets cooled, she wrapped them and put them in the fridge and thought about the other fish she required.

Molly faced a dilemma. She thought she needed a further eight herring, and they would be fresher if she caught them in the morning, then cooked and prepared her pie to serve in the afternoon when the men arrived. *But*, she wondered *what if I leave it till then, and the weather turns bad, or for whatever reasons, I don't catch the required number?* She would have insufficient time for another alternative. Molly knew she couldn't risk it and grabbed her warm jacket, some more bait, and bread for burley and then left for the jetty carrying it all in her trusty bucket. Providing she was back by four for the radio check-in, all would be well, and if she only caught some of the numbers she required, it would mean less to do tomorrow.

Molly needn't have worried; she caught her eight herring almost immediately. It was almost as if, she thought, they were lined up waiting for her to return; willing to donate themselves to have a successful meal for her new friends.

She stopped at the vegetable patch on her way back and dug up some potatoes; enough for her dinner that night, and to make the mashed potatoes for the topping on the pie. She decided to leave the other vegetables she would need, so they were even fresher in the morning. She whistled a tune all the way back to her home and made it in plenty of time to speak to Rachel and tell her she had nothing to report.

Molly felt wonderfully content at nine that night, as she sat down on the couch, with *Moby Dick* in her hands to read a few pages before bed. She had enjoyed her dinner of salted roast pork chop, and a large baked potato served with steamed carrots and Brussels sprouts. Molly enjoyed another long luxurious bath and even sipped a small glass of red wine from her father's wine store, while she soaked. Laid back in the steaming water, Molly thought about the meal she was going to serve the next day and felt confident it would all turn out well. She looked forward to playing host and having someone to talk to who wasn't in her mind, or over the radio.

She read avidly of the developing friendship between Ishmael and the harpooner Queequeg ahead of setting sail on what Ishmael thinks will be an ordinary whaling trip but will be far from that. Once again, she forced herself to stop reading, knowing if she did not, she would finish the book in a single sitting, or two at most. By ten, she wearily carried her Tilley lamp to her bed and was asleep within minutes.

****

In the morning, Molly doused the lamp, grabbed the binoculars, and went out onto the balcony to do her usual check for boats in distress. The sun was shining, but she noticed way off to the North, a long line of clouds on the horizon, though the waters were calm and the usual shade of blue. The reefs were clear of shipwrecks, as per usual, and to her joy, the family of whales were back basking and jumping. One was a huge monster of the deep, so graceful for one so large, repeatedly coming all the way clear of the ocean to come crashing down, raising a mini tidal wave radiating outward. Through the viewfinders, she could see the barnacles encrusted on its flanks, and she smiled in delight at its antics. *How can they get so far out of the water when they are so big, and weigh so much?* She wondered.

Once her visual search of the surrounding waters was complete, she went back inside. The windows and prism didn't require cleaning, so she topped up the tank of fuel, checked the wicks, and left the watch room, knowing her daily tasks upstairs could be ticked off her to-do list.

Molly found herself skipping down the steps to her room, where she hastily put on her day clothes, intending to clean up, and put on something more suitable for receiving guests later. In the kitchen, she made a pot of tea and an omelet filled with some of the leftover salt pork, onions, tomato, and grated cheese, and read two more pages of her book while she ate.

At ten, she radioed in her report, and after she finished, Rachel said, “Molly, we think you need to batten down the hatches, there is a storm heading your way, and it looks like a big one, over.”

Her first thought was of disappointment that it might mean her visitors wouldn’t come, rather than any fear for her safety. “When will it arrive, do you know, over?”

“The best estimates vary from between sometime during the night, or early tomorrow morning. Mr. Harpington has asked me to go through some things with you, Molly, as it’s your first storm alone there, please take notes, over.”

“Pencil at the ready, Rachel, fire away, over,” she replied, glad the storm still might allow her guests to come for a while. She had intended to carry water down to the vegetable patch later, that was one less job to do with rain coming, which was more good news.

“All right, most importantly, you should not leave the lighthouse in inclement weather, this is a ruling now, especially after what happened to your father. This storm looks to be quite a big one, so you should make sure you have sufficient fuel for a week inside with you, is that clear, over?”

“A week it is, Rachel, that’s what I’ve been doing anyway, as my dad did before me. Is the forecast that the storm will last for that long, over?”

“Three days, four maximum for this time of year, but it always pays to be prudent. So, to be clear, this means no trips to your vegetable patch, the jetty, or anywhere else. Make sure you have enough supplies inside. I’ve been told to make sure I have impressed this upon you, Molly, over.”

Understandable, she thought, *especially considering the circumstances that brought me here.* “Receiving you loud and clear, no leaving the lighthouse until the mighty tempest has passed, for any reason. Anything else, Rachel, over?”

“Yes, during times of low light, typically during a heavy storm, leave the light burning to aid any ships out in it. It means you will need more fuel stores kept in the watch room. The rule is: when in doubt, leave the light burning. That could conceivably mean you use three times the amount of fuel as normal per day, over.”

Molly nodded, it made sense, *better bring some more drums up, just in case*. “Okay, I understand, Rachel, over.”

“The last item, please make sure you radio in twice a day, at ten and four. Mr. Harpington is concerned and wants to know you are safe. He also says if you do not adhere to these rules, he will have to relieve you, over.”

“Thank him for his concern, please tell him not to worry, I won’t break the rules, I won’t leave the lighthouse, I will keep the light burning all day if the weather is gloomy, and I will radio in twice a day, over.

“I will pass that along, Molly. Stay safe, and I will talk to you in the morning, over and out.”

Molly sat back in the chair and marveled at her calmness. She had matured a lot in the last few days, she realized. Alone, on an island, with a storm coming, and she felt calm about it. Back in Perth, she flinched at a clap of thunder, and almost screamed with every flash of lightning, but now she wasn't concerned. She understood their concern for her wellbeing, and the threat of replacement if she broke the rules. Doing so would not just mean her being fired, but her father would be out of a job, too, and she couldn't allow that to happen. So, she was determined to enjoy the day, knowing she would be cooped up as of tomorrow. She had to prepare.

She changed frequency, and pressed the button on the side of the microphone, "*Morning Dawn*, this is Forbes Light, do you read, over?"

"Yeah, I hear you, Forbes. Good morning, Molly, and how are you on this fine day, over?"

"I'm feeling tickety-boo, thanks, Derek. I'm told there's a storm coming and just wondered if you were still stopping by today, over."

"Yep we are. We started early today to allow more time, so I hope to be there around one. It's a bloody big storm coming by the looks, but it won't hit before midnight, so Mikey and I will still visit, as planned. Are you going to be all right on your own, Molly? Mikey has offered to stay and keep you company if you're worried, over."

He didn't click the microphone off quickly enough, and she heard him guffawing. She shook her head, his gentle ribbing was relentless, but she still knew the more fuss she made, the worse it would get. "I will manage just fine, thank you very much. Did you see

Dad last night, over?"

"I did, and he's doing all right, but climbing the walls with boredom, and he is worried about you, over."

Well, once you see how I'm going gangbusters here on my own, you can report back he's got nothing to worry about. I've put all of his writing stuff in a box; if you would be so kind as to drop it all off for him. He can do some work on the book, that should give him something to do, over."

"Can do. See you around one, Molly, over and out."

****

As the radio conversation ended, two hundred and twenty-nine miles away, on William Street in Perth, a brown Chevrolet pulled up into a loading zone. A young man named Hank Drage, with chestnut-colored short, curly hair was in the driving seat, and he kept the motor running while nervously looking around. From the back seat, two men got out, both carrying large ex-navy haversacks as they walked across the pavement. They were dressed for winter, wearing long coats and woolen beanie caps, and gloves. As they stepped through the door of the Commonwealth Bank, as one they jerked down their beanies to reveal the caps were ski-masks and completely obscured their hair coloring and faces.

From the bags, they simultaneously yanked out sawn-off shotguns and separated from each other. *"This is a hold up, everyone stand still and no one will get hurt,"* one shouted. To reinforce the order, he fired his gun at the ceiling, which brought down a cloud of plaster around him, which would be comical if the situation wasn't so dangerous. Amid screams from the customers the other robber screamed, *"Get down on the floor now."* He waved the shotgun from person to person as they scurried to lay down.

The man who fired into the ceiling pumped another shell into the chamber then tossed his bag toward the other, who deftly caught it one-handed. He sprinted to the first teller, threw one sack over the barred barrier, and said in a gruff voice, "Fill it and pass it along." He walked briskly to teller number four, which had a closed sign on the counter, and did the same with the second bag.

Mable Dorrington had worked at the bank for twenty years and had never been involved in a robbery. She was a senior teller, which was why on that day, it was her job to make up the payroll wage packets for three hundred and eighty-five Jay-Col Manufacturing company employees.

Suddenly, an elderly guard rose to his knees when the robbers looked away from him and clawed at the flap of the holster over his revolver. Both heard the scuffling noise, and as the guard yanked the gun free of its confine, the nearest robber turned and pulled the trigger of his shotgun. The blast hit the security guard in the chest, sending him jerking backward, arms flailing, and blood exploding through the front his tunic.

The man who fired the shotgun bent and picked up the dropped pistol and tucked it into his belt as if he had just swatted a fly while the customers screamed hysterically, creating a cacophony of noise. *"Let that be a lesson to the rest of you."* He snarled in a wheezing sounding voice.

At that moment, someone pressed the button of the alarm and the building reverberated with the harsh sound of a ringing bell.

"Move, move, move," the masked man nearest the counter shouted while aiming his gun through the bars at the tellers while the second man covered the people sprawled on the marble floor.

In the car outside with its engine still idling at the curb, Hank heard the shot, and then the bell, and suddenly realized he had never felt more scared in his life. He knew the second gunshot meant most likely they had killed someone. At the rehearsals, when they discussed the possibility, Nick shrugged while smiling at Barry, as if to say anyone stupid enough to test their resolve and try to stop them would regret it. Neither seemed too worried about taking lives.

It all sounded so easy and straightforward when the two seasoned criminals convinced Hank to be the driver for a one-off job which would get him enough money to follow his dream of becoming a professional speedway driver and buy a boat big enough to run a charter operation for deep-sea fishing in the racing offseason.

They had heard of him through a mutual acquaintance they told Hank when they introduced themselves to him in the public bar of the Busselton Hotel. At heart, Hank was a simple country-boy, who loved life and driving speedway cars around local tracks on weekends, and one day hoped to break into the big time. A bank robbery seemed like such a good idea at the time, an easy way to make the kind of money he needed to kick start his dream of international motor sport stardom. But he never seriously considered the possibility someone would die, and by proxy, he would then be jointly responsible for the death.

The two men were from Melbourne, and they told Hank they did that sort of bank robbery twice a year in different cities around Australia. “We’re straight in and straight out, three minutes tops. We go on a Friday when they are making up the payrolls, and your take will be thirty to fifty thousand, cash; easy money,” they assured him in turn, though Nick did most of the talking.

After the gunshots and alarm, he wanted to drive away and leave them to their fate, but if he did, and they didn’t get caught, they would hunt him down and kill him. They warned him of that eventuality if he lost his nerve and left them high and dry. Barry said even though they might get locked up, they had associates and family, who would avenge them, and Hank believed they were telling the truth. The plan was simple; they would stay at Hank’s house in Busselton, drive to Perth on the day in his car, steal another from a busy car park and use that for the robbery. In and out in three minutes, then swap cars back at the car park, and go back to Hank’s house where they would stay for one week until the fuss died down. They needed a local driver, who knew the streets and could drive fast, in case there was a silent alarm, and the cops turned up. When the waiting period was up, Nick and Barry would go back to Melbourne, leaving Hank with a full one-third share, they promised. Hank could buy the boat of his dreams and fund his racecar team for years to come, including a tilt at a US title. It all seemed so easy, but sitting nervously in the car, made him realize he had been stupid, and thoughtless.

He sat in the Chevrolet, frightened and biting his thumbnail, feeling sick that someone had been shot. He wished he had said no to joining them. At the time, though, he knew that if he refused after they told him of the plan, they wouldn't hesitate to murder him to keep him quiet.

He heard another blast. His nerve crumbled, and he was about to drive away when the two men came running out of the bank. In six bounded paces, they were at the car, yanked the door open, tossed the bags and shotguns in, then dived onto the back seat. "Drive, drive, drive," Nick yelled, then laughed. Hank gunned the motor, and with wheels fishtailing the car down the street, and rear passenger door flapping, the car sped out into the traffic, and away. The sight of the bank and the people who came running out receded in the rear-view mirror.

****

Molly raced around and got all her jobs done within an hour. She brought sufficient fuel up to the watch room, visited the vegetable patch, and cleaned up in readiness for her guests. By twelve, the fillets were steaming, the potatoes were boiling, and she felt a nervous excitement in the pit of her stomach. There was a lovely odor permeating through the lighthouse, and her mouth was salivating at the thought of eating the pie a little later.

She had a record going on her father's wind-up gramophone, an orchestra playing some Mozart, and she hummed along as she worked. She set the table and had a bottle of beer cooling in the fridge with two glasses for the men at the ready.

Molly had worked all morning tirelessly. She

cleaned, tidied, brought a mountain of firewood in for the stove, made sure the water tank was full, and every other job she could think of. Molly was confident that once the storm hit, she would not need to leave the lighthouse, as instructed, save for visits to get eggs from the chicken nesting boxes. As that was less than a dozen paces from the front door, she didn't think it applied.

Periodically, she went up to the watch room and looked around with the binoculars. She told herself it was to keep an eye on the approaching storm front and not to keep watch for *Morning Dawn*, yet there was no denying she felt a growing sense of excitement as one o'clock drew closer. The band of clouds didn't seem to be getting nearer, but she noted the shade of gray they were earlier seemed a touch darker, blotchier somehow, yet it still hugged the horizon. *I'm imagining things*.

At her twelve-thirty visit, finally, she saw the unmistakable shape of her guest's boat, carving its way through the waves, still some distance away, but making a beeline for the gap in the reef.

Perfect timing, she thought and raced back down the spiral staircase to the kitchen. Her fish pie stood resting on the benchtop in a glass casserole dish. Its mashed potato top had been layered and forked, with a smattering of grated cheese to help it brown. She opened the oven door, and slid the dish onto the middle rack, then took one last look around to make sure everything was neat and tidy.

The breeze was stiffening, though the sky was still blue as she walked down the path toward the dock to meet her visitors. If she didn't know the forecast, she would have no idea there was a massive storm coming.

The cloud band still stuck to the horizon, though now it was definitely taking on a darker, more forbidding color. She felt a shudder as she realized the last time a big storm came through Forbes it gave her father a broken leg as a gift. That would not happen to her, as she had no intention of leaving her sanctuary.

She arrived at the jetty as the *Morning Dawn* rounded the headland inside the reef and turned resolutely toward her. She took a hand from her jacket pocket and gave a little wave to Mikey, who stood on the bow, rope held in a loop. She couldn't see Derek in the wheelhouse as the sun was glinting off the glass, but she assumed he could see her, so her wave was to both men. A sudden long drawn out wail from the foghorn confirmed he had, and she giggled as Mikey jumped in fright at the sudden noise.

Molly marveled at how effortlessly the skipper guided the huge boat against the small jetty without so much as the slightest jolt. Mikey stepped across the gap and quickly tied off the bow rope, then with the ghost of an embarrassed grin, walked in front of her to the cockpit to secure the stern. The engine was turned off, and she realized she was watching two men who worked like a well-oiled machine and had done the same maneuver many times before, but Molly still found it impressive.

"Hi, Mikey," she said warmly with her best smile to show how happy she was to see them.

He acted schoolboy like, as he looked from the boat to her, then back to the *Morning Dawn* again. "Hi, Molly, you look good." With that, he stepped back into the cockpit, busy with the chore of making sure everything was secure, though Molly thought it was to get away from her too.

She stifled a grin when he had his back to her. *I look good?* She questioned. *I look no such thing, but what a lovely thing to say.* It was true she had washed her hair during her bath the night before, and she brushed it till it shone that morning, but she wore denim jeans, sensible shoes, a brown pullover jumper and over that a long anorak jacket with fluffy hood, which granted wasn't up, but she couldn't accept she looked good by anyone's definition. *Oh dear, I think Derek was right, he does like me.*

Derek strolled out of the cabin, with two muslin cloth bags in his hands. "Hey Molly, how're you doing? Young Mikey hasn't shut up about you all week; I swear if you give him a kiss hello, he will faint."

Out of the corner of her eye, she saw Mikey suddenly become even busier, but she noticed his ears look bright red from behind, so she knew he was blushing. She shook her head. "Hi Derek; it's good to see you, please stop having a go at Mikey; you're embarrassing the poor lad."

"No way, I can't do that; I'm having way too much fun." He climbed out of the boat, one hand holding the bags and the other on one of the railings. "Here you go, present for you, lass. What with the storm coming I thought you could do with some fresh meat, there's a leg of lamb in one bag, and a couple of good size crayfish in the other, careful they're still alive. The crayfish that is, not the lamb." He cackled with laughter at his humor.

"Aww, Derek, that's so kind of you. Thank you very much." She delighted in seeing it was his turn to blush. "I've cooked lunch for us, and I have to admit, cooking is not my forte, so I'm very nervous about it."

"We've been at work since five a.m., lass, you could make soup out of my old socks, and so long as you serve it with a bread roll, it would taste good."

She smiled as Mikey joined them. "Oh, I think it should taste a bit better than old sock soup, at least I hope it does."

Together, they headed off up the track to the lighthouse, with Molly between the men. They chatted about things in general, such as the weather, that day's catch; which Derek said was a good one, and how she was coping being alone so much.

When they stepped inside, the smell of the pie hit them all at the same time. "Yep," Derek said, "that smells a lot better than sock soup," which made Molly's heart soar.

She took her jacket off and hung it on one of the hooks on the wall, and waited while the men did the same, then she led the way up the spiral staircase. Halfway up, she had a sudden thought that in part thrilled her, and part shocked. She felt the unmistakable stare of Mikey directly behind and below her, looking at her denim-clad bottom from inches away. Then it was her turn to blush as she knew there was nothing she could do about it other than keep walking upward. Being a nurse, she was aware when patients looked at her in a leering lustful way, but at least Mikey was shy and innocent, not like dirty older men in hospital beds who made her feel like a burlesque dancer.

Molly settled them at the dining table, and poured them a glass of beer, then got busy in the kitchen. She had earlier part cooked some vegetables, and she put the saucepan back over the heat to warm them through.

Mikey asked her what she found to do with her time, and she listed her chores, her fishing expeditions, and her daily walks around the island. She even told them of, what felt like to her, her secret cave, where she sometimes took a lunch break.

"You know, Molly," Derek said, in a hesitant voice, "I'm not sure if I should tell you this, but back when they built the light on Forbes, one of the workers discovered a skeleton in that cave. No one knows how long the poor soul had been there, he must have washed ashore from a shipwreck, and there he stayed until he died."

"Oh, that's so sad. Well, at least he had a beautiful spot to end his days," she replied. Molly recalled her first day there when she had wondered about a shipwrecked sailor stuck in there. *Nothing more than a coincidence*, she told herself.

"Did you not feel a presence in there, Molly?" Mikey asked.

She shook her head, then bent to take the fish pie from the oven and set it on the benchtop, "No, I don't give a lot of credence to ghost stories."

"I hope you never do, lass, but we seamen respect the dead, and the spirits they sometimes leave behind. You'd do well to mind that, and don't go to the cave at night," Derek murmured.

Molly glanced up, unsure whether he was joking. He had often shown his irreverent side, but he looked deadly serious. A chill ran down her back, and she shivered. Damn the man; she felt suddenly shocked at the acid in her thoughts. *The cave is my secret happy place, and I won't let him spoil it for me.* "Derek, I am not scared of the boogeyman, and while I have no intention of being in the cave at night, I won't be frightened of old wives' tales about spooks and demons. I'm a nurse, and I've held many a person's hands as they've passed away, and I know there isn't much beyond, except heaven and hell, depending on your faith."

He grinned, showing the gap in the front of his teeth. "You are your father's daughter and no mistake; you've' got plenty of spunk, girl. 'Taint no need to snap my head off, all I can tell you is there is a tale to do with the cave, and over the years, I've learned to respect those who die at sea. No need to get your knickers in a knot."

She drained the vegetables and tipped them into a serving bowl, telling herself that these were her guests and to mind her temper. She could lose that at the drop of a hat, and Molly knew she was so typical of a redhead; she'd been told that on several occasions, even by her father.

Molly put on her oven mitts and carried first the bowl over, then the casserole dish with the fish pie in it. Then she grabbed the bottle of beer from the fridge and topped up their glasses then put it on the table. "Sorry, Derek, I didn't mean to snap; of course, everyone is entitled to their beliefs. Tell me the story you've heard of about the cave." She served the fish pie with a large spoon on each of their plates, then the mixed vegetables with another.

Both men looked at the meal, as the steam twirled upward and the room was filled with a wonderful smell. "For someone who says she doesn't cook well, this looks amazing," Mikey said as he picked up his knife and fork.

That brought a smile to Molly's face. She had to agree it smelled and looked terrific. "Derek, I'm not one for saying grace before a meal, but if you are, please feel free," she said.

"If my good wife were here, I would, but I'm happy to let it pass if you are." He took a forkful of the pie, and nodded his encouragement while he breathed in and out, trying to cool it down. He swallowed just as Mikey took his first mouthful, breathing deeply to cool it too. "Sensational, Molly, it's sensational. What fish is that?"

"It's the humble herring; half of it's smoked, the other steamed. I've become quite adept at catching them from the jetty. I'm so pleased you like it, seriously I'm not a good cook at all." She had to admit, though, as she took her first nibble, it was seriously tasty. *Must be the freshness of the fish,* she decided. *It couldn't possibly be my cooking skills because I don't have any.* "Now, Derek, please tell me this ghost tale."

Derek took a few more bites, alternating with sips of beer, and looked thoughtful as if deciding how to tell his story. "My family has been farming, woodcutting, and fishing in the southwest for five generations, and this story has been handed down, since 1875, when the light was built and commissioned. You must understand, construction didn't start till 1872, and landing the men and supplies here was no mean feat of seamanship. That gap in the reef we use now is not for the faint-hearted, and it was those brave souls who charted it using longboats while the mother ship stood off under anchor who found the way through. Of course, there was no dock to tie up to as there is now, so it was quite a job to unload the men and everything they needed to build what we now sit in, eating an excellent lunch." He raised his glass to Molly, who toasted back with her glass of water.

"It would have been a cold and dreary place to be here all those weeks, living in tents, putting up with dreadful weather and conditions back then. I'm told one or two of them went mad, but that's another story. A man named Leslie Hampton, who was the draughtsman and senior builder, complained about an unearthly wailing noise on the morning following the thirteenth night they were here. At first, the others thought he was going insane because no one else heard it, not at first, anyway. For a few days, he accused one of the workers who had an ax to grind with him, for playing some hideous sick joke on him and threatened to send him back to the mainland, despite his denials. Hampton's tent was apart from the others, as his station allowed, so it might have been understandable he heard a noise when the others didn't. The men tried to assure him that they were not trying to keep him awake by making weird noises in the night."

Derek took another mouthful of pie and licked his lips before sitting back in his chair, seemingly warming to his task of being a storyteller. "By the third week, Hampton by all accounts, was a shadow of the man he was before, and there were a few concerns for him. He couldn't sleep because he said, he would no sooner close his eyes, and he'd hear the noise again. On Hampton's order, his foreman Nigel Woodstock moved his tent alongside his, and that night, he too heard the screaming. They woke up two others and using lit torches, set off in the direction from where the noise emanated. They almost got to the water, but because they were above and behind the cave, and they only had torches, it was invisible to them, and they almost gave up. Then the noise came again, from just in front of them, and though they were to a man, scared out of their wits, they went down to the water's edge, and only then, found the mouth of the cave."

Again, Derek paused for effect and ate some more of the fish. "This is delicious, Molly."

She nodded, frantically. "Go on; what did they find?"

"Up against the back wall, on a large rock, there sat a skeleton. Whatever clothes he once wore, had long since rotted away. His flesh had been eaten from the bones by birds, or crabs, so there was no way to know how long he had been waiting, wailing away at night, trying to attract attention.

"The next morning, they placed the bones in a box and gave the poor man a Christian burial up near the bushes on top of the cliffs in a crevice. All the workers said a prayer for him, and interestingly, the wailing noise was heard no more. But I still think it's not the place to be at night, just in case."

Chapter 6

The Storm of the Decade

People who have lived for a long time in the south and southwest of Western Australia know there are three types of storms that can hit the area. This generalization includes summer cyclones and gale-force winter tempests of the most severe.

The first type is the kind that comes along reasonably regularly in winter. It can hit pretty much anywhere and anytime and was the kind of storm that took Malcolm's leg.

At the other end of the spectrum are storms which grace the area once in a hundred years and can be catastrophic with king tides bringing severe flooding.

Then there is the storm that comes on average, once every ten years. This can be destructive, lengthy, and can bring flooding, extensive damage to property, and death.

****

The first clap of thunder rattled the windows and woke Molly from her sleep around one-thirty in the morning. The noise was so loud and unexpected she screamed in shock and fright. Her terror intensified with the flash of lightning, which streaked through the small window above her bed. It bathed her in harsh light, brighter than that put out by the lamp up above in the watch room.

It was as if the storm front had crept up on tiptoes to Forbes Reef, and waited until Molly was fast asleep before unleashing its full fury. She thought, just for a moment, the lighthouse was shaking until she realized it was she who was trembling, not the building. Molly never felt so alone and so frightened in her life as at that moment.

****

Earlier in the afternoon, the three of them finished lunch and talked as if they had been friends for years. Even Mikey seemed to be more relaxed and at ease in her presence and complimented her several times on her cooking skills. Molly had to admit, it did taste good, and the evidence was that both men went back for seconds and there wasn't any leftover for her supper, but she didn't mind that.

Molly had fun serving her two new friends lunch, and she looked forward to the next Friday when they promised to visit again. She walked them back down to the dock around three thirty with Mikey carrying the box of her father's work. The men stood on the jetty and said their goodbyes. The threatening clouds were still a long way off, but the light was different somehow, and the breeze a little stronger, and Molly had no doubt the storm was coming.

"Molly," Derek said as Mikey climbed aboard with the box to get the boat ready. "This storm looks like a big one; you mind yourself out here alone. Don't go doing anything daft like your dad did, will you?"

She sighed. "No, Uncle Derek, I don't intend to leave the light for any reason. I'm fully stocked up, and I have strict instructions from the powers that be to stay inside, so trust me, that's where I'll be, no matter what."

****

Molly sat up in bed cringing, with the bedclothes wrapped around her as the thunder cracked furiously across the sky. She remembered her earlier promise to Derek and agreed; there was no way she was going outside the building with a storm directly overhead.

It's just a storm, calm down and grow up, Molly. She knew the lighthouse was sturdily built and wasn't going anywhere; it had stood for nearly eighty years and she was safe while inside. Just as her heart slowed back to normal, she heard the wailing noise for the first time.

She snapped her head up and listened to the sad, soulful sound which ebbed and flowed with the wind. *Someone is out there and needs my help*, she thought. Then she assured herself it wasn't; it couldn't be that. *It's just my imagination after that horrible story Derek told me of the skeleton in the cave. No one is outside, making that noise, it's the wind under the eaves, or howling through the lean-to.*

She had to check; she knew she had to. Her logical internal voice did not convince the more dominant panic-stricken side of her brain which assured her it was a ghost, or a shipwrecked sailor washed up on the reef, perhaps injured.

Molly thought it had been all well and good promising not to leave the safety of the building, but what if someone who needed medical assistance washed up on the island? It certainly sounded like that, or did it? Was it just the wind after all?

Molly threw the bedclothes off, turned up the

Tilley Lamp, and struggled to put her dressing gown on with trembling fingers. Part of her; a huge part of her, wanted to hide back under her blankets until the storm passed. *Surely it would be better in the morning? Why is everything so much more frightening in the dark of the night?* She asked herself.

There was a compromise, Molly realized with a grateful sigh. She could check the surroundings for anyone injured, and stay inside, well, kind of inside. Another flash of lightning lit up the room through the window, and an enormous clap of thunder rocketed across the sky directly overhead, traveling from left to right. Then she heard the rain. Maybe it had been raining before and she hadn't noticed, or possibly it started at that moment, but it sounded like huge drops were smashing onto the stone walls driven by gale-force winds.

Yet, with all the other noise going on, still, Molly could hear what sounded like someone screaming in pain. She suddenly had an image of what it must have been like for her father, out there, in a storm with a broken leg, screaming for help that wasn't going to come. "Well," she uttered in a stern voice, "If someone is out there, I *will* go and help them."

"And, Miss Molly, what of your promise not to leave the lighthouse for any reason?" she asked. Even to her, she could hear the fear, bordering on hysteria in her voice. Usually speaking aloud gave her comfort, but she was shocked at the sound of her nerve-wracked words. She cleared her throat, and began again, "If I go to the balcony on the watch room, I can probably see who is making that noise, and if someone is hurt, I'm sure Mr. Harpington won't object to my leaving to go and help. Isn't there some unwritten law of the sea that a mariner cannot refuse aid?"

"You're no a mariner," she replied in her father's Scottish brogue, and hearing her father's voice, albeit imagined, gave her comfort. "You're a young slip of a girl, minding the light. Your first duty is to yourself, and to keep the light going." She shook her head, choosing to ignore her father for the first time in her life, got up, and went downstairs.

Molly took the oilskin poncho, which was three sizes too big for her, from the hook near the entrance door and nearly dropped it. *It's so heavy,* she realized. Molly pondered whether to bother, but the sound of the torrential rain bucketing down outside made her understand if she did go out on the watch room balcony to check for someone in trouble, she would get drenched in seconds without it. Again, Molly considered going back to bed and not bothering, but then the wailing sound came again, if anything louder than before, which strengthened her resolve.

She put down the lamp and shrugged the weatherproof garment on over her top half. As if to taunt her, the moment her vision became obscured, another clap of thunder roared across the sky and made her jump. The night was rapidly approaching being the worst of her life; second only to the night she lost her mother in the air raid, though this was worse because she was here, living it, but had been in the country when her mother died alone when the bomb exploded.

Molly felt the weight of the world was on her shoulders wearing the poncho. She groaned, knowing she had to climb the spiral staircase having gained twenty pounds.

Before she could change her mind, she picked up her lamp and headed back up the stairs, determined to get her check done as quickly as possible, and get back to bed. *Perhaps the worst of the storm will be gone by morning*, she hoped.

Molly was panting by the time she stepped up into the watch room. She placed her lamp on the floor, then grasped her knees as she bent at the waist and took several deep breaths.

Molly looked out of the windows and saw an incredible sight. Forbes Reef was instantly lit up by three forks of lightning, which simultaneously streaked from the sky. They snaked across the darkened clouds and hit the reef and ocean all around her.

In the harsh, blinding flash, she could see the rain being driven at a forty-five-degree angle by the wind, and as the glare died down, it was replaced with the sweeping beam radiating outward from the light in the watch room.

"Wow, Molly, my girl, that is some sight," she uttered.

As her eyesight followed the beam, in the murky distance beyond the shoal, she could see the waves were mountainous as they rose and fell upon themselves to boil and bubble then rise again. It was as if the howling wind was stealing away the white caps from their tips to add to the torrential rain.

Molly no longer felt scared. The fear was replaced with awe and appreciation for nature's beauty and wrath. Her eyes followed the revolving ray of light, loving everything illuminated in its glow, as thunder crashed overhead again. This time it didn't make her jump. Molly realized she could no longer hear the wailing. *It was probably just the wind through the lean-to all along,* she thought.

A lightning fork flew from the clouds and disappeared into the heaving seas to her right. Then came another to her left. "Oh, my goodness," she exclaimed, "I'm so glad I'm here to see this; it's the most beautiful sight I've ever seen."

Molly felt warm wearing the oilskin and shrugged it off; it had become superfluous because she didn't need to go out on the balcony. Molly could see all she needed to from inside. And there was still no sound of screaming. For a moment she hoped that wasn't because whoever made the noise had died or passed into unconsciousness. *Nature's light show will show me all I need to see, especially with my binoculars,* she decided.

Molly unhooked the Weiss Glasses, strung the lariat around her neck, and raised them to her eyes just as another obliging explosion of light flooded out from a twin fork. Under the magnification, everything became more evident, and even more visually spectacular, as she scanned the three hundred and sixty degrees around the island. Using the recurring lightning flashes and rotating beam from beside her, Molly's vision was crystal clear in the harsh, stark black-and-white view.

Molly was diligent and pleased with her sense of responsibility as she studied every rock and crevice on the island and surrounding reef her from her vantage point. She paid particular attention to the rocks around the cave knowing full well she was only doing that because of the ghost story she'd heard over lunch. Once completed, Molly turned her attention to the reef, her gaze traversing across it slowly as she allowed for the waves to subside so she could see behind them when they receded. She took her time, enjoying the task, and had no idea how long her vigil lasted. When she finally lowered the binoculars, she was satisfied there was no one in trouble. There was no shipwrecked boat that had run aground, and no one lay injured on the rocks screaming for aid, so the wailing noise was nothing more than a trick of the wind.

After breathing a long sigh of relief, Molly turned and hung up the glasses. She realized she was no longer tired and made a spur of the moment decision to stay for a while longer.

Molly went back down to the kitchen, put the kettle on, and while she waited for it to boil, she carried the heavy oilskin back downstairs and hung it on the hook. As she did so, she heard the wailing once more, but it sounded different; as if whatever was making the noise knew it had lost the battle in luring her outside, so it no longer had the same intensity. "Yeah, go on you stupid sound, go back to where you came from," she murmured, then smirked as she headed back to the kitchen.

When she poured out her mug of tea Molly climbed back up to the watch room. She sat cross-legged in front of the floor to the ceiling glass door, leaned back against the mounting which was the mercury bath for the lamp. Molly stared out at the unbelievably beautiful sight of Mother Nature's full fury. She knew she was safe, she was under no threat whatsoever, and the thunder and lightning show from her point of view was spectacular.

She had long since finished her tea when she

thought perhaps it was time to leave the show. Her own call of nature was making itself known as Molly realized the tea she had drunk now required an outlet. Molly also thought she should get some sleep because she needed to make her radio schedule in the morning, for which she dared not be late.

Molly thought probably a storm as violent as she had been watching would blow itself out soon enough. She stood up and stretched her legs to ease the pins and needles, then took a long respectful bow toward the window. "Thank you for the entertainment," she whispered, then turned and headed back downstairs.

****

Molly glanced at the alarm clock as she climbed into bed; it was four fifteen. She didn't think she would sleep, but the next thing she knew, the same clock was ringing its welcome tone to get her up. The wailing hadn't returned to keep her awake, and as she lay there listening, it didn't come again, thankfully.

The wind and rain appeared just as powerful, but without the sound that had terrified her the night before. Maybe, the wind changed direction through the night? She wondered but didn't know for sure. Whatever the reason, she was delighted not to hear it and smiled as she remembered observing the sheer beauty of the lighting effects before she finally went to bed. *Good job I'm familiar with working night shifts at the hospital*, she thought, as she should by rights feel a lot more tired than she did.

She got up and got dressed, feeling very pleased for having got through the first night of a significant storm, and while yes, she acknowledged there was a time she had been frightened, she had got through it maturely. No doubt her father and Mr. Harpington would be proud of her if they had seen her in action.

As always, Molly's first job was to check for boats that had come to grief during the night. She was keen to do it; Molly wanted to see the storm in daylight, having enjoyed its fury during the night.

Molly glanced at the stairway window as she passed, which was running with rainwater rivulets; it looked very gray outside, so dim she decided to keep the light going. "When in doubt, don't let the light go out," she parodied Mr. Harpington's officious voice.

In the lamp room Molly again had a three-hundred and sixty-degree view. She marveled once more at what was going on around her. The ordinarily blue seas were ashen gray, and fiercely angry, rising and throwing up its whitecaps to be snatched away by the screaming winds. By the angle of the rain, Molly didn't think it was quite as strong as it had been earlier when she sat watching the flashing of the lightning forks. She realized since she woke up, she had not heard any thunder. *Well, at least that's something,* she thought as she reached for the binoculars.

She scanned the reef in an almost cursory fashion, having done so in minute detail just a short time before, and as she expected, saw nothing out of the ordinary. As she was about to go and make breakfast, something caught her eye way out in the ocean. It was just a speck, but the revolving light caught it momentarily. She had gone past the spot before her brain registered something was amiss, but when she went back to where she thought it was, it was either gone or was hidden by the mountainous waves. *What was it?* she wondered, *or did I imagine something?*

Molly kept watching, then saw a flash of orange before it disappeared again. *Hmm, what's the difference between flotsam and jetsam?* She shrugged and hung the glasses back up, not concerned; it just seemed to be something floating.

Molly skipped back downstairs to the kitchen; her first cup of tea for the day was calling her name. She poked and prodded the firebox on the stove and added more wood, then filled the kettle, still mulling over what she had spotted, and put it on the heat. If she recalled it right, jetsam was something thrown overboard, or from a wreck, while flotsam was something floating but not from a boat. She remembered seeing a pile of milk crates at the local deli once; they were bright orange. Maybe that's what I saw, a milk crate bobbing along, minding its own business, or perhaps it was a fisherman's marker buoy from a cray pot.

The time slipped by as she made breakfast of eggs on toast, which used the last of her bread, so she decided today would be the day to bake a new loaf. She tidied her bed; her nursing training forbade her to leave it messy. As she worked, Molly decided dinner that night would be the roast leg of lamb, thanks to Derek's kindness. There would, of course, be lots left over, but she could think of many uses for it. She could have it with grilled cheese on toast, make a casserole of some and have it with rice, or even have it sliced with fried eggs and chips. That night, Molly decided, she would have it with roast potatoes and fresh vegetables. But what to do with the crayfish Derek had given her? *When will I use them? Sometime, I suppose.* Derek had said that kept in the coldest part of the refrigerator, they would go into a state of hibernation for at least a few days, or even weeks. So, they should be fresh to cook in three or four days, which should see off the last of the lamb.

At ten o'clock on the dot, Molly treadle powered up the radio and checked in with Rachel, who seemed pleased to hear from her. "How was the night, Molly?" she asked, "The blooming storm is ferocious here, causing damage all over the place. People lost their roofs, fences were blown down, and all sorts, over."

"Oh, Rachel, it was magnificent here, thunder right overhead, and the lightning was fantastic. It was the most spectacular night of my life. I sat up for a few hours and thoroughly enjoyed it, over," she replied, smiling again at the memory.

"You mean you weren't scared, over?"

"Oh, I admit I was at first when it woke me up. There was this weird screaming noise, so I went up to the watch room, just in case someone was hurt and washed up on the reef, but it was just the wind. Then once I was up there, surrounded by the lightning, it was magnificent, over," she replied with total sincerity.

"I'll take your word for it. I stayed huddled up in bed with my husband, hoping we wouldn't lose our roof, which, fortunately, we didn't. Our dog Max suffered badly. He wouldn't stop howling all night, which didn't help us get any sleep, over."

Molly smiled. She had no idea about the circumstances of Rachel's private life, but she had assumed from the sound her voice she was young and single. "You know, Rachel, I rather think if I had been back in Perth, in a house, I would have felt the same. The nurse's quarters at Royal Perth are in one big solid building, so I dare say it wouldn't have bothered me in there, but in a house, it would have been very frightening. I felt safe in the lighthouse, though, and I'm glad you didn't suffer any damage, over."

"Mr. Harpington will be pleased with your report, but he did ask me to remind you of the rules of being in a lighthouse during a bad storm. I don't think I need to remind you how serious it is though, do I, over?"

Molly raised her eyes to the ceiling, "No, Rachel." She bit her tongue as she realized she was answering in a sarcastic sing-song voice. "I've no intention of going outside in this weather. I'm well stocked up, and I will ride it out. Any idea how much longer it's going to last, over?"

"Yes, bad news, I'm afraid. The Bureau of Meteorology says two more fronts are coming behind this one, so this is going to continue two to three more days, over."

"Well, it's a good excuse for me to get my studying done, which I've been putting off, and I'm rather enjoying a book at the moment. I will have time to finish it, over."

"All right then, stay safe, and I will talk with you this evening. Over and out," Rachel said.

"Bye, Rachel. Forbes out."

She put the microphone down, stopped pedaling when the pointer touched the green band of the gauge, and sat back, to think. There would be no point calling Derek; he would not be out in this weather. He said as much the day before during his visit.

Something was niggling in the back of her mind, and with the spare time she now had, she tried to think what it was. Then it came to her. "That flotsam can't be a milk crate; it had to be bigger than that, surely, Molly?" she asked out loud, still finding comfort in the sound of her voice.

The orange crates she remembered seeing held twenty-four one-pint bottles. Yes, they were orange, but when she held out her hands to prove the sizing, it dawned on her that at a distance from her to where she had seen it bobbing between the waves, it would be considerably larger than that. The Weiss binoculars were excellent, but no way could they magnify to that extent. And another thing, she thought, even if the size was correct, would a milk crate stick out of the water that high? Wouldn't it be more submerged?

She leaped to her feet, unsure why, but she felt concerned she had made a mistake. Molly bounded up the stairs, taking two steps at a time, her mind racing. The direction had been almost directly into the wind; therefore, *it should be quite a bit closer to the reef by now,* she thought.

She stepped into the watch room and snatched up the glasses and stopped in her tracks. "Yikes, Molly, that's no milk crate, you idiot. That's a bloody inflatable dinghy."

There, only two hundred and fifty to three hundred and fifty yards from the outer reef, heading straight for her island, rode the unmistakable shape of a covered orange life raft. Molly jerked the binoculars to her eyes and brought the dancing, weaving craft into focus. That was no mean feat because no sooner did she have it in view; the waves would snatch it away again. After three minutes, it was giving her a headache trying to look at it with maximum magnification as it bobbed and weaved between waves. Her eyes became tired and watery trying to keep up with it, so she lowered the binoculars again. As far as she could make out, there was no one inside it. At least, if there was they were not sitting up that she could see, there was no sign of life at all. The problem with that was, there was some sort of tented roof over it, so Molly couldn't see inside to be one hundred percent sure if it was empty.

"What the heck am I supposed to do about this?" The first thing to decide was whether to report it or not, and so began a two-sided conversation on what Rachel or Mr. Harpington might say if she did:

"An empty life raft, Molly, and what do you want us to do about it in the worst storm for the last God knows how many years?"

"Well, I don't know if it's empty, I just can't see anyone in it."

"Don't you think if there were someone there, they would be waving to get your attention?"

There was the crux of the matter. *Yes,* she thought, *if it is manned, knowing they were approaching a reef and a lighthouse, they would surely be trying to get help before they were smashed to smithereens on a rocky shore by the massive waves*. Then there was the other issue; *if there are people on board, what can anyone do about it? There is no time for a boat to get here, even if a captain was mad enough to try. It's a treacherous reef in good weather, let alone in this storm.*

She did have her boat tied up at the dock, but to go out in this weather with her lack of seamanship skills would be madness. And, even if she could navigate out through the passage, which she seriously doubted she could do even on a calm day, there wouldn't be enough time to get to the dinghy in trouble. It was doomed. Then, the final nail in the boat's coffin dawned on her; she had been forbidden to leave the lighthouse, so to do so for what looked very much like an empty life raft, she would be fired if anything went wrong. If she lost her job, so would her dad, and she could not permit that.

"Molly, my girl, stop worrying. It's a blooming empty boat, and there is nothing constructive you can do about it, so go and make a cup of tea, then come up and watch its demise."

That sounded very harsh, but realistically Molly knew it was correct; there *was* nothing she could do about the situation, no matter how much she might want to. She raised the glasses again and tried to see any movement inside, but it was impossible. She hung them up and went back down to pour her tea.

Within minutes she was back watching the slow, rag-tag, violent approach of the dinghy. As she stood and sipped from her mug, she mused what she was doing was akin to people slowing down when they drove past a car accident. *Sometimes you can't help but watch something potentially bad happening*, she thought. Urged on by the wind, riding the waves like a demented surfer, the boat edged ever nearer to its destruction on the rocky outcrops along the reef.

"Oh, hang on, just a cotton-picking minute, is that…?" She put the mug on the floor and grabbed the glasses again. "Go, little boat, go; you can do it, go, go, go!"

Molly had noticed the subtle change in the waves ahead of the life raft, which, she realized, must be the opening in the reef they had brought the *Morning Dawn* through. It looked to her, miracle upon miracle, as if the dingy was heading for it. Could it be that lucky? “Oh, I do hope so, c’mon, little boat, you can do this!” she cried with glee.

It was like watching a one-horse race as the craft careered around, rising and falling as it was herded forward by the constant force ten gale toward the impossibly tiny gap in the reef and potential safety. Thirty yards, then twenty-five, closer and closer, dipping and diving, sometimes disappearing from sight entirely, then reappearing as it was blown to the top of a wave.

“No, no, noooooo,” she wailed as it seemed to change course and headed for a prominent rock half-exposed when the waves receded. That was the port-side marker, she knew, for the safe passage through purgatory, as Derek had named it, and it looked as if the boat was going to hit it head-on.

Molly realized she was sweating, and her knuckles were white with exertion holding the binoculars to her eyes, using all of her will power to help guide it to safe waters. “Come on, you bloody thing, sort yourself out, aim for the bloody gap!”

She gave a small laugh as she realized she had sworn twice in one sentence, which was most unlike her. In a flash of memory, she recalled her mother once threated to wash her mouth out with carbolic soap and water if she ever said a naughty word in her presence. “Sorry, Mum,” she whispered.

Five yards to go, and as if God reached down a helping hand, the little boat was picked up by a wave, and the wind pushed it spinning away from the rock. “Woohoo,” she yelled at the top of her voice. The life raft had entered the slightly less turbulent waves; maybe it did have a chance after all. The words less turbulent was, of course, a relative term, even in the channel it was rough that was true, but not quite as wild as outside. She gave a silent prayer; it could make it, but just then, the wave it was riding dropped, and the left-hand side hit an exposed rock. Molly winced as if she could feel the pain, but the inflatable hull survived and didn't burst on impact. Instead, the collision recoil sent the craft lurching out into the passage proper again, where the wind gusted once more and propelled it further toward where she imagined the middle to be.

When she was a child, one Christmas, she was given a gift of an inflatable snowman with a rounded base, which was as tall as she was. The idea was if she punched it, it would bounce away, then come back to be hit again. She and her best friend Doris used to play for hours laughing as they took turns thumping it. Strangely, as she watched the tiny boat, in the mountainous seas, she was reminded of the snowman, bobbing and weaving from side to side.

"C'mon, little feller, you can make it," she shouted, though why she was cheering an inanimate object to make it through the dangerous reef, unaided, was beyond her reasoning. Wherever the small boat had come from, it had made it this far, and it would be tragic if it were destroyed at the last hurdle.

The break in the reef acted like a funnel because suddenly, the raft shot forward; aided by the current and the wind. As it lurched to the left-hand side, something brown colored inside just for a moment caught Molly's eye. Now the boat was closer, and not jumping and jiving as much; she could see more detail. It looked to her as if the tiny boat had a tent-like roof over it, which was the same color as the hull. That had aided in its survival as it had not only kept the worst of the rain out but the flying spray from the waves as well, which helped keep it afloat. That was why she had been unable to see inside. With it jerking all over the place in the mountainous seas, the open flap had often been facing the wrong way. Now it was closer; with the aid of the glasses she could see through the opening, and just for a moment, before it had spun around once more, the gap faced the magnified view of the Weiss lenses. Molly thought she saw what looked like a large tree branch, which made no sense. Much more likely, she realized, it could be a human leg.

Before she had been sweating with the excitement and the thrill of hoping the dinghy would make it through the reef, now she felt ice cold with worry for fear if it didn't. Was someone inside, and if so, were they alive or dead? If they were alive, she might be forced to watch the occupant drown when it had come so close to safety.

It seemed to take forever, but in reality, it was only a few more minutes, and the little boat made it through the channel into the calmer waters on the inside of the reef. It was going to come ashore, fortunately not on the cliff side of the island where it would have been dashed to ruin, but on the rocky shore near the secret cave.

Once again, Molly was gifted a second view of underneath the tent-like covering, and then she saw what she thought of as a person's leg, wearing brown trousers. But then it could just as easily be a pile of rags, a parcel, an oar, or heaven knew what; but it was something.

Molly hurried back downstairs to the study. She was about to turn on the radio to tell Rachel about the raft when she stopped. Molly still faced the same dilemma; she couldn't report it until she had more information. Was the boat empty, and if it wasn't, was the person alive or dead? There had still not been any movement she could detect, she had to go and see, and if she had something to report, do it then. She nodded, that was the only plan that made sense; if the boat was empty, Molly could avoid telling the powers that be she had left the haven of the lighthouse, but if there were a survivor, surely they would understand, and she wouldn't be discharged for breaking her orders to stay put? Molly recalled one of her father's maxims that sometimes it was better to seek forgiveness than permission, and that determined her decision.

Without a second thought, she went to her father's room and grabbed his medical bag, then down the spiral staircase to the entry hall. Outside, the wind howled, and the rain still fell in sheets that rattled the door and windows, so she needed the oilskin, as heavy as it was. But, she wondered, what if someone is alive in the dinghy? She would need something warm and dry for them, too, but there was only the one oilskin coat.

She shrugged, then put on her anorak and hood, then put the oilskin over that. She would get quite hot walking over the rocks, but better than being cold and wet. Molly kicked off her slippers and stepped into her hiking boots. Lastly, she pulled on her sheepskin mittens, and she was ready to go.

Molly opened the heavy oak door, and it was almost ripped from her grasp by the screaming wind. She dropped the bag so she could use both hands to stop it being torn from its hinges, then stepped outside, and shouldered it closed. The rain teemed down in sheets as Molly pulled the hood over her head and tightened the drawstring to hold it in place. She picked up the bag once more and headed off into the wind, toward the cave.

Molly knew the way well enough, which was a good thing because she needed to keep her head tilted down to watch her footing. Visibility was dim at best, though each time the light rotated, she got a view of the terrain before her in its shaft of brightness. She had no intention of breaking a leg and ending up like her father, so she slowly stepped from rock to rock, as the gale buffeted her, and the endless rain tried to drown her. She thought she was lucky the wind was head-on. No doubt, it would have hit her father from the side, which caused him to lose his balance. Though it was close to midday, the light was poor with the sun behind thick gray and black cloud cover. Periodically, the illumination from the beam swept over her as it turned three-hundred-and-sixty degrees before coming back around again. The sky was twenty different shades of gray, though fortunately, there hadn't been any thunder and lightning for a while. Molly wasn't sure she would have had the courage to make the walk if there had been.

The medical bag wasn't heavy, but the wind and weight of her overcoat made it feel worse than it was, so she frequently changed it from hand to hand. Molly thought she was well over halfway when she was deafened by an enormous clap of thunder directly overhead. It was as if the gods wanted to taunt her having lulled her into a false sense of security. "Oh, for goodness sake, give me a break, will you. I'm trying to save a life," she cried in frustration when her heartbeat slowed back to normal.

As if her plea was answered, the storm decreased, even the wind dropped a little, and she grinned under her hood, and carried on more determined to get to the life raft, and then back to the lighthouse as quickly as possible. Suddenly she stopped in her tracks when a thought hit her like a personal clap of thunder. *What if it's a dead body in the life raft, what the heck do I do then? Get it out and radio it in,* was the answer. But that could be problematic too, she realized, as she argued with herself in the comfort of her mind, while the rain poured around her. *Then I must admit I left the lighthouse, and I risked Dad's job for a dead body. Yeah, but you didn't know it was a blooming corpse did you, assuming it is, of course.*

"Molly, get your act together, you don't know anything right now, so let's check out the boat, and worry about what we find when we find it, all right?" She shook her head at the absurdity of the situation and started her trek again. *And to think*, she mused as she jumped across the gap between two boulders, *only a few days ago I was snug and warm, working twelve-hour shifts at the hospital, and just look at me now.*

But then, Molly realized, she couldn't remember a time when she had felt so happy and satisfied as she had since moving to Forbes. She would be disappointed when her time was up, and her father took back the reins, and she headed back to Perth to resume being a nurse. Another thought hit her, like a slap in the face, which made her stop once again. She had always wanted to not only live up to her father's expectations;

she had wanted to follow in his footsteps. That was a revelation, like a light turning on in her mind. She loved him with every fiber of her being, admired, respected, and wanted to be like him. He was a doctor—she became a nurse with ideals of medical school, even though for women, it was practically impossible. He moved to a lighthouse, and she followed him and found peace and harmony in doing so, as she did when she took over from him. No matter she did it to save his job, and, in the confines of her mind, bemoaned doing it, once she took up the post, there was no denying, she loved it. "You are your father's daughter," she said aloud, and smiled at the truism, then started again across the rocks.

Molly was panting from exertion when she crossed the rise and could see the ocean, and the raft bobbing thirty yards from the shore. She looked up, and a rain squall hit her full in the face, driven by the wind which nearly knocked her off her feet, yet she smiled. Soon she would know if anyone was alive in the boat, or if she had been on a fool's errand.

Chapter 7

The Man in the Dinghy

Molly reached the rocky shore, where waves as tall as she was crashed at its edge and shot up shards of white foam spray to be flung in her face by the wind. The life raft ducked and dived only a few yards away and was coming closer by the minute. She propped the medical bag between two large boulders, determined to keep it from being washed away in the angry surf, then wondered what she could do next.

The dinghy's opening in the tent-like awning faced away from her, no doubt acting as a wind tunnel, which helped drive the boat ahead of it, but that meant she still had no idea if anyone was inside or not. She cupped her hands around her mouth. *"Hello, is anyone there?"* she screamed, trying to be heard above the howling wind, but she feared she wasn't.

There was nothing, no sound or movement from within, but the boat was coming closer, and she had to decide what she would do when it hit the rocks at her feet. *Try to grab it and pull it ashore, I suppose, then look inside the damn thing.*

"C'mon little boat, you've made it this far, don't fail me now," Molly murmured.

The next moment the rounded bow hit a protruding rock, and the wind driving from the rear nearly tipped it end over end. Without a thought for herself, Molly took five steps into the icy cold waves and grabbed the ropes strung along the side. She tried to pull it into safety. *"If anyone is in there, get out, I can't hold this forever,"* she screamed, as loudly as she had ever shouted in her life.

The next few seconds were frantic as Molly tried to hang on to the boat, while the wind and sea frantically tried to rip it from her grasp. Meanwhile the water had seeped through her lower clothes chilling her to her very soul. Bravely, Molly decided to try and pull the dinghy by the side up onto the safety of the rocks, but the storm and breakers had other ideas. She felt something substantial inside the hull shift its weight toward her, which upset the balance, and the wind got underneath the flat bottom and lifted it. Molly felt unable to stop herself falling backward as the boat reared up, and the undertow snarled her feet. The next thing she was aware of was something heavy rolling inside, then hitting her upper body, though cushioned by the inflated hull. The boat rose in the air, and the shift knocked the breath from her lungs. The momentum sent her backward into the freezing cold waves as they broke on the rocky shore.

She saw stars and felt dazed both by whatever hit her chest and the impact to the back of her head on the rocks. Suddenly, Molly was pinned by the dinghy, which the wind flipped upside down on top of her. Something inside the hull was extraordinarily heavy, which pinned her down. Another monstrous breaker came through and pushed the life raft down on top of her even harder. But it also streamed over her, getting inside the oilskin and washing over her face. Molly choked and tried to catch a breath, but only sucked in more ice-cold seawater. *Oh my God, I'm going to drown!* She panicked and desperately attempted to shift the weight on top of her so she could sit up. Through the thin roof of the canvas canopy, she realized it was a body lying on her, and she put both hands on it and shoved as hard as she could. Just then, the wave receded, and she spat the water out and took a deep lungful of air, which made her cough, and she heard the unmistakable sound of a man groaning.

She found more strength, and frantically pushed him again. *"Wake up and move, damn you, you will drown us both if you don't,"* she screamed and was rewarded with another deep soulful groan.

Then the next wave hit, and Molly realized the mistake she had been making; she shouldn't try to push the raft back down her body, against the force of the sea and wind, she should use its momentum to help it up and over her head. Before the surf covered her face once more, she took a deep breath, wriggled her body into the stones, lifted her knees, and placed her feet flat on the ground. Then, Molly used her hands to half shove and half roll the body backward, up and over her head with the incoming wave.

Just when she thought it wasn't going to work, and she would surely drown as freezing saltwater flowed over her face, the boat and man inside it suddenly lurched off her chest, over her head, and she was free.

Molly struggled to sit up and get to her feet, gasping and spitting out saltwater, but her troubles weren't over. The receding wave and undertow now tried to reclaim the boat and pull it back out to sea. She felt the weight against her back as it shoved her headfirst into the turbulent waves face down. Her oilskin ballooned out and acted like a sail working in reverse. Full of water, it weighed her down, and relentlessly pulled her into deeper water.

Molly was in trouble, and she realized her actions in the next few seconds would determine whether she lived or died. She forced herself not to panic, but to act calmly and get out of the dire situation she faced. Suddenly, miraculously, Molly was in the clear again when the weight of the boat passed over her and headed back out to sea. Molly struggled to find the rocky bottom with her feet and stand up. She burst free of the surface and took another deep, life-giving breath of air. The orange boat was out of her reach, but she knew the wind would soon blow it back to her if she didn't get out of its path. Her first concern was to get out of the water before she was dragged further with the severe undertow.

As she turned, another wave hit and knocked her off her feet, but it helped because it pushed her back toward the shore and shallower water. She struggled to her knees, then feet to stand unsteadily, and that was when she saw the man's body face up in the water, moving groggily.

She splashed six staggering paces over to him and gripped the left arm of his brown windcheater jacket, jerking him with all her strength. He was lying in barely six inches of water, and she thought she could get him out, but the wave took that moment to decide to recede and began pulled him back into its deathly clutches.

"Oh my God, will this nightmare never end? Wake up and help me!" she screamed while trying to shake him awake and stop his body, being dragged into deeper waters. The wash flowed between her legs and over his head and filled his mouth, but thankfully it was enough to rouse him. He coughed and spluttered, kicked his legs, and, as if drunk, he tried to stand up.

Molly thought his feet found some purchase on the rocky bottom, and the pressure eased with his help. Together, they struggled out of the force of the waves and up onto the shallows. She helped him turn, first onto his knees, and then his feet as he lurched with her aid several paces out of the clutching grasp of the sea, to safety where he collapsed on his face, retching and vomiting saltwater.

Molly sat down slowly, on a pile of rocks, exhausted, cold, wet, and shivering, but so glad to be alive. Her heart pounded and felt as if it would burst through her chest, and her head ached agonizingly. There was the horrible taste of seawater in her mouth, and just for a moment, she thought she might faint.

Come on, Molly, wake up, girl, you've got a patient who needs your care. She coughed deeply, turned her head, and spat out the briny mucus. When her eyesight returned to normal, Molly looked at the man who had come so close to inadvertently killing her.

Hs seemed to be a similar age, perhaps a little older, but not by too much. His brown curly hair was matted and stringy; he was cleanly shaved though he did have some stubble like he was two days overdue for a shave. His clothes were bedraggled and sodden but looked like they were of reasonable quality. He wore light brown pants, a darker windbreaker jacket, and a red checked flannelette shirt. His shoes were brown leather and scuffed, but not dreadfully so.

As her gaze swept upward, she noticed the gash

behind his ear, which, while it was not bleeding, clearly had been by the staining in his hair and clothes. It looked ugly, and as if needed stitching.

Molly shook her head; she had to get him moving. The rain was teeming down worse than ever, the gale-force winds still blew, and she felt chilled all the way to her very soul. Her patient couldn't be faring any better; in fact, with the blow to his head, he could be concussed or worse. She wriggled across the stones and reached for his shoulder and shook it vigorously.

"We need to get going, or we could freeze to death out here, can you walk?" He groaned again. "We've got about half a mile over rocks to get to safety," she urged. "Can you make it?"

"Who are you, where am I?" he asked in a voice so croaky she could barely hear over the wind and wave noises of the storm.

Molly placed her lips close to his ear. "My name is Molly, and I'm the lighthouse keeper on Forbes Rock, your lifeboat somehow made it through the reef, and you've come ashore on the island. We got a rocky terrain to walk over, but we can't stay here, we need to get you to warmth. It looks like you've had a nasty blow to your head, how do you feel?"

He didn't answer, and she noticed his eyes were closed; he'd passed out again. *Oh, my giddy aunt, what am I going to do?* She had to get him off the rocks and out of the weather, but how? He seemed concussed, and Molly knew she needed to get him warm and dry, but she could hardly carry him; he must help her, help him, concussed or not. She got up and crossed the rocks and grabbed the medical bag from where she had left it. Kneeling back at his side, trying to shelter his face from the driving rain, she opened it up and found what she was looking for.

She unscrewed the lid off the bottle of smelling salts and held it under his nose. Soon enough, he flinched, and his eyes opened again. "Wha, whah, whaaaaat?" He shook his head and then grimaced with pain. Molly watched his eyelids flutter.

"What's your name?" She demanded, with a firm tone of voice, knowing she had to take charge of the situation.

He frowned, blinked several times, and seemed to be trying to concentrate. Their gazes locked, and Molly noticed his eyes looked dilated, a sign that not all was right with him. He shook his head. "I don't know who I am," he whispered.

Hmm, Molly thought, *Short term memory loss. That can be common with a severe blow to the head.* "All right," she replied, "Well then I'm going to call you John. Now don't worry, you've had a knock on the head and your memory will come back, but the most important thing is we must get out of this weather, you have a concussion, do you understand me?"

He nodded, slowly, and she continued. "You can lean on me, but I can't take all of your weight, and we have quite a distance, over wet rocks, to get to safety. I don't care if I have to give you smelling salts every other step you take, but you must walk. Other than your head, are you feeling any pain from anywhere else, any broken bones, stomach, or chest pains?"

He seemed to consider the question, and moved his arms and legs, testing them. "I feel sick in my stomach, dizzy, and my eyesight is sort of cloudy. My rump and knee are sore, but I think I can walk if you help me, and we go slowly. Keep that smelly bottle close." He gave a crooked grin and showed his perfect teeth. Molly realized in other circumstances, he would be handsome, but she forced such thoughts from her mind.

"All right, well we're going to go slowly, the wind will be behind us, pushing us along so the rain won't be in our faces at least. If you need to stop for rests, say so, and we will. So long as we keep moving when we can, we will stay warm enough, and before you know it, we will get there. You can carry the smelling salts; I've got the bag to take, and I want my free arm around you to help guide you. Every few seconds you will see the light as it turns, that's where we are heading. Can you get up?"

She stood and gripped his right hand with both hands, then helped him stand into a crouching position. He almost fell straight over and wobbled terribly, but she hung on and encouraged him, "C'mon, you're doing great, focus on not falling over, all right? That is the hardest bit done; getting up, everything else will be plain sailing."

That was a lie, of course; the walk would be challenging in any circumstances, but a concussed man in a howling storm? She shuddered.

"Whoa," he mumbled, and placed both hands on his knees, bent over and took three very deep breaths. He retched, suddenly, and seawater spewed from his open mouth. Molly held him as best as she could until he recovered.

She held the smelling salts close to his nose, but not right under it once more. He flinched, but it seemed to help. "How are you doing, John?" He nodded once, seemingly trying to concentrate on not diving face-first into the rocks. "Great, now, if you start to get woozy, say so, and we can stop for a breather. There is no rush, but there is another storm front coming through, and we need to be back inside before it hits this evening, so slow and steady, and we will win this race."

Molly picked up her father's bag as he stood to full height, and she realized how tall he was. She gave him the bottle of salts and then slipped under his arm, snuggling in. She placed her right arm around him and held his side. Together they took the first step, and miraculously, Molly thought, they stayed upright.

The trip would not be easy, she knew, and she hoped concussion was the only problem he had. If John had an aneurysm, or worse, any brain damage, she would not be able to save him. Her teeth were chattering from the cold, which seeped through to her bones. Her best hope was to get him back to the warmth and safety of the lighthouse, then keep a close watch on him, get him warm and dry, stitch his wound, and radio in she had a survivor from a shipwreck. She would be in trouble, she knew, but surely, they would understand why she left the damned building? Molly hoped so.

With the wind at their backs and the rain lashing them, they stumbled and weaved their way back. Molly had no idea how long it took, and they had three rest stops when John sat on a convenient height rock. By the time they arrived at the entry door, Molly was exhausted. They almost fell inside, and she closed the heavy door, so glad to be out of the rain and wind. Molly propped him against the stone wall and pulled off the oilskin poncho, and anorak dropping them on the floor. Then followed it up with her sodden woolen jumper.

Feeling stronger but still cold, she helped pull his jacket off, and for the first time, noticed he too was shivering uncontrollably from the cold. “Let’s get you upstairs, and out of those wet clothes.”

He looked like he couldn’t walk a further step, yet somehow, he nodded, gripped the iron railing, and took his first step. Molly slipped in behind him, holding his hips, assuring him by her touch, and slowly they climbed, step by step to the living quarters.

She could hear the radio, calling for her to answer as she entered the sitting area. “Sit down on the couch, that’s my bosses wondering why I missed my scheduled check-in. I need to answer them and report you’re here so they can send a boat or helicopter to get you to hospital.”

He suddenly grabbed her arm tightly, which made her jump in shock. “Whatever you do, please, please don’t tell them I’m here,” he gasped.

“What, what do you mean, why not?” She frowned bewildered.

“I, err, umm,” he looked lost as he seemed to struggle to find the words, and her heart melted because he seemed so helpless. She wanted to agree, but she needed an explanation. He sighed, and shook his head in evident exasperation, “I’m sorry, Molly, I don’t know why. I just have this terrible feeling I’m in danger. You said memory loss is usually temporary; please give me a day or two for it to come back. I know it sounds strange and melodramatic, but I know in my heart, I’m in terrible danger if anyone finds out I’m here.”

She gazed back, trying to understand, and failing. *Is it possible to lose one’s memory, but know you are in danger, or is this strange man lying to me?* She wondered. The radio squawked again, and she could hear a strident sounding Rachel calling again for her to respond. "All right, I will give it twenty-four hours, and then I really must advise them you're here."

He squeezed her hand warmly and smiled. "Thank you, Molly."

She took her hand out of his and went to the study, began working the pedals, and waited for the dial to show she had enough power to transmit. The capacitors retained only enough charge to receive for a short time for emergencies.

"This is Forbes receiving. Hi Rachel, please forgive me being late for checking in, I was up most of the night watching the storm. Then, wouldn't you know it? I fell asleep on the couch this afternoon and slept through my sked. I'm so sorry about that, over."

She waited a few seconds until a very relieved sounding Rachel came back. "Molly, you had us very worried, one more hour, and we would have sent a chopper to check on you. Mr. Harpington has been having kittens, over."

Molly looked up at the clock. Hell's teeth, she thought, I'm only forty-seven minutes late, thank goodness we got back when we did. "I am sorry if I gave you all a scare; I just fell asleep, that was all. Oh, by the way, I seriously doubt a helicopter could land in this weather out here; that's another reason I slept so heavily, the storm hasn't abated at all, and I got almost no sleep during the night, over."

"Stand by Forbes, Mr. Harpington is here, he wants a word, over."

Oh, Gawd, now I'm for it, maybe I should just tell

them why I'm late and ask them to keep John's arrival here secret? She looked up, and the man was standing, shivering as he leaned against the doorframe, watching her. *There goes that idea*, she decided, knowing she couldn't let him down. Why she felt that way she hadn't had time to figure out, but Molly thought if he was in some kind of danger, she didn't want to be the one to get him hurt. She gave him a slight smile. "I'm in trouble because of you," she said, making sure she didn't have her thumb anywhere near the transmit button.

"You've saved my life twice," he said in a serious monotone.

"Molly, this is Darcy Harpington, do you read me, over?"

"I do, Mr. Harpington, I'm not sure if you overheard, but I do apologize for making you worry. The storm came in so fierce overnight. I didn't get any sleep, and then I nodded off on the couch at the wrong time this afternoon. I am sorry, sir, over." She gave a shiver, she was still wearing wet clothes, and while it was warm inside because of the heat the wood-burning stove gave out, there would be little more than embers in the firebox because she had been gone for so long.

"Your voice sounds different, Molly, are you sure there is nothing wrong? You haven't been outside, have you, over?"

She gulped and tried to quell her shivers, hating the fact she was lying, which went against everything she believed. "Mr. Harpington, this is the worst storm I've ever seen. I promise you nothing short of a life or death situation would tempt me outside. If I sound different, it's just that I only just woke up, and I know I made you all worry, and I'm upset for doing so, over."

There was a long pause before the speaker crackled again. "All right, Molly, now please listen. I know you are very new to this life, so I'm going to make an allowance on this occasion. There are not too many responsibilities to being a lighthouse keeper, and ensuring the light is burning is obviously paramount. But adhering to your radio schedule, so we know you are safe and healthy is also vital, so that we know the light is going to get lit each night. If you don't radio in, how do we know you haven't had a fall down the stairs, come down with food poisoning, suffered a heart attack, or whatever? If you are going to have a daytime sleep, it's your responsibility to set an alarm clock to wake you up. Please make sure this doesn't happen again. Do you understand, Molly, over?"

Molly felt aggrieved. *I've saved a man's life for goodness sake,* she thought*, but here I am being scolded like a naughty schoolchild.* "I do, Mr. Harpington. I won't let you down again, over."

"It's Rachel again, Mr. Harpington has gone now." She said, a few moments later. "Forgive him, Molly, he really was worried; he's like a bear with a sore thumb over you because he stuck his neck out to keep your father's job. Now, the weather forecast isn't going to get any better for the next day or two, or even three. So, sit tight, and keep to your radio skeds. Over and out."

Molly tossed the microphone down, feeling unfairly chastised. She looked up at the man she only knew as John, and suddenly a shadowy sense of fear crept in. Molly was alone, on a remote island, with a strange man who had convinced her not to report he was there. She felt a fear she hadn't experienced before.

What if he was evil? She was well and truly on her own.

****

You're being stupid, Molly, don't be so melodramatic. She smiled at John. "Let's get you out of those wet clothes, and I will have a close look at the gash on your head. I am a nurse, by the way, in case you're concerned. I will get you some of my father's things for you to put on and poke the fire to get this place warmed up too." She stood up and crossed to the door, but he didn't move, so she stood in front of him.

"You're a very special person, Molly, thank you for having faith in me. I don't know what's wrong with me; everything is like trying to look through thick fog in my brain." He looked so forlorn, her heart melted, and again was struck with how handsome he was, but then realized this was not the time to have such thoughts.

Molly took his arm and led him to her father's room, grabbing one of the towels on the way. I'm going to help you undress so I can check you over for any other injuries, then help you put some of my dad's clothes on because I don't want you to fall. Are you all right with that, John? Once again, please be reassured; I am a qualified nurse."

He nodded, and she noticed he looked very pale as if he could pass out. "Lean on me, you look like you could topple over any moment, but we need to get those wet things off you and into something warm and dry. We also need to get you to drink some water; there's no telling how much salt got into your system." She began with his shirt, and he placed both hands on her shoulders to keep himself as steady as he could.

The flannel shirt was so wet it clung to him, and it was as if she had to peel it from his skin. His ribs area on his left-hand side was severely grazed and bruised, but she didn't think any were broken. Without an x-ray machine, she could only feel for any damage, which was never foolproof. She threw the shirt across the room, back toward the door, and threw the towel around his back and draped it over his shoulders. "That looks ugly, and I need to see if you have any fractures, hold on to me tightly; this may hurt."

She touched the ugly purple area and tried to feel for anything out of place. John flinched and flung his head back but seemed to accept she had to do it. "How did this happen, John, do you have any memory at all?" She asked, trying to keep him conscious by making him think and speak.

"I, umm, have some vague recollection of running, like I was being chased, and falling over, but that's all I can remember."

She glanced up at his face, intent on reading his honesty, which for some reason, she didn't completely believe. "John, please tell me the truth," she asked quietly, but in her most serious tone of voice. "Are you some criminal who is on the run from the police? Having saved your life, I deserve to know if you are." She realized she was incredibly naïve, but Molly was torn between wanting to believe him, and distrust, so all she could do was ask and gauge his truthfulness.

His impossibly blue eyes shone back and held her gaze. "I believe I'm a good person, I don't think I'm capable of breaking the law, but I can't remember how I got hurt, and how I came to be in the lifeboat. I know I'm not a bad man, you're safe from me, please believe that."

Something was niggling in the dark recesses of her mind, should she believe him? *Why would he lie?* She wondered, other than wanting safe refuge both from the storm and whoever might have chased him. *But he had been unconscious on the boat*; she was sure of that. *Is his memory loss real? He certainly has had a bad blow to his head, so it's more than possible.* She nodded her acceptance of his word and took the ends of the towel and rubbed his chest and arms. "I'm pretty sure you haven't broken any ribs, let's get a warm top on you, then get those pants and underwear off, and check your lower half."

She reached for the chest of drawers, opened the top one and took out a white cotton T-shirt from the left, and a gray fleece-lined windcheater from the right. "Let's be careful of that cut on your head, I'll be dressing it soon, but we must get you warm," she murmured as she helped him put them on.

"Look, umm, I think I can do my pants and underwear myself," he said, and she could see the embarrassment written all over his face and grinned. They were after all in a bedroom, not a hospital, and she should try to show some decorum.

She nodded and opened the lower drawer and removed a pair of her father's underwear and track pants, which looked like they would be warm enough. "Perhaps you're right. Two things though, firstly I want you to check over your legs for cuts or anything you feel might need medical attention, remember I am a qualified nurse, and I don't want you getting infected from a cut I don't even know you have."

He clutched the pants in front of him and gave a

slight nod signifying he understood her concern. "What's the second thing?"

"You've suffered a blow to the head, you are pale, and your eyes are dilated, all of which tells me you are concussed. You are standing up now, but you are not steady on your feet, which is why it took us so long to get back. If I leave you alone, to dress, do it perched on the side of the bed, so you don't fall. A second bang could be fatal, and you're too big to carry down those stairs, deal?"

He showed the ghost of a smile at her attempt at levity, which she realized was weak at best. "Deal."

"Right, I'm going to go and get changed into dry clothes myself, then stoke the fire, get some hot water, iodine, and things to stitch and dress that gash on your head and bring you back a glass of water to drink. Call out when you're decent." Molly turned and left the room; leaving the door open, so she could hear if he fell.

In her room, Molly hurriedly stripped everything off, toweled dry, and noticed she was covered in goose bumps. Grateful to be dry once more, she threw on a thick jumper and canvas pants over clean underwear and rushed to the kitchen.

Molly busied herself getting everything together she needed, when she realized she was hungry. *That's no real surprise, is it?* She asked. *You've not eaten since breakfast.* Because she had been out in the rain most of the afternoon, she hadn't made the bread. I will make the dough tonight and bake in the morning.

She got the fire going without too much trouble and lit the small kerosene heater to get the place warmed up. "Are you decent yet, John?" she called out and was rewarded with a loud grunt which she took to mean yes. Molly was in the habit of leaving a full kettle on the warming area of the stove so there would always be water to make tea available within minutes. She poured some into a metal bowl and decided they both needed something to warm their insides up, so moved it onto a hotplate to boil. She also drank a full glass of water to rinse the brine taste from her mouth and filled another for John.

When Molly returned to the bedroom, she found him fully dressed, lying on his side on her father's bed, but his pants were pulled down at the rear, and she saw why. He had an extended angry-looking cut across his buttock. It appeared as if he had been whipped with a very thin cane to such an extent it had opened up a gash or slashed with a sharp knife. Like his head wound, the cut had stopped bleeding though it looked to be weeping. She perched on the edge of the bed and looked closer. "I don't suppose you remember how you came by this, John?" She asked, while her fingers gently prodded around the wound.

"No. I thought it was just a bad bruise because it hurts, but when I took my pants off, I saw blood, though the sea washed a lot of it off. There are a couple of holes in my trousers, but I still can't remember anything. What's wrong with me, why don't I remember?"

She scrutinized it, ignoring his question for the moment, and noted it had begun to knit back together. Molly hadn't ever seen a cut quite like it before; it was as if rather than be a slice, or graze; it was more of a groove. She shrugged; being young and fit his healing powers would be good. Depending on what caused the wound, it could still be infected, but she didn't think it required stitching.

"You'll have quite a scar to impress your future wife," she said, "and try not to worry about the loss of memory. I'm sure it will all come back soon, maybe as soon as you've had a good night's sleep." She opened the bag and pulled out some cleaning swabs and cotton wool, then began.

He groaned when she touched it, and positively flinched when she rubbed the iodine laden swab over it. "Try to keep still; I need to make sure you don't get it infected, though that would be unlikely with all the saltwater you've been in, but still as we don't know what's caused it…"

Once it was clean to her satisfaction, she covered it in gauze, then using the stainless-steel scissors cut lengths of adhesive plaster to hold it in place. "When is the last time you had a tetanus injection?"

"Umm," he let out a loud explosion of air, "I don't remember, school, maybe?"

"Listen, John, you must understand I'm not a doctor; but I am a nurse, who hopes to get a scholarship into medical school soon, and in my opinion, because we don't know what's caused this cut and the one on your head, I would urge caution. I can give you a shot to be safe, but it has to be your choice. That's because, well, like I said, I am not a doctor, so I shouldn't be prescribing anything. I'd hate to see you survive all you have, though, and then die from an infection. You won't be leaving Forbes anytime soon, not until the storm passes, and we get you some help, so unless I radio in and get advice from a doctor, I'm the best you've got."

He hesitated for a moment before speaking. "How come you've got a doctor's bag?"

"My dad was a doctor; he was a chief medical officer for the Navy during the war. Then, we came to Perth afterward to begin a new life. My mum died in an air raid, and Dad wanted to get me out of the country for a fresh start. He was with the Royal Perth Hospital until he chose to give it all up to work here at Forbes, so he could find enough time to write a book. The bag is his."

As she spoke, she took out a vial marked tetanus and a new syringe, to which she attached a sterile needle from a sealed container. She knew John would say yes, he just wanted to have some idea she knew what she was talking about.

"Well, that explains why he came here, but not where he is now, or why you're here, though thank God you are."

She inserted the needle through the rubber seal and drew back the plunger until the bottle was empty. Patiently she explained the fall and how she came to volunteer so he could keep the job he had come to love. "So, that's answered your questions, now what do I do with this syringe in my hand?"

"Molly, you saved my life, if you say I should do it, of course, I will. I think if you get your scholarship, you will make an incredible doctor. I hate needles, though, so do it before I change my mind."

Molly smiled; that was perhaps the biggest compliment he could pay her. The next second she ensured there was no air left in the syringe, then injected him into his buttock.

"Ow," he yelled. "You didn't say it would hurt."

"Don't be such a baby," she replied as she pulled the needle out. "Right, pull your pants up and turn over, let's look at your head wound. You can drink this glass of water I brought you too."

Slowly and clearly in discomfort, he wriggled over until he was looking up at her. She noticed his eyes were still dilated, his skin was pale, and he was sweating slightly. Her heart melted at his vulnerability, and once again, she saw that he was a very handsome young man. *Blooming hell, I've got butterflies, what is wrong with me?* She wondered. To distract herself, she took a thermometer from the bag. "Under the tongue," she demanded, and he obliged. While waiting, she delved back in the bag and removed the blood pressure band and stethoscope.

She held it out for him to help thread his arm inside it. With practiced ease, she fastened it, jammed the earpieces into her ears, and pumped up the bladder while listening to his pulse. He tried to speak to her, but she shook her head, concentrating on measuring the high and low reading. When Molly saw his result was acceptable, she took his pulse properly, watching the second hand sweeping through, reasonably normal, thank goodness. Then Molly looked at the temperature on the thermometer she took from his mouth. "What did you want to ask me?" she queried.

"I was going to say how lucky I was to be washed up on an island with you here. Of all of the places I could have come ashore, how fortunate am I to be rescued by a beautiful nurse who is going to look after me?"

She stared, trying to understand if he was being serious about her being beautiful. Of all the words she could think of to describe herself, beautiful would be last on the list. Oh, she never thought of herself as ugly, but a red-headed, freckly faced woman could never be called beautiful so far as she was concerned. Not that her beauty or lack of it had ever been important. On the rare occasions she thought about her looks, she would have used the word average, unremarkable was another, and plain was another. The list could go on endlessly. *He's lost his memory*, Molly reminded herself, for him*; I'm the only woman he's ever seen, so of course, he thinks I'm beautiful. Shame he's going to get it back, maybe I could keep hitting him over the head to make sure he doesn't*. She almost giggled, but that wouldn't have been right after he had said something so lovely.

"John, thank you for saying so, but no way in the world would anyone in their right mind call me beautiful. Yes, it was very fortuitous the wind blew you onto Forbes Rock, and that I saw you coming and was able to save you. You very nearly drowned right at the last hurdle. It was nothing short of a miracle, I thought, as I watched your raft threading its way through the gap in the reef. Hell's bells, when the supply boat comes through its all hands-on deck with everyone being vigilant, but you? You just breezed through like it was a walk in the park."

He blushed, just a little, and looked down at his hands clasped on his lap. "Molly, you may not think you are beautiful, but I do."

She shook her head, playfully. "Well, let's blame your lack of good judgment on that head wound. Your vitals seem to be all right, so talking of that blow to your head, let's have a close look at it and clean it up. Here, drink this."

He sat and took the water, downing it in several large gulps before handing the glass back. "Thank you, Molly." He then inched further down the bed and turned his face away. Like a lot of head wounds, his cut looked worse than it was because of the bloodstains. Most of it had washed away in the saltwater, but the rest had congealed and crusted in his hair. The gash itself was around two and a half inches long and appeared deeper than it was because of the raised lump it bisected. Molly cleaned it with cotton swabs dipped in the warm water before dabbing another ball in iodine. "This will sting but try not to move; I think we can get away without stitching it."

The second the iodine touched the cut, he yelped and wrenched his head nearly off his shoulders, and the violent movement seemed to make him woozy. For a moment, Molly thought he might pass out or at the very least vomit.

"Obviously," she said quietly, "Our definitions of trying not to move are vastly different." She smiled when she thought he had recovered. "I have to disinfect it, John, and I'd like to do it sometime tonight, but if you keep moving, that's not going to happen, is it?"

His eyes were watering, and he looked deathly pale, but he managed a grin. "I'll try," he whispered. "But no promises."

"Well, any more of that sort of escapology, and I will go down to the shed and get some rope and tie you down. Now, shall we try again?"

He turned his head to the side and gritted his teeth, silently giving his consent. This time, though he gave involuntary flinches, she was able to disinfect the wound to her satisfaction. She took some gauze and a roll of bandage from the bag. Molly slowly wound it around and around his head to hold the pad in place to protect the cut. "We're done," she said, eventually.

He lay back and closed his eyes, a single tear slowly crept its way down his cheek, and her heart melted even more for him. "John, how is your pain level on a scale of one to ten? I'm not authorized to give you a morphine injection without a doctor's instruction, but I could give you some aspirin if you need it."

He took a slow, deep breath. "I feel sick, and I'm worried if I do, I will bring it straight back up, but my head hurts, and my eyesight is still cloudy."

"I think you need to drink some more; you've swallowed a lot of seawater, and I think that's what is making you nauseous and dehydrated. I can't put you on a saline drip, which I believe they would in hospital. I will go and make you some soup, which will take me fifteen to twenty minutes to warm up. When is the last time you had anything to eat?"

He seemed to be taken by surprise and stammered a response. "I, err, umm." He shrugged. "I don't know, I can't remember."

She stood up and left the room only to return with a full jug of water. She poured some into the tumbler and put the remainder on the bedside cabinet and held the glass out. "Come on, John, drink up."

He lifted himself onto his elbow and took the glass, finishing it in four gulps before falling back into the pillows. Molly watched as his eyelids drooped, and within seconds, his breathing became deeper, and she knew he was asleep.

Chapter 8

The Lure of Allure

Molly cut some of the meat from the leg of lamb into small cubes and using that as a base for her soup added onions, diced carrots, potatoes, and two large spoons of stock powder with water and put the saucepan on the stove to boil. Next, she went to the watch room to check fuel levels and the state of the wicks. She also took a cursory look around with the binoculars.

The weather had cleared somewhat, she noticed; the rain was down to a fine drizzle, and the wind had abated. Obviously, the calm before the second storm, she thought. The seas were still gray and angry with whitecaps being thrust up and along with the swell, which was still mountainous.

With the coast clear, and the light set for the night, she went back down the spiral staircase to the living quarters. Molly stuck her head around the corner and noted John was still asleep. *The best thing for him, I think. Maybe he will recover his memory while he's out.* That thought led her back to once more wondering if he was sincere with the loss, or whether he was making it up because he had something to hide. On a whim, she picked up his discarded, soaking wet clothes intending to put them in the washing basket. It was as she picked up her own to add to the pile she thought about his pockets and what might be in them; *Possibly something to identify the mysterious stranger*? With a glance over her shoulder to make sure she was alone; she ran her hand through each of them but found nothing other than a silver shilling coin.

So much for that idea; I didn't think it would be that easy. It was as Molly bent to put everything in the wicker basket, she had another idea. She put everything else in but held up John's trousers and stared in disbelief at what she saw. The holes John had referred to were two perfect circles, with ragged edges, slightly less than half an inch diameter, and around four inches apart. It took a moment, but it dawned on her she was looking at two bullet holes, which formed an entry and an exit. Molly decided that when she imaged the pants on his rump, the holes would line up with the start and finish of the gash, and the only thing she could think of that would have caused such a situation was a bullet.

He said he had been chased, but was whoever doing that shooting at him too? Then, she recalled his palpable fear she would report his presence on the island. Did that mean he was a criminal on the run from the police and lying to her, or was he innocent and in trouble with some hoodlums? She shook her head, dropped the trousers into the basket, and went back to the kitchen; it was time for a cup of tea.

The soup had come to a boil, so she added some herbs and tasted it on a spoon after first blowing on it. Molly nodded. *Not too shabby*. She exchanged the pan with the kettle so it would simmer. Once she brewed the teapot and poured out a cup, Molly went to the couch, sat down and picked up *Moby Dick* to see what

Ishmael was up to, but she nodded off to sleep after only one page, the cup of tea undrunk on the small table by her side.

****

Molly woke to the sound of an enormous clap of thunder overhead, and a split second later, John screamed out in apparent fear. The storm had returned with a vengeance. The room was gloomy; she had neglected to light more lamps earlier, and through her exhaustion, had slept like a baby. She sat up, the book on her lap fell to the floor with a clatter, and she realized she had a stiff neck. Just then, a flash of lightning lit up the room through the tiny window, and without a thought, Molly crossed to where the Tilley lamp was. The matches were always alongside, and she struck one and used its light to open the glass shroud to light the wick.

"It's all right, John, you're safe, I'm lighting the lamps, and I will be there in a minute," she called out.

Soon the room was bathed in the soft, warm light from the three lamps, and then she fed more wood into the firebox because the flames had died down while she'd been asleep. Molly poured another tumbler of water and took it through to her father's room just as another peal of thunder rocketed across the sky. Molly entered to see him sitting up, with a confused look on his face. His curly hair was mussed up so much that in conjunction with the bandage around his head, she thought he looked adorably vulnerable.

"How are you feeling now?" she asked as she handed him the glass of water.

For a moment, the man she could only call John looked as if he had no idea where he was and who was offering him the water, but then his face softened, and he gave the ghost of a grin and took the glass. "Like I've been run over by a herd of wildebeest," he muttered. "Thank you for the drink, Molly." He swallowed half of it, then wiped his mouth with the back of his hand, as a little boy would, and she smiled.

"Your eyes look clearer, is your headache easing?"

"No, it still feels like there is a football game going on in there, but I don't think I'm going to throw up anymore. And, umm, I feel hungry." He said sheepishly.

"Well, that's a good sign. Soup is ready, though today was supposed to be the day I baked a new loaf of bread; however, certain events meant I didn't find the time. I do have crackers, though, and I can open a can of peaches for dessert. Come on, let's go and eat."

He finished the water and put the glass back on the cabinet, then swung his legs over the side of the bed and paused before going any further. "I'm okay," he said slowly, "Touch of vertigo; that's all." He stood up, teetered just for a moment, and she reached out for his arm to steady him. "Whoa, maybe I'll just lean on you until we get to the dining table." She felt him lean against her.

In one fluid movement, she slipped under his arm and put hers around him, gripping his side while his hand held her shoulder. Despite knowing he was unwell, suddenly, she experienced a flush of attraction run through her body. Molly felt his strength, and for the first time, she didn't feel like it was a nurse and patient relationship, but more boyfriend and girlfriend; and she liked it. He stood a good six inches taller than her, and he was well built. Because of his circumstances, he was vulnerable, which appealed to her mothering nature and increased her desire.

Pish posh, she thought, *there is no way he is attracted to me in real life, he only said what he did before because of the injury, so steady on girl, and don't let your feelings run away with you.*

Together they wiggled through the narrow doorway, and Molly heard a loud clacking noise like she imagined a machine gun would sound. "And that will be hailstones, goodness me, can this storm get any worse?" she asked rhetorically.

She guided him to the head of the four-person table to sit down. To hide the blush which warmed her face and shake off her feelings of attraction, she busied herself, by making a new pot of tea, and when ready, poured them both a cup. "Do you have sugar, John?" she asked, with her back to him.

There was a long pause before he eventually answered with an odd-sounding voice. "Do you know," he began, "I don't know. I know I do drink it as well as coffee, but for the life of me, I have no recollection of the taste to know if it's sweet enough by itself."

She turned with his mug in her hand, smiling, happy this was further proof that her earlier doubts of his sincerity were groundless. "Well, try it without, and if you'd like some, add it then, no problem."

He took the proffered gray china mug, cautiously took a sip, and grimaced, which made Molly giggle. She passed him the bowl and a spoon, "I think that face you pulled means you like sugar, help yourself."

She turned back to the bench, a smile still on her lips, and concentrated on the soup. She gave a cautious taste, hoping her very meager cooking skills would pass muster, and decided it needed seasoning. She added a generous amount of salt and pepper, then as an afterthought added just a touch of powdered cayenne and tasted again; she nodded her approval. Next, Molly opened a box of crackers and put some in a bowl which she placed on the table.

John smiled at her. “Molly, the smell of that soup is making my mouth water,” he said eagerly.

“Well,” she replied, unused to compliments, “Let’s hope it tastes as good as it smells.”

“May I ask a question, Molly?”

“Umm, yes, you can ask anything, but that won’t guarantee an answer if it’s too personal.” She retorted, feeling just a little nervous knowing if someone thought they had to ask for permission to ask a question, it was because the answer could be tough.

“Well,” he began nervously, “Back in Perth, do you umm, have a boyfriend, you know, are you seeing someone special?”

She burst into laughter, and then stopped as she saw doing so had embarrassed him. Oh my God, she thought, he really does like me! Her heart melted a little more. “John, gee, I hope that is your name now I’m used to it. I’m a nurse at Royal Perth. I do twelve-hour shifts that sometimes turn into fourteen or fifteen. I live in the nurse’s quarters, and while yes, I do go out with friends now and again to see a film or something, I do not have a boyfriend. How about you?” she asked as she carried two steaming bowls of soup over and put them down on the table. “Is there someone special in your life?”

She stared pointedly and watched him open his mouth to speak, then pause before shaking his head slowly. "I don't know. Should I know that? I mean, I'm attracted to you, and if I did have a girlfriend and an emotional attachment, you'd think I'd remember that, wouldn't you?"

Molly sat opposite him, picked up some crackers, and crumbled them into the soup in front of her. "I'm far from an expert in head trauma, being a nurse rather than a doctor. I think there is a lot we don't know about the brain, for example, how can you lose your memory for things like who you are, and things like that, but still remember how to speak, and eat. You'd think a loss of memory would be a total loss, but it isn't. I think, and I could be way off the mark here, but the head wound isn't your only problem. I think you've had a traumatic experience, too, and your subconscious is trying it's best to protect you from that by making you think you've forgotten everything."

He took a cautious sip of soup and smiled broadly. "This soup is sensational, Molly. Tell me why you think there is some sort of psychological cause?" He followed her example of crumbling a handful of crackers into his soup.

She put her spoon down and with her elbows on the table interlaced her fingers so she could rest her chin on them. "John, you had a recollection of being chased, and you were quite stressed when I was going to tell the authorities you were here; there has to be a reason for that. Plus, there is the bullet wound you have."

He jerked his head up suddenly, but then closed his eyes with pain. When it eased, he asked, "What bullet wound?"

Molly was watching him like a hawk; still, some

part of her doubted his memory loss, and she did not want him to take her for an idiot in some game he might be playing. Molly believed she was nobody's fool, even if she liked him. But, however much she worried he was lying; she had to admit if he was hiding something from her, he was the world's best actor.

"The cut across your behind isn't a cut; it's a graze from a bullet fired at you, no doubt while you were running away from your attackers. If you put your pants back on, you will find there are two holes in them which line up with the two ends of the gash. One hole is an entry, the other an exit; you were fortunate indeed."

His mouth stayed open in apparent shock. "I want to remember, Molly, this not knowing is killing me. If I go back to the mainland with no idea who is after me, what's to stop them from getting to me without being able to defend myself? Please don't let anyone know I'm here until I remember."

There was no doubt in her mind he was sincere, and she had to agree, clearly, he had been in danger, and whoever had been after him, might still be when he returned. She could not condemn him to be hunted down by persons unknown by reporting he was in the lighthouse. She had to keep him safe, at least for a few days, she felt she owed him that much.

"John, you can't stay here forever, you must accept that. However, this storm is going to hang around for two or three days more yet, so no one can get here. I have two friends who visit me every Friday, weather permitting, so if your memory hasn't returned by then, they can at least take you back without fanfare. They will be able to get you to hospital for medical assistance, and they will help you remember far better than I can. There is no rush, relax, get over your concussion, and who knows, you may wake up and remember everything."

****

"What do you think, did he make it?" Barry asked for what seemed to Nick the hundredth time.

Nick shook his head. "No way in the world, not in this storm. Mind you, if you'd learned to shoot straight, he wouldn't have made it to the boat and got out of the marina in the first place."

"Yeah, I shoulda used the shotgun, not that bloody revolver I took from the guard, but I thought someone would have heard the blast if I did. Christ, he ran like a rabbit once he knew we intended to bump him off and keep all the money. I was lucky to hit him at all. And where were you, why didn't you grab him, or bash his brains in like we planned before he overheard us?"

Barry shook his head in resignation. "What's done is done; the bastard had a premonition, or maybe even just lost his bottle and wanted to run out on us. He won't get far with that hole he bashed into the side of his boat when he hit the rock wall on the way out of the marina. Either it sank, or the storm finished it off and then it sank. Either way, there's no way he got back to shore. You searched north, while I went south, and there was no sign of him landing. Plus, no one has come knocking on his door, which they would have if he ratted us out, so he couldn't have got away."

"Well, when this bloody storm passes, we will steal, hijack, or hire a boat and go searching for him. We know the line he took when he cleared the breakwater, and with the water, the boat was taking in through the hole in the hull, he wouldn't have got far.

I'm betting we find wreckage or hear about it on the radio; we don't have a thing to worry about, I'm telling you. Now stop asking me the same bloody question over and over again."

****

Late that night, Molly lay in bed thinking about the mysterious man who had washed up on her island. Earlier, the evening had been lovely until he had wearily gone to bed; one of the nicest she'd ever spent in a man's company. It was a shame John had no memory, which was so very troubling. What if she permitted herself to fall for him, and he then remembered he was married or engaged?

He isn't wearing a wedding ring, Molly reassured herself, she knew because she looked and there was no tan line from its removal, but that was hardly proof. Molly had to accept the possibility he was on the run from the police. If so, it was they who shot him. That was the most sobering worry of all.

Molly had always respected the law. That notion was drummed into her by her father, whom she idolized, for as long as she could remember. Molly couldn't afford to lose her heart to a criminal, no matter how cute he was. Yet, they had five nights to spend together until Derek arrived, and she could hardly avoid him inside a lighthouse.

As she drifted toward a troubled sleep, knowing he was doing the same thing only yards away, she unintentionally fantasized that his memory returned. In the half-awake dream state she was in, he didn't have a girlfriend, and the wounds were all a misunderstanding and a case of mistaken identity.

The storm raged all night, and Molly woke several

times to the sounds of alternating thunder, rain, and hailstones rattling on the windows and howling around the stone walls. She didn't hear a murmur from John and at one point, got up and crept to the open doorway of her father's room to find him in such a deep sleep she had to watch the rise of fall of the blanket to make sure he was still alive. *Well, that's one good thing,* Molly thought. *He's not a snorer*. She smiled and went back to bed and slept through to the alarm clock's shrill tune calling her to wake.

****

Molly was in the watch room, tending to the wicks when John joined her and made her jump as he appeared at the top of the stairs. "Sorry," he said, "I didn't mean to startle you."

"Oh, that's fine, don't worry about it, I'm too used to being here on my own. You look much better today, how's the head?"

He did look brighter; she noticed his eyes seemed less bloodshot, and the pupils had returned to more normal size.

"Just a dull ache now, thanks, but still no memory, unfortunately. I've been lying in bed trying to remember things, but it's all just blank still. The most painful thing I've got now is my bum; that is really stinging."

"I'm not surprised; bullets can do that to you. I will have a look for you in a while; I need to make sure it's not infected. Sometimes lead projectiles can leave nasty bugs behind. The weather looks like it's clearing up a bit; I might turn the light off for a while."

The morning was brighter than the last two days had been, with occasional breaks in the clouds letting sunbeams through, which weaved and danced over the whitecaps. The wind appeared to have dropped too, though the ocean still looked gray and angry. Molly doused the wicks and checked them; they needed a minor trim. She gave them a haircut as her father had shown her quickly and effortlessly while John leaned against the railing, watching her work. "Molly, can I do anything to help?" he asked.

She turned and smiled. "Well, yes, thanks, you can top up the tank with one of those drums over there, if you would," she replied, nodding at the neat stack of containers.

They finished at the same time, and Molly took the Weiss glasses off the hook. "Now to check for any boats that came to grief on the rocks during the night. That's was how I spotted you. Forbes Reef is around six miles long and about one and a half at its widest; lots of places to run aground."

"I know," he said.

Molly's head snapped around. "How do you know?" She demanded in a more authoritative voice than she intended.

He looked flustered for a moment, and then he blushed, which at any other time would have been boyish and cute. "I'm not sure…I just know it is. I suppose the fact that I washed up here from a boat, I must know something about the local waters, mustn't I?"

She nodded encouragingly. "John, from what little I've read about head injury memory loss, it's likely to come back in bits and pieces. Like little flashes of unrelated recollections, so don't fight them, let them come and explore each one when they crop up. Yes, it does make sense you would know local waters and conditions, but then again, if you did, I wonder why you would put to sea with a major storm coming."

He opened his mouth to speak and then clamped it shut again. John shook his head after a while. "I don't know any more than that, but I do know about Forbes, and I also know I was being chased. I recall running, and being frightened, I mean seriously scared, but not why."

"Okay, well that's something at least, let's do a little experiment, do you mind?" He shrugged and nodded for her to go on. "All right, so lean against the railing, like you were before, we don't want you losing your balance and falling over. Now, close your eyes, and think back to when you were being chased, can you do that?"

John closed his eyes as instructed and waited. "Now," she said in a soft voice. "Breathe slowly and deeply, concentrate on long drawn out breaths. In and out, slowly, gently, we have all the time in the world. Think back to when you were running, what can you see? Where are you?"

His brow furrowed, clearly concentrating. "I don't know. I can't see anything; it's foggy."

"Is it nighttime, is that why you can't see?" she urged, but he merely shrugged his shoulders. "What can you hear, listen carefully?"

"My footsteps, running, they sound hollow."

"Hollow? What do you mean by that?" She leaned forward; she knew this could be a vital clue.

"Like, I'm running on something…wooden, yes, wooden."

Molly shrugged, unsure what that meant. "What

can you smell, John?" She watched his nostrils flare.

"Seaweed, the ocean, like its low tide. I can hear lapping, gentle; it's before the storm, the water is calm with just ripples breaking on the poles."

A sudden understanding came over her, and she grinned, this was a breakthrough. "You're running along a jetty or a pier. You can smell the ocean, and it's dark. You're hurrying to get to a boat, why?"

There was a long-drawn-out silence. "I have to get away; they're going to kill me; I heard them planning it. I can't use the car; they took the keys." Suddenly, he stood up straight and clutched his rear. "Argh," he yelled, "it burns." His eyes flew open, and then he seemed to realize where he was.

"What happened?" she asked, but he looked blankly back and shrugged. "Who was going to kill you?"

"I don't know, Molly, it's gone. I had a sudden stinging, burning pain, and the rest is gone."

She reached out a hand and gripped his arm. "It's all right, John, don't fret, it will come. We've learned a lot. You were trying to get away from some people who were planning to kill you. You tried to get to a boat by running along a jetty or pier. That must be when you got shot. What I suspect is the gunshot made you fall, and you hit your head, so it's a combination of the physical and mental trauma that's caused the memory loss. I'm guessing you got to the boat, and dazed and confused you escaped them, but headed straight into the storm. The boat sank, you made it into your life raft and ended up here. I think it's time to tell the police you're here so they can protect you."

"No," he insisted, "I don't know why, I can't

explain it, but I know the police are part of this, somehow I won't be safe with them, but I know I'm a good person. Please give me a few more days; maybe as you said, I will remember more in time."

He looked so frantic; there was no way Molly could deny him another day or two. *Besides, no one knows he is here, and he is stuck with me till the seas drop anyway—unless they were to send a helicopter and I don't think they would do that for a man whose only medical emergency is he has no memory.* Molly nodded her acceptance and relief washed over his face. She drew the binoculars to her eyes once more and scanned the violent ocean for any sign of life.

"Well," she said five minutes later. "No one else has taken to the seas; even the freighters have given us a wide berth. Time to bake that loaf of bread, it would have finished rising by now, then I can make us some smoked bacon and eggs, I have some in the refrigerator just for special occasions; I think we can justify today as being one of those."

Together they went downstairs to the living quarters where Molly stoked the stove fire and put the bread tin on the middle shelf. "Right, even though I'm not supposed to leave the lighthouse, we need some eggs, and the chickens will need feeding, come on, you can keep me safe."

Ten minutes later, they returned with eight eggs in a basket, the kettle had boiled, and Molly made a pot of tea. "Molly," John asked from the table, "how do you stand the solitude? I love your company, but honestly, I think if I were here alone, I'd go mad in no time flat."

She placed a steaming mug in front of him and grinned. "Good question. I thought the same before I came here. They tell me that over the years, many lighthouse keepers *have* gone mad, and some even took their own lives. That's why radio check-ins are so important. Generally, they have married couples, or families do this job on remote lights. My dad volunteered because he wanted the solitude to write a book, and he says he found utopia. Me, I'm only here because the silly bugger went to check the moorings on the escape boat at the jetty in the middle of a storm and broke his leg. He was fortunate to survive, which is another reason why usually they don't let people do this alone. But you know what?" she asked as she took the piece of bacon from the fridge and picked up a sharp knife to slice it.

"No, what?"

She glanced up to make sure he was sincere, and she thought he was. "I found my rhythm and discovered I quite like my own company. I sometimes have conversations with myself out loud, which I've always been told is the first sign of madness, but I'm genuinely enjoying the peace and quiet. I've re-discovered reading; I'm halfway through *Moby Dick* and loving every word. I also do some studying. When I get back, I have a chance for a scholarship to get into medical school, so I have a heap of textbooks I'm wading through. And, best of all, I love fishing, so each day I go down to the jetty and catch some fresh herring for my dinner. Some I smoke, but otherwise, I love eating it fresh." She smiled and noted his eyes were sparkling.

"I think you are an awesome woman, Molly," he said quietly, and she was shocked by the admiration in his voice. "I always had a dream to own my own charter boat business, but I know I will never have the money for that, so I work as a deckhand part-time on a tuna boat."

She jerked her head back to him at the revelation; another fragment of his memory had come back. He looked equally startled. "Oh, my God, Molly, you were right, little bits and pieces are sneaking back to my consciousness, I do have a dream of owning a charter boat; I know I love the sea."

"Fantastic, don't force it, let it come. I suspect soon; it will be like floodgates opening, then we can solve the mystery of who was trying to kill you, and why." She smiled but noticed his face darkened from the happy puppy dog look he had to one red with anger.

"Well, maybe that's one memory I could do without. I think I'd rather stay here with you and enjoy your company and the rugged beauty of Forbes," he scowled.

"Oh, I'm sure you would tire of me very quickly, right that's the bacon ready," she glanced up at the clock, fifteen minutes, and the bread should be ready, forty-five, and she would radio in. "Are you hungry?"

He nodded earnestly. "Yes, I am. May I ask a question, Molly?"

Oh gawd, here he goes with asking permission to ask a personal question again, but she didn't mind really; she was impressed with his polite manners. "Sure, fire away; I can take it." She placed the cast iron fry pan on the heat, not wanting to face him in case she blushed with him, asking too intimate a question.

"Why do you keep putting yourself down, and why would you think I'd tire of you? I think you're the most amazing woman I've ever met!"

Okay, this has to stop, Molly decided. She turned

her back to the stove and leaned against it, then moved quickly away as the heat got to her. John looked expectantly at her, and just for a moment, her heart melted before common sense took over. “Well, John, firstly we don’t know that’s your real name, do we? We also don’t know if you are married, single, in love, or whatever. You have no memory of a relationship to be an expert on how you genuinely feel about me. Then, there’s me, I mean, look at me, I’m a ginger top, I’m not one of the beautiful ones like some of the girls I work with, I’m very average. I’m not putting myself down; I’m realistic. I can’t do a blooming thing with my hair; if I let it grow long, it goes frizzy, too short, and I look like a man with freckles. Granted, I’m not overweight; I work too hard at nursing to ever be fat. But trust me, John; men do not beat a trail to my door to ask me out for dates. So, let’s get real, you think what you think because I’m the only woman here. Were there three of us, you’d choose me last.”

“Can I kiss you? You’re even more beautiful when you’re mad at me.” He stood up, and Molly jumped like a startled rabbit. In three paces, he would be in front of her if she didn’t stop him. If she wanted to stop him, that was.

Oh, my good God, he wants to kiss me. “You most certainly may not. Sit back down before you get another blow to your head, and this one you may not recover from. I’m not some floozy.” She waved the frying pan in his direction as a threat.

He burst into uncontrolled laughter, and the sight of him almost falling back to his chair in hysterics made her smile too. That grew into a laugh, which only made him laugh louder when he saw her giggling. Eventually, he found his voice: "God, Molly, you should have seen your face," but that only set him off again.

He wiped tears from the corner of his eyes and slowly brought himself under control. "As much as you're right, you're also wrong," he began. "Firstly, I am very, and I do mean very attracted to you, so therefore no matter how you think you are an ugly duckling, I see you as so much more. Secondly, you saved my life, and more importantly, you risked your life to save me in wild weather. You waded into the ocean to get me to safety, which naturally created an emotional bond between us. Thirdly, I like your red hair, because it's you. More importantly, if three women were here right now, I would still choose you first, never last. Oh, and one last thing, who says floozy anymore? That's the kind of thing my grandmother would say, if I could remember her, that is."

She stared at him, trying to decipher if he was truthful, or just playing with her emotions, but before she could come to a decision, she jumped as she smelled the unmistakable odor of the pan overheating. "Eek, I forgot the frypan with all this nonsense." She turned back to the stove, grateful for the distraction from trying to figure out how she felt about him, and more importantly, how he really felt about her, despite his words.

She finished preparing the meal in silence, but she could feel his eyes on her back with every movement she made. *Is he serious?* She wondered but forced it from her mind. She popped the bread out of the baking tin and onto a cooling rack and then turned to cook the hand-cut rashers of bacon to a golden crispy brown before putting the eggs in to accompany them.

****

After breakfast, Molly suggested John use the bathroom first and shower while she cleaned up, then she would do the same. She gave him fresh underwear and a T-shirt and told him her father's spare razor was there, and he could use it to get rid of the dark stubble on his face.

When he came out, clean-shaven and red-skinned, she redressed his wounds and then went in, with fresh clothes under her arm, and closed the door. Molly felt nervous undressing, with a man in the next room and only the thickness of the door separating them, but she told herself not to be stupid. She took her time washing her body, then shampooed and conditioned her hair, and then later sat on her bed, brushing it dry. Molly tried to make sense of her feelings for John and failed dismally. She had never felt more confused in her life, but there was no doubt in her mind; she was not only attracted to him but could quickly lose her heart. If she stopped to think too long and hard, Molly realized she already had, but she must not let him see it. For all she knew, John could be married, or deep into a relationship with a woman who could be growing frantic at his disappearance.

She had to keep a rein on her emotions until his memory returned, no matter what, she knew she must.

****

At ten on the dot, Molly treadled up the radio and called Rachel while John did the dishes, at his insistence, in the kitchen. She had warned him to do it silently; she could not afford for the sound of a clattering plate be transmitted to Mr. Harpington.

"Hello, Molly, thank you for being on time today,

Mr. Harpington was here but left the moment he heard your call sign. How's everything out there, over?"

"Things are just fine and dandy, thank you, Rachel. Nothing to report, we got through the storm last night in once piece, and no one came to grief on the rocks, over."

"Who's we, Molly, over?"

Damn! She realized she had said we, meaning her and John, and not me, for her alone. She had to think quickly and fortunately had a brainwave. "Just me and the chickens, Rachel, I thought they might have died of fright with the thunder and lightning, but we all survived, over." She bit her lip, hoping her lie would fool the vigilant radio operator.

"You had me worried there for a minute. I thought you might have smuggled a boyfriend over there with you, over," she laughed.

"I wish I had; I'm getting cabin fever stuck in here not even being able to go outside for a walk, can you send me one of your spare men, over?" Molly hated lying, but now she had made her particular bed, she had to lay in it.

"Don't tempt me, or I'll send you my husband, and trust me, Molly, you won't like that, over."

Time to change the subject, she decided. "What's happening in Perth, Rachel, anything exciting, over?"

"Albany copped the brunt of the storm, lots of damage there, roofs ripped off, fences were blown down and the river is in flood, Perth missed most of the nasty stuff, though it hasn't stopped raining for two days now. Only another thirty-eight to go, and we will need an Ark. Talking of the weather, you've had two fronts, the third one should come through late this afternoon, or tonight, but the weather bureau says it shouldn't be as bad as last night, over."

"Well, that's something, at least. I might be able to get outside the lighthouse tomorrow, then, God willing, over." Molly glanced up, John was leaning in the doorway again, with the tea towel draped over his shoulder, and once more, she was struck with how handsome he was. She smiled and held a finger over her lips, urging him to stay silent, lest their secret became exposed.

"Probably be all right by late tomorrow, Molly, for sure the day after if it's still iffy. Oh, hey, did you hear about the big bank robbery, over?"

"No, I didn't, do tell, over."

"Well, Mr. Harpington doesn't like clogging up the airwaves with gossip, but the Commonwealth Bank on William Street got held up on Friday. They say they had inside info because they struck when a big payroll was being done up. Oh, and a guard was shot, he's in critical condition, no one is saying if he will pull through or not, but the feeling is he is going to die if he hasn't already, over."

"Wow, that's my bank, thank goodness I wasn't there, they might have got my meager savings. I hope the guard will be all right. Are they closing in on the culprits, over?" She looked up at John, but he was gone.

A massive search is on as we speak, Molly. The papers are saying they know who the men are, two men from Melbourne working with a local driver; real bad guys, apparently, known for their violence. They got away with nearly a hundred and thirty thousand, in cash, so I don't think they'd have wanted your savings, over."

"I hope they catch them, scum like that don't deserve to be free, I reckon, over."

Chapter 9

Falling and Catching

When Molly found the man she had come to know as John, he was sitting on the couch, and he looked ill. She dropped to her knees in front of him. "What's wrong, I thought you were doing so well, but you look like you've seen a ghost." She touched his forehead, but his temperature seemed normal.

"I don't know, I was just watching you at the radio, and suddenly I felt like I was going to pass out," he replied. A thin grimace crossed his face as he shrugged.

"You have concussion, recurring dizzy spells are common, and it's nothing to worry about. Do you have a headache?"

He slowly shook his head. "No worse than it was before. I'll be okay; it will pass; it was just…a momentary thing, I think. What do we do now, when do you have to check in again?"

"Not till four. We've tended the fuel and wicks, so they're ready to light later, that's it for work for now." She craned her head to the side and glanced toward the window. "Looks like it's brightening up outside, and the wind has dropped, but Rachel says another storm will come through late this afternoon. About now, I'd generally go for my walk, tend the vegetable patch, and catch some fish for dinner. But, thanks to my friend,

Derek, who is the skipper of the supply boat, I have a roast leg of lamb for dinner tonight." She got up from her knees, satisfied there was nothing seriously wrong with his health, and sat alongside him.

"You said earlier, you had an escape boat, and your dad broke his leg while checking it was tethered to the jetty, is that the same one you catch your herring from?" His eyes seemed to bore into her, with an intensity he hadn't shown before. Suddenly her suspicions came roaring back.

She nodded. "Yes, follow the path, it will take you all the way to the boat, if that's what you want, I won't stop you. But I would like to know why you feel the need to steal it and run out on me."

He looked as if she had slapped him. "You think I would do that; I would steal your only means of escape?"

"You tell me John, all of a sudden you seem to have changed, what's caused that?"

He sighed loudly, then lowered his head as if caught by the headmaster trying to play truant. "I wouldn't do that; I owe you my life, I was just interested, is all. I was surprised you had a boat and wondered what sort. It was like an overpowering urge to find out, and I don't really know why."

She relaxed, he looked so hurt by her implied accusation, and she softened. "I'm sorry if I offended, sometimes my foot is an ideal size to fit in my mouth; that's the redhead in me. The boat is a twelve-footer, with a Biggins and Stratford outboard motor. But a fat lot of good it would do me, or you, unless you knew the way through the reef, which I don't. I suppose a mariner like yourself could work out the passage by watching the waves, but it's no mean feat, let me tell you. According to Dad, it's one of those silly government rules that say if they put you on a remote island, you must have the means of getting off it in an emergency. You can go and have a look if you want to, the weather has dropped, and it's not raining. I'll come with you for a walk if you like."

He looked up during her speech and held her gaze. "Molly, when I said I thought you were awesome and asked if I could kiss you, I was serious. No matter who I turn out to be, I'd never do anything to hurt you, or cause you to be hurt, I'd rather die than have that happen."

For what seemed like long seconds on end, she stared back, hoping he would kiss her. "I believe you. But John, what's happened, you've changed?"

"I don't know, I'm not sure, but I have a terrible feeling about those two men who robbed the bank Rachel mentioned on the radio, and I don't want to be responsible for putting you at risk in any way. How many shootings do we get in Western Australia, not many I bet, yet I was shot sometime after the bank robbery, two within two days, is that a coincidence?"

Oh my God, it must be a coincidence, undoubtedly, she thought, but her hackles still rose. "Tell me the truth, John, and look me in the eye when you do. Do you remember anything you haven't told me, especially since you heard about the bank robbery?"

"I do not; I'm not lying to you, Molly." He did not look away, or give any indication he wasn't truthful, and she wanted to believe him, more than anything.

"Okay, well, that's good enough for me. I think it's important you don't do anything silly out of unnecessary chivalry. You don't know your wound is anything to do with those men. The bank robbery was in Perth, and we are something like two hundred miles away, so it may be just some bizarre coincidence. Maybe you got shot during a rabbit hunting accident or something innocent; you don't know. So, until your memory returns completely, be careful of false memories, and don't go risking your life by taking the boat and trying to find the route through the reef because you think in some way you are saving me. Especially in seas as we have at the moment; even the supply boat won't risk it in anything less than perfect weather."

He didn't answer, he just stared back, seemingly mesmerized by her, as she was with him. Molly thought she had said all she could, she had convinced him, or she hadn't. If he chose to steal the boat, she could hardly stop him, but she wanted him to stay with her. Slowly, agonizingly so, they came together, and he kissed her. Her arms reached around him, and she kissed back with a passion and need she didn't know she possessed.

Molly had never felt so alive as she did in John's arms. It was far from the first time she had kissed someone, there had been once during her last term at school, behind the bike shed with Maurice Barrington. Then there had been two very short-term boyfriends afterward. But, if she was honest, she felt the kissing and petting were expected of her on those dates. It hadn't been something she had done because she wanted to. She wasn't sure she had even genuinely enjoyed those experiences, looking back. But with John, being wrapped in his arms, repeatedly kissing, tasting his tongue, feeling his hands roaming up and down her sides; it was as if she were lost in a cloud of sensuality. Her breath came in short gasps as her senses came to life. She allowed herself to be pushed back into the couch, her fingers interlaced around his neck as he nuzzled her bare shoulder, kissing, licking, and sucking, driving her wild with passion.

Molly's eyes opened wide as she felt his hand closed over her breast. No one had ever touched her there, and while she loved the feeling, she knew she had to stop him. Her hand closed over his, and pressed it harder against her body momentarily, before firmly removing it. He broke the kiss and stared questioningly, but she shook her head. "I said I'm not one of your floozies, John. When I give myself to a man for the first time, it will be because I love him, and I decide he is worthy of that gift. As much as I feel for you, I don't even know your name."

He nodded slowly, and she noticed his eyes were twinkling.

"I respect you for that, Molly, but I hope you don't blame me for trying; I do think you're amazing."

"Well, I didn't say we had to stop kissing, and no, it's fine; I took it as a compliment."

****

The weather continued to improve, with patches of blue sky growing more abundant, and the wind velocity dropping every hour. The rain had stopped altogether and didn't look like it was returning anytime soon. Molly cooked one of the crayfish Derek left her, as per his instructions, and made lunch of it with the freshly baked bread with cheese and pickles. After his first taste, John lifted his head and grinned. "How bizarre," he stated.

"What's bizarre?" Molly asked, afraid she had undercooked the seafood.

"I just had one of those flashes of remembrance hit me like a slap on the back of my head; I don't like crayfish, and never have. But this is delicious; how weird is that?" He held up a forkful and popped it into his mouth as if to prove his point.

Molly smiled back. "Well, either it's my amazing culinary skills, or, and this is the more likely; between the last time you tried it, and now, your taste buds have changed." She whispered the next thing she said as if it were a secret, "I suspect it's the latter; I'm not known for my cooking."

"Why do you always put yourself down, Molly? You have so many good qualities, and you know how much I think of you. It's no fun to hear you rubbishing yourself all the time."

At first, she was angry with him for rebuking her; she was not at the lighthouse to provide fun for him. But she stifled her temper and desire to put him immediately back in his place and bit her tongue. She put her cutlery down and thought about what he'd said. Yes, he had criticized her, but he'd also paid her a compliment, and she should at least acknowledge that.

Her father had often told her she was far too quick to find fault in others and she had inherited her mother's red hair and temper; that had always been her excuse. "John, I was being honest. In my life, I've probably only cooked a handful of meals, if you don't count making an omelette, frying bacon, or toasting bread. First, my mum always cooked before she died in an air raid during the war, then my dad looked after me, which included doing all the meals. I didn't have a mother there to teach me homely skills, though we did have a part-time nanny for when Dad worked late shifts. Then, I moved into the nurse's quarters, where we have a canteen to eat our meals. So, when I say I'm not known for my cooking, I most assuredly am not. We've discussed my looks, which are average at best, but not my personality. I consider myself more of a realist than someone who, as you say, puts themselves down for no reason. I think I have a good heart, high morals, and being a nurse has taught me to care for people. I don't suffer fools, and I have a very long memory for people who do wrong by me. But overall, I'm happy with who and what I am. I don't criticize myself for no reason, but neither do I hand myself bouquets when I don't deserve them. This," she pointed a thumb back at herself, "is who I am, John, and when your memory comes back, for us to have any emotional entanglement, you need to accept that. My mother had a saying that my father reminded me of once. She said she was not in this world to live up to his expectations of her. My dad tells me I'm very much like my mother was."

He stared, and she realized it was probably the most extended statement she had ever made to him. "I think you're wonderful," he said eventually, "and I hope when I get my memory back, I'm the sort of man you will want to be involved with."

"So do I," she whispered, more to herself than him, but she saw he had heard her.

****

After lunch, they tidied up, kidding each other, seemingly wanting to stay away from any serious conversations. John broached the subject of going for a walk. “In fact, how about showing me your jetty, and if you have two fishing rods, I challenge you to a fishing competition.”

“Well, that’s hardly fair, is it? You’re a professional tuna fisherman,” she joked, but in the back of her mind, Molly wondered if his real reason was to see the boat and his means of escape from her. That thought saddened her, more deeply than she imagined possible. “Let’s go up top and check out the weather first. If it’s bad, I’m not supposed to leave the building. If we do go, we must be back by four for the radio check-in.”

“I think you’re making excuses because you know I will beat you at catching herring, c’mon, let’s go, it’s not raining, and you can hear the wind has dropped. If it’s too rough when we get there, we can come straight back.”

He is determined, she thought, there’s only one way to find out if he is going to steal the boat, and that’s to show it to him. “All right, you win,” she smiled to hide her fears. “You can wear one of Dad’s jackets, and there is a spare rod in the shed, the other I keep down there on the boat, so I don’t have to carry it there every time I go.”

They dressed appropriately for the cold after Molly checked his head wound and changed the bandage. She also insisted on checking the bullet wound for infection, and both appeared fine. Molly took some bait from the fridge and a slice of bread from the pantry. Once outside, they found the spare rod and took off for the jetty. The sky was filled with broken cloud cover, letting the sun mostly shine though, and the wind had dropped to be a solid breeze as opposed to the gale-force it had been. Molly was glad to be outside the confines of the lighthouse in the fresh air, and as they walked the path, they joked who would catch the largest herring and the greatest number of fish.

She stopped to show him her father's vegetable patch, which had taken a battering, but predominantly the plants looked healthy. Weather permitting, she would venture back there tomorrow to tidy up, she determined, but with the third and hopefully final front coming in that night, Molly knew she might not be able to get back until the day after that.

She smiled and sighed with relief when they crossed the final rise and saw what she had come to think of as her jetty. The dingy was still tied up securely and bobbing as if it was glad to see her. The canvas covering the protective steel frame had stood up to the ravages of the wind and had done its job of keeping the hull from filing with rain, while the hawser ropes had held it from bashing itself to pieces against the pylons. For some reason, she thought of the book she was reading, *Moby Dick*, how they put to sea in smaller boats to sink the harpoons into whales, and she shivered throughout her body.

"Clinker built," John said, admiringly, "looks like a good sturdy hull, the perfect boat for threading its way through the reef. Anyone with half a brain should be able to get out of here if they had to, and they picked the weather, and took their time."

"Well, the point is I can't even imagine a situation where I had to leave the island when I could just radio for a bigger boat to come and get me. So half or full brain, I can't see it's relevant," she replied a little testily. She felt he had insulted her lack of seamanship skills; didn't he understand she was here only temporarily?

He glanced at her. "I'm sorry, Molly. I didn't mean that to sound the way it came out; I meant no disrespect. All I meant was in the event of danger, or a catastrophe, like a fire, for example, you could get off the island. I can see why they insist you have the means to escape; even though, yes, you would hope never to need it." He reached out a hand and gently squeezed her arm, and her heart melted; once again, she realized she was far too quick to temper.

"I suppose," she began slowly, casting her eyes downward. "You're right. If the lighthouse burned down before I could radio for help, I would have to use the boat, and it's good that it's here. The supply boat only comes once every three weeks, and once a year they come and tow the dingy back to Augusta. There they take it out of the water and coat with something to stop the barnacles growing on it, so it's always in good shape."

"Anti-fouling."

"What?"

"It's called anti-fouling, the goo they paint on the hull to stop growth. We have to do the tuna boat every year too."

"Is that another memory come back, or is that general knowledge?" She looked up again, interested that he remembered something else.

He grinned. "Yeah, I suppose it's both, I remember another bloke and me doing it, and he never stopped complaining the whole three days the job took. I remember I wanted to punch him to stop him whining, but he was a bit burlier than me."

"Anything else come back to you now, we are on a jetty, and you're looking at a boat?" she asked, studying his face and trying to read how sincere he would be when he answered.

He went vague for a moment as if thinking deeply. Molly squeezed his hand for encouragement. "I'm trying, Molly," he replied after a while. "But nothing more about the night it all happened. Just running, the sound of footfalls on timber, echoing back, the smell of the sea, and being scared out of my wits."

Momentarily, his eyes darted to the left, and for the first time, she thought he was lying; he had remembered something but didn't want to tell her, she was sure of it. *Why is he not telling me the truth, what is he hiding?* She wondered. In her heart, Molly knew the best thing was not to let on she suspected him.

Molly liked the man she had only known of as John, and that was the rub; she had never felt like that about any man before she had known. She had even let him touch her breast and had enjoyed it wildly while he had, and that was a first. But now she was sure he was hiding something from her, and that could only mean it was terrible. Another thought crossed her mind. He could be lying because he thought he was protecting her, but protecting her from what? "Are you sure, there is nothing else?" she said gently, desperate to hide her doubts from him.

John shook his head and gave a forlorn look as if he had just received bad news. Molly debated whether to press further or wait for him to tell her whatever was upsetting him of his own volition. Some inner sense told her not to push him, that whatever it was would be better for them both if he told her of his own accord. Suddenly, she had an idea. "John, I'm not really in the mood to fish today, and we don't need it for dinner tonight; we have roast lamb. How about we leave the gear here on the boat until tomorrow, and I show you somewhere that is very special to me instead?"

His eyes opened wider as he smiled. "Molly, I'd genuinely love to see anything, or anywhere you think is special. I'm up for it, let's go."

Molly took his fishing pole, and bucket, and crossed the jetty to the boat. Her fingers were cold, and she fumbled with the zip on the canvas cover until she finally got it open. As Molly worked to put the things out of the weather, she felt happy again at the lovely thing John had said. It almost, but not entirely, balanced out the nagging doubt she had that he was lying to her. *He must care to say such beautiful things to me*, she thought. *If he didn't care, he didn't have to be so lovely to me; he could have just stayed.... aloof. I so want to believe in him.*

She got everything into the boat, and tugged the zipper back down, then turned back to him. "C'mon, let's go." She held her hand out, and he took it, interlacing his fingers through his. "It's a bit of a hike, and over rocks, though none of them are dangerous if you watch your footing. But I think you will agree; it's worth it when we get there."

He pulled her to him and whispered, "I'm not going anywhere until you kiss me, then we can go."

She melted into his arms, his lips met hers, and again she was transported to utopia. Her lips parted as the tip of his tongue gently but insistently invaded to meet hers. *Oh, wow,* she thought, *I could do this for hours and hours, and hours.* Time seemed to stand still while the sound of the breaking waves and seagulls wheeling overhead went on all around them.

When they finally broke, Molly leaned back and gazed into his eyes. "John, please, no matter what, never lie to me; I couldn't bear that."

"I won't, Molly, now take me to your special place." He smiled deeply and warmly, and Molly doubted her earlier belief he was hiding something from her. Maybe, she conceded, she had been mistaken.

"It's this way." She led him away from the jetty, not wanting to let go of his hand.

The breeze was stiff and cold and it bit through their clothes. It was a reminder to Molly the storm hadn't finished; it was just in respite. On the horizon, to the North-West, very dark clouds amassed, and she realized they were the harbinger of the third front due that evening. They rounded the point, hopping from boulder to boulder, laughing and joking with each other. Suddenly, a giant whale leaped from the water outside the reef, breached, and slammed back into the depths sending spray fifty feet skywards. Half a minute later, a second did the same, so close she could see the glistening of the water on the barnacle growths that encrusted it, so they resembled diamonds. "Aren't they beautiful?" she asked John.

He nodded enthusiastically. "Yeah they are, we see them all the time on the tuna boat, especially this time of the year."

He's had another memory return; they're coming thick and fast now. "John," she said slowly, "do you think your boss will be wondering about you; I'd hate for you to lose your job because you're here?"

The vague look returned, rather than the happy wondrous face he showed when the whales appeared. “Umm, I don’t know, but I have a feeling, nothing more than that, so I don’t want to trust it, but I think I quit that job or took some leave. If I did, I have no idea what I do now; maybe I’m on holiday.”

Molly smiled encouragement. “Don’t push it, and they will come flooding back, don’t worry.”

They watched the whales frolic for a few more minutes until they slowly made their way out to sea. John nudged her and nodded off to their right. She looked where he was pointing and saw the deflated life raft that had delivered him to her, hung up on some exposed rocks on the inside of the reef. She could see torn flaps that had been ripped underneath on the shards of limestone outcrops, and she shuddered at the thought of what would have happened to John if he hadn’t miraculously made it through the opening in the reef.

“C’mon,” she said to distract them both from morbid thoughts of what could have been. “Time to move on.”

“Are we there yet?” he asked in a child’s sing-song voice, ten minutes later.

“Soon, little boy,” she joked back.

“Is it on top of the cliffs?” he asked, sounding a little breathless.

“No, before the cliffs; it’s very close now. The incredible thing is that we are almost on top of what I wanted to show you, yet you can’t see it. We need to get closer to the water, and then you might spy what I’ve brought you to. I sometimes bring a picnic lunch here and sit looking at the ocean for an hour or more. I find it so therapeutic.”

"What, sitting on the rocks?" he asked incredulously. "That's bonkers, Molly, you can do that from the lighthouse, or while sitting on the jetty, come to that."

"You'll see," she replied with a smirk.

Four minutes later, after veering closer to the waterline, Molly stopped and faced John. She held him by his upper arms and asked, "Are you ready?"

He looked like he was about to burst into laughter. "Ready for what?"

She turned him around and nodded to direct his gaze. "Oh," he exclaimed, "A cave? I see what you mean; it's just about invisible. I doubt any boats wouldn't come this way after coming through the gap you pointed out; they would go around to the jetty."

She smiled, he liked it, she could tell, and her heart swelled a little more. She led the way, and they stepped inside. John had to duck very low to avoid banging his head on the overhang, but Molly did it with just a stoop. At the back of the cave was her favorite rock, and she sat down, tugging his arm, so he sat beside her. "Now, do you see why I can sit and do this for hours?"

He stared out through the craggy opening, and she watched as his eyes moved from right to left, taking in the vista. The water stretched out over the reef, where whitecaps dominated all the way to the horizon. "The mouth of the cave does something to the perspective, doesn't it?" He asked, "It's like a beautiful picture frame on a work of art, but this work of art is continually moving. It's quite simply breathtaking, Molly."

She beamed her happiest smile because he saw it in the same way she did. Molly pushed her right arm through his left and squeezed. It dawned on her in doing so, his arm pressed against the side of her breast, and it thrilled her realizing she had never been so brash and naughty. He seemed in no mood to move it either, and they sat silently, just soaking in the view, and enjoyed each other's company.

****

They made it back to the lighthouse with thirty minutes to spare before the radio check-in time. Molly's cheeks were rosy, and her fingers numb from the cold wind, which had picked up considerably while they sat in the cave. She estimated a tailwind of forty plus knots drove them once more back to warmth and safety, ahead of the approaching rain front. They had kissed some more; she couldn't stop him, not that she wanted to, and Molly loved that he respected the boundaries she had stipulated. His caressing hands stayed on her back, sides, and thighs, but secretly, she wanted them to travel further; she was breathless with desire, and she came to within a hair's breadth of taking his hand in hers and cupping her aching breast with it. Common sense prevailed, but she knew her will power was weakening by the hour.

After closing the door tightly, she peeled off her topcoat while John did the same. "A cup of tea is long overdue," she suggested with a grin.

He nodded sagely. "'When all else fails, make a cuppa' was always my mum's motto." He stopped suddenly as if slapped. Molly saw he had another flash of recall. Silently she waited for him to tell her more.

He shook his head, as if coming out of a daze, saw her watching him and grinned. "My mum, I can remember her wearing a purple apron, damn, she always wore a purple apron. Sometimes I wondered if she slept in it. I can remember her gray hair, her damned apron, and scones, fresh out the oven on a cold day after school with hot tea. She used to dollop fresh whipped cream and homemade strawberry jam on them. Oh my God, Molly, I can taste them, how's that for a memory?"

She laughed at his happiness and her own. Everything was coming together; he was honest, his fractured memory was returning one shard at a time, and at that moment, she believed she was falling in love with him. "Maybe," she said softly, "I could try to bake scones for you, though I doubt they would be anywhere near as good as your mother's."

"They were pretty darned special," he grinned, "but I'd be happy to sample yours and be a one-man judge." He placed his hands on her hips and tilted his head to one side to kiss her, but she raised a hand to his chest to stop him.

"I can't now; we don't have fresh cream. We have chickens on the island for eggs but not a cow to give milk, so we have to make do with condensed and powdered. I could radio for Derek to bring me some, but on his next visit, he will be taking you back to safety to make sure there is no permanent damage from that head wound."

He didn't continue his attempt to kiss her. Instead, he held her gaze and tucked his lower lip between his teeth as if thinking. But, while he didn't advance any closer, neither did he let go of her hips, and his hands seemed to get hotter with every moment. Eventually, he spoke and what he said shocked her: "Molly, what if I don't go back? What if I stay here with you, just the two of us, caring for the light and each other? I think I love you, Molly. Whatever my past is can stay buried for all I care; right here is where I want to be, with you."

"I, err, umm. John, I don't know what to say; I'm staggered. You know that can't happen though, don't you? No matter how much we both might think that would be wonderful, there are probably a hundred reasons why we can't stay here together."

He stared back, in a half pleading, half challenging way. "Give me five," he said quietly.

"Five what?" She didn't know what he meant.

"Five reasons why we can't stay here, together, forever."

She laughed, but it died in her throat when she saw he was serious. She waited a minute to think by raising her hand and tucking an errant strand of hair behind her ear. "How can we ever build a future if we don't know the past? I believe the whole point of having a past is so we can learn from our mistakes before moving on. No matter how attractive you might think to wipe the blackboard clean and starting again would be, until you know who you were, how can you know what you want to be?"

He let go of her, clearly disappointed and sat down on the third step of the spiral staircase. "I don't agree with what you say. I could debate that with you, and I still might, because I think it's a debate I could win. However, that's one reason, what are the other four?"

Oh, my freaking good God, he is serious, she worried. Molly paused to gather her thoughts. "I have an employer, two really including the hospital, but this job calls for one person, not two, I'm not sure Mr.

Harpington would allow someone to stay here permanently without a thorough background check, and you don't know yours."

"Okay," he nodded. "That's valid; I will give you that. But of course, who says we have to tell him I'm here? I could hide in the cave when the supply boat comes in."

Molly felt a sudden burst of frustration; he was being silly. But he couldn't see it, and if she carried on, it might lead to a row. *Well, maybe it's a row we need to have,* she decided. She put her hands on her hips and knew she had taken on her dominant, threatening pose as her mother used to when she was angry. "So, you want me to lie for you, do you think I don't have honor and principles?"

He kept his voice calm and soft when he replied. Perhaps, Molly thought, he saw she was close to becoming an erupting volcano of rage. "No, Molly, I would never ask you to tell lies. But there is a difference between not telling the whole truth and lying, don't you agree? Just don't report I'm here."

She shook her head in exasperation. Her temper at his foolishness slipped another cog on the capstan of logic she prided herself with owning. "John, I'm only here temporarily. In a month or two, my father will be back to take up his post again, and I will return to Perth to enter medical school, if I'm lucky, or back to the nurse's quarters if I'm not. You running away from whatever is haunting you might be good for you, but what about me? What about what I want from my life?"

He looked down at the stone floor, like a child who had just learned Father Christmas wasn't real. "Yeah, Molly, I get it. I'm sorry, for a while there; I thought you had fallen for me the same way I had fallen for you. Forgive me, I'm stupid."

Now she felt her temper rising to burst point, and she could not stop it. "Oh for goodness sake John, quit with the guilt laying martyrdom bull shit. I don't even know who you are, yet you expect me to throw the rest of my life away to live in hiding on a lighthouse because you're too gutless to face your past? Get real. For your information, I have fallen for you, more than anyone in my life, and damn you; I want it to work out. I want for you to remember who you are, what you've done that warranted getting shot, and free yourself from it. When you're clear of your troubles, I want you to date me. I want a man to woo me, court me, wine and dine me, introduce me to his family, and for him to meet my father. To respect him and for him to ask me to marry him, and for me to be so much in love, that I say yes. Perhaps that's a pipe dream but hiding in a lighthouse for the rest of my life would be a nightmare for me, despite how much I might have fallen for you." She was breathless and trembling with anger. How dare he put her into a situation where she had to defend her beliefs and dreams?

In an instant, he jumped to his feet and took the two paces separating them. He wrapped Molly up in his arms and hugged her, despite her not wanting to be held by him at that moment. "I'm sorry, please forgive me, Molly. Of course, you're right; I was stupid. I got carried away with the beauty of your secret cave and your beautiful heart. It came to me in a flash of irresponsibility that I wanted you in my life, for the rest of my life, and not for one moment did I think of the practicalities of that desire. You're one hundred percent right, and I was wrong. Can I tell you I love you when you're angry though; your cheeks glow, and your eyes are like burning embers?"

She bit her lip, forcing herself to calm down, and slowly she felt it recede, like the tide going out. "John, it's not enough to love and want someone. True love means respecting that person, and a relationship should be built on the foundation of mutual love and respect. I want to know you, who you are, what you like, and what you don't. I want our relationship to grow and mature, and when the time is right, I want you to go to my father and ask him for my hand before you ask me. Maybe I'm a traditionalist, but I am what I am. I love it when you kiss me, but kissing isn't enough. What about children? And if we had any, how would you support us, and how would they know who their father is if you run away from finding out?" The levee wall that was her anger was crumbling, and in its place, she felt like crying. He had spoilt a perfect day, and she couldn't remember the last one of those she'd enjoyed.

"You're right, Molly," he whispered in her ear as he stroked her back. "I love you, and of course, I respect you and what you want from a relationship. I just got caught up in the moment is all. I felt like all the emotion I feel for you had to be released, like a pressure valve, but it was a dumb thing to think, let alone to suggest, and even worse to then try and justify. Forgive me, please."

Eventually, she pushed away from him and with her index finger, wiped the single tear away that had formed from her right eye. "I'd better radio in, and then get things ready for dinner," she said softly, "that leg of lamb won't cook itself." She rewarded his pained expression on his face with a smile, a sad one, but a smile nonetheless to let him know she had forgiven him. “John, we’re running a bit low on firewood, would you bring some up from the lean-to please?”

“Sure,” he replied quickly, and Molly thought he seemed eager to move on from what was their first official argument. She turned on her heel and began the trek up the staircase. Once in the living area, Molly glanced at the clock; she had four minutes to go. Molly wondered how Derek and Mikey had been. Knowing they had not been fishing, she had not bothered to try to radio them. That thought made her wonder how Mikey would feel about John; Molly smirked as she imagined the jealousy he would probably portray. *I bet he sulks, she thought, he seems to me like he’d be a sulker, rather than a fighter, but…then again, you never know; still waters run the deepest.* She checked the kettle, topped it up with water and placed it over the heat to make the tea, then poked and prodded at the firebox, and fed in two more logs.

“Whiskey Delta Oscar one zero, this is Forbes Light, are you receiving, over?” she said, gently treadling the pedals, once she sat down at the radio.

“Forbes, this is Rachel, receiving, how are things out in the Southern Ocean, Molly, over?”

“Oh, just more of the same, Rachel; nothing untoward to report. The weather eased during the day considerably, enough to let me get outside the building for a change, so I checked the lifeboat’s moorings and made sure the jetty hadn’t been dragged away in the storm, over.”

“Well, the weather guru says tonight’s storm will be a baby compared to what you’ve been through, and tomorrow it will start clearing. By the day after, it should be fine; not enough to get a suntan mind, but enough to go from three pullovers and a jacket down to one, over."

Molly grinned and looked down at how she was dressed; a thin jumper would be good. "I can't wait for that; I miss my hikes around the island, and fishing from the jetty. Rachel, is there any news about my father, over?"

"Yes, Mr. Harpington must have known you'd ask; he phoned the hospital around lunchtime. He is doing well. The infection appears to be easing thanks to the penicillin; he is eating like a horse, demanding rum for medicinal purposes, and driving the nurses mad, by all accounts. He asked us to pass on to you his love, and the doctor says he should be back on his feet in six to eight weeks, though he will be limping for a long while after that, over."

Molly's heart sank a little even though she had expected it would be that long. She supposed her viewpoint had changed somewhat with John's arrival and her growing feelings for him. Once he went to wherever he was going, she would be able to see him only if she was on the mainland. That wouldn't be for at least two months, which could equate to never, depending on what his memories contained when they returned. A saying of her father's echoed in her mind, which always sounded silly when she was a child, but it made sense to her then. "It is what it is, lass," he would say when something happened to upset her, that neither of them could change. John had to go to the hospital and get checked out. He could need medical help to regain his memory fully, just in case there was a lingering blood clot or something.

Then there was still the bullet wound to contend with. John had gotten into a situation, which he'd tried to run away from, and been shot. The police needed to be involved; she was as sure as she could be John was a decent man. The most likely situation she could think of was that he must have got caught up in something, maybe he had witnessed a burglary or an assault, and when he tried to intervene, he had been attacked. That scenario made sense to her; he seemed like such a kind and decent person. She could well imagine John wading into a fight to help someone out and biting off more than he could chew in the process. Yes, she decided, that situation sat well with her impression of his nature, as she interpreted it. With or without memory, undoubtedly, the essential man would be the same.

The radio crackled back into life, "Are you still receiving, Molly, over?"

She shook herself out of the malaise and grinned. "Yeah, sorry Rachel, I was wool-gathering there for a bit, thinking of my dad giving the nursing staff hell. Trust me; there is no worse patient than a doctor. As I said earlier, there is nothing to report here; everything is tickety-boo, over."

"All right, well, at least tonight's storm won't be as bad as you've had. They are saying on the news, especially down south where you are, there are millions of dollars' worth of damage, even some boats torn free from their moorings. Mr. Harpington asked me to ask you to keep an eye open for any that might still be afloat and drifting your way. As you know, this channel is always monitored, so if you do see anything, radio in and we can organize a rescue boat to go out, the seas will have dropped enough by tomorrow, over."

"Will do, no worries. I'm not surprised there was damage, the wind screamed through here like an out of control freight train rolling down a hill. Is there any news on the bank robbers, over?"

"Not that's made the papers or radio. Apparently, the robbers are known to the police by reputation, but they don't have identifications for them. They've been credited with seven robberies all over Australia, and three shooting deaths in the last three years. No one knows where they will strike next because they move from state to state. The bank has posted a twenty thousand dollar reward, and the airport and train stations are being watched. They've put roadblocks on all highways out of Perth to check ID, and the cops say they won't rest until they catch them, but most people think they will be going without sleep for a very long time. The government says they will hold an inquiry, and the banks will increase security at branches, but it's all a bit stable door after the horse has bolted if you ask me, over."

"Probably left the state already, I think, they'd be mad to hang around, wouldn't they, over?" Molly couldn't imagine a situation where they would still be in Western Australia, and if no one knew who they were; there were a hundred ways to get out.

"No idea, hon. Anyway, I better move on, can't sit here gossiping with you, as much I'd love to. I will talk to you in the morning, sleep tight, over."

"Rachel, just one last thing, with the worst of the storm passed, can I go back to daily check-ins, or do I have to stay at two, over?" The four o'clock schedule was a pain, and she would be delighted if she didn't have to do it anymore.

"Personally, I'd be happy with once-daily check-ins, but I do know Mr. Harpington worries about you being there alone, so young and inexperienced. I think he loses sleep, so how about give it another couple of days to make sure this storm is well and truly past, and then I will ask him on your behalf. Is that fair, over?"

Molly knew well enough, not to argue. She had to admit she was young and inexperienced, and Molly supposed if she were in Mr. Harpington's position, she would be the same. "Fair enough, Rachel, thank you for that, I will talk to you in the morning, Forbes over and out."

She tossed the microphone down, not so much in a temper, but disappointment. Only she knew the lengths she had gone to rescue John, and how reliable at the job she was. If others were aware, she was sure she would be appreciated more, but she had agreed to keep John's secret, and Molly never broke her word.

She went back to the kitchen to find John pouring out two cups of tea, and the remaining anger she felt toward him vaporized. He had his back to her, and she paused, leaned against the doorframe, watching him from behind. John had taken off his jumper, and her father's shirt was tight across his broad shoulders. His muscular arms, where he had rolled up his sleeves, looked lean and hard. She nodded, yes he did look like a deckhand on a Tuna boat, fit and healthy because he would have to be to haul the fish from the stern and flick them over his head. She had once seen a short documentary on a newsreel at the cinema, which showed Australia's burgeoning tuna trade with Japan. It featured film of how frantically the men worked to pole the fish, which appeared to be in a feeding frenzy, and she remembered how the sea seemed to boil with giant tuna.

He is so darned country boy handsome; she thought and realized she felt the stirrings of sexual excitement once more. As he worked, a horrifyingly naughty thought raced through her mind: *What if I never see him again? Do I want to make love with him before he goes?*

He turned to see her there and grinned, "I was just about to bring you a peace offering and thought I could get it done before you finished on the radio," he said. Molly noticed a tinge of red creep into his face as he acknowledged he had been silly earlier. She postponed the thought of whether she should give him her virginity until later, with a touch of relief, and walked across the room to the dining table.

"Thanks, I'm gasping for one of those. John, I'm sorry, but I'm not much of a cook or a baker; if I were, there would be biscuits and cakes and things to enjoy at times like these. But without a mother to teach me to cook growing up and going into nursing as I did at a young age, well, as I said before, I'm just not much of a homebody, as you might call it." She sat down at her usual place and smiled at him to let him know she had forgotten the earlier upset.

"Well, it seems to me, if the burst of recall I just had is true, we could be a match made in heaven." He placed her cup and saucer in front of her, and then sat down opposite her with his.

"Why, what have you remembered?" she asked with a raised eyebrow.

"It's the darndest thing," he began earnestly.

"Making the cuppas, I had a sudden vision of working in a commercial kitchen, and I was the one doing the cooking. I recall the wonderful smell of cooking pies and pastries, and I'm pretty sure it was the Busselton Bakery. I have this feeling I worked there. Qualified or not, I can't say yet, but I think I might be able to cook; I felt very at home in the kitchen doing this. If we do end up together, and I hope more than anything we do, I could do the cooking, while you look after our children."

She felt her mouth open in surprise. "A baker? I thought you thought you were a tuna fisherman?"

He nodded enthusiastically. "Both memories are equally strong. Maybe I did cook part-time after or before school, or when I left school, I did an apprenticeship. Possibly I left one job to do the other as I said, the memories aren't solid enough yet, but slowly things are coming back, though haphazardly. I'm sure I know how to cook, and with you keeping harping on about how you can't, even though everything you've done for me so far has been great, I see it as a positive, don't you?"

She had to agree; the thought of a husband who could cook was a dream made in heaven. But it jangled just a little that here she was talking about a future life with a man who firstly didn't know who he was, and secondly, she had only met two days before. *It was madness, surely*? But she couldn't deny how much she was attracted to him, and she believed he was to her, but…*will he when he remembers his past fully?* She wondered. Shouldn't she try to protect herself from hurt if he was married or promised to someone, and she got dumped the moment he realized that he was? She sighed and sipped her tea to give her a moment to process it all.

"John, it's wonderful that things are coming back to you, and I suspect now it's begun, the floodgates will open soon, and everything will return. You say so many nice things to me, and I love hearing them, but I must keep reminding myself you could be married or engaged. I feel a mixture of pleasure and guilt when you kiss me; in case I'm doing it with a man who is promised to someone else. I must protect myself from being heartbroken if all this turns out to be just one of those things caused by your amnesia. You will be fine when you leave to go back to your wife or girlfriend, and I will be stuck here for another two months alone and hurt. Surely you can see I must be careful?"

He looked thoughtful and nodded his agreement. "Molly, I can promise you I'd never hurt you intentionally, and I do believe if there was someone special in my life, I'd at least have an inkling. But yes, I agree, you must think of yourself first and foremost—just in case." He lifted his cup, winked at her, and drank from it.

Why does he have to be so thoughtful? She wondered as she gratefully drank her tea. *I almost wish he'd do something horrible so that I won't like him as much. God, I ache to be held by him.* Her gaze locked with his over the top of her cup, and just for a moment, she imagined being naked and John touching her intimately. She felt a blush creep up her body from her chest to head and was stunned by the vivid image. "I've been asked to keep a close watch out," she said to disguise her immoral feelings.

"What for?"

“The storm has done a lot of damage on the mainland; it’s also ripped boats from their moorings. If I see anything drifting this way, I’m to radio in and report it in case they become shipping hazards.” Molly finished her hot drink and stood up. “Thanks for making the tea, I might go and have a look around up top and get the light ready for tonight, then come down and make a start on dinner, roast leg of lamb tonight.” She smiled.

Just then, she heard a clap of thunder, but it sounded a long way off, so it seemed it was more of a warning of things to come later than an imminent deluge. “I’ll come with you, I love being up in the watch room, the view is spectacular, and I can help be a spotter for floating ghost boats.”

Chapter 10

The Calm before the Real Storm

Barry and Nick sat at a well-worn wooden round table in the corner of the Augusta Hotel's public bar, sipping from frosted pint glasses of beer. They tried to keep a low profile and sat hunched down but had taken the opportunity of the lull in the storm to check out the marina and a potential boat to steal. They were also going stir crazy being cooped up in Hank's home and needed to get out for a while.

Everyone they encountered talked about the storm that had been, and when it was likely to ease. Some houses lost their roofs, fences were blown down, and there had been a hive of activity as everyone pitched in to help those who had suffered damage.

"Mate," Barry began softly so as not to be overheard, "you sure you can handle a boat well enough? The locals say the reef systems around here can be dangerous."

"Yeah, piece of cake. I grew up in Southport, and I've been on boats all my life. Don't worry about the reefs; I've been studying Hanky-boy's nautical charts. The way I see it, if he didn't sink from the hole he put in the hull, he couldn't have made it any further than Forbes Reef. It could be the wind from the storm when it hit, blew him right onto the shoal. This pissy tail end will ease overnight according to the locals, so we will pinch the boat at dawn, and the owner might think it broke free from its mooring. It will be a bit uncomfortable at first, but I reckon as the day goes on, the sea will flatten out. If we don't find his wreckage or him washed up on that island out there, we will dump the boat and piss off to Albany in Hank's car, just to be safe. But if we find him, we kill him and dump him out at sea as shark bait. Then go back to the plan of lying low a few more days. Then fly to Darwin—they'd never expect that, from there to Brisbane, then home to Melbourne. Piece of cake, like I said."

"I still reckon I winged him, so maybe by now he's bled to death," Barry added.

Nick finished his beer in three gulps, "Well, let's hope so. It's your buy, this WA beer is as weak as piss, so I might have a double scotch, then get some fish and chips for tea and go back; we have an early start tomorrow morning."

****

Molly and John returned from the watch room forty minutes later, laughing and joking with each other. There had been nothing much to see, other than an approaching wall of rain on the horizon. The increasingly darkening sky with angry tufty clouds and lightning in the distance heralding its advance like a marauding troop movement. Molly was reminded of the light show she had been treated to on the first night of the storm, and John was impressed with the view of the far-off spectacle Mother Nature provided for their entertainment.

By six o'clock, the smell of roasting lamb permeated the lighthouse. John had helped with peeling and preparing the vegetables, which were cooking, and the table was set for two. Molly remembered her father's small collection of alcohol. "John, do you drink wine?" she asked, which seemed to catch him unawares when he sat at the dining table.

He jerked his head toward her with a questioning look in his eyes. "I'm not sure, I think so, why do you ask?" He licked his lips as if by doing so, it would bring back a memory.

"I feel like drinking a glass, but if you won't help, there's no point opening a bottle for me to drink alone. I seem to recall an article I read somewhere that said when trying to regain lost memories; all senses can be a trigger, including taste, so I thought...."

"Well, let's give it a go. I'm game. Let me do the honors, where is the wine?" He grinned like a schoolboy, and just for a moment, Molly wondered if it wasn't due to a mental image he had of getting her drunk and lowering her morals and inhibitions. A thrill ran through her body all the way to her toes.

"In the cupboard in the radio room come study, pick one out you think you might like, while I find two glasses and a corkscrew." She turned away from him so he wouldn't notice how flushed she felt her cheeks had become as some very naughty thoughts rattled around within her.

Two minutes later, he returned with a bottle in one hand and a pack of cards in the other. "Hey, look what I found in the drawer, do you play cribbage?" he asked cheerfully.

"More importantly, do you?" Molly asked and raised an eyebrow in inquiry."

"Yeah," he replied eagerly, "The second I saw

them, I remember I used to play with my dad on cold winter nights. I can even picture what he looked like when we played. It's like you said, Molly, everything is coming back one piece at a time, but all jumbled up." She stayed silent; her eyebrow still cocked and waited for him to answer her unasked question. "No, he said with a shrug, "Still nothing about a girlfriend, fiancée, or wife."

She handed him the corkscrew and pointed to the glasses on the table. "Pour us a drink while I go up and check the wicks and have one last look around. It's almost dark, but I will sleep better knowing there are no boats out there; the storm will be here any time now."

Once she was in the watch room, she leaned her forehead against the cold window, closed her eyes, and gave herself a good talking to. *What are you doing?* She screamed silently. *Red wine, a nice meal, a game of cards, and then what? You want him to make love to you, don't you?* She didn't answer; it was self-evident. *Consequences, Molly, think of the bloody consequences, what would Dad think? And what if John makes you pregnant, what then? You're a nurse, you know, you're not some young girl who doesn't know better.* Then the killer thought hit her again; *You have no idea who he is, how can you give your most precious gift to someone when you don't even know his name?* She sighed, long and slow. There were a hundred reasons not to do it, but she still wanted to, she had fallen for him, and she couldn't help that. *But you've fallen for who, Molly? You know nothing about him other than three of four fragments of memory that had seeped back into his consciousness. At least wait till he remembers something more concrete.*

It made sense; it was perfectly logical. In the past, when she had been so undecided about something, Molly always relied on her father's guidance. But this was one time she couldn't go to him, and not just because of geographical reasons. He would be horrified she was contemplating such an irrevocable step. If he ever found out, and for one moment thought John had taken advantage of her good nature, he would kill him, or hurt him very badly. She wasn't the only McLaren with a temper, and he had always been so lovingly protective of her.

Her face suddenly lit up in a blinding flash of lightning; the storm was coming closer now, then a slow, menacing roll of thunder crossed the sky. The rain began, and the whole sequence broke the spell of her fantasy of making love with John. The cold, rational side of her being, took over—*one glass of wine only, Molly. Not two and three are out of the question. You have dinner, clean up, play cards, and go to bed - alone.*

She nodded to her reflection in the glass, her resolve restored. *And if I weaken? Recite passages of* Moby Dick *until it passes,* she replied, and that made her laugh aloud.

By the time they sat down to eat, John had filled her glass with the Margaret River Cabernet for the second time before she could stop him. The first one had gone during her meal preparations and making gravy while John carved the meat from the joint. It just appeared full again magically, and she had taken another sip before she remembered her earlier pledge. Molly was not and never had been a big drinker. One glass of wine, usually white, but on rare occasions, a red, with her father was her limit. She was entering uncharted territory.

She served their meal on the white china plates and sat down. “John,” she began nervously, “will you make me a promise, please?”

He looked up, knife, and fork in his hands. “Of course, anything, name it.”

She took a deep breath, steeling her courage. “Well, I’ve never had two glasses of wine in my life, but I’m enjoying this, so, if it goes to my head, promise you won’t take advantage of me, please?” *Bless him; he looks like I’ve slapped him,* she thought.

“Molly, do you think I’m that sort of a man? I’d never do anything like that.”

She reached out a hand and covered his with a gentle squeeze. “No, if I thought you were, I wouldn’t be drinking at all, and I’d have a big stick by my side to beat you over the head with if you tried. But, that said, maybe it’s me I don’t trust, and of course, while I might think you are chivalrous, I don’t know anything about you, not really. There is also the fact that I’m still trying to save your life; my dad is fiercely protective of me, being an only child whom he raised after Mum died, so…” She grinned, the threat silent, and was pleased to see he smiled back.

“Message received and understood. Molly, I vow and declare not to take advantage of you, even if you get drunk and want me to, scouts honor.” He crossed his heart, knife in hand, so it looked like he was slashing at his chest.

“How’s the lamb?” she asked, to change the subject. “I’ve never cooked a roast before.”

Silently he cut a piece off, dipped it in gravy, and

slipped it into his mouth. His face was impossible to read, and Molly's anxiousness increased. He shook his head. "It needs mint sauce." He burst into spontaneous laughter as she felt her jaw drop in disappointment. "That was a joke, Molly; it's gorgeous. You know, I live alone, so I only get roast meals when I visit Mum or have Sunday Roast at the pub for lunch." He dropped his knife, and it clattered on the edge of the plate. "Wow, there's another memory; I live alone, Molly. No wife at home who is waiting for me. I can picture my house; it has timber walls and an iron roof, and it's close to the marina, a two-bedroom ex woodcutters shack. No idea where my keys for the front door are, they must have gone down with the boat, but I remember where I keep the spare, under a rock near the garbage bin."

She beamed at him, not doubting his sincerity for a moment, and a wave of relief washed over her; he was single. Molly raised her glass. "Well, I'll drink to that." She grinned.

As they ate, her glass of wine slowly diminished, and their table talk flowed. They spoke of John's recollections of the house, and slowly he remembered more and more details right down to the color of the carpeting and style of the furniture. John seemed animated, enthusiastically remembering things, and adding one after the other. As he put the last piece of meat into his mouth, he stopped chewing and looked troubled for the first time. "What's the matter?" she asked.

"I have a feeling I've got someone staying with me that I don't like, but I have no idea who or why. It's like, a sense of impending doom; that's the best way I can describe it."

"You mean like a distant family member you don't get along with? You know, the kind of person you invite to stay for a couple of days to be polite, then they don't want to leave, and you can't get rid of them without a scene." She queried.

He shrugged. "Maybe. What else could it be? It's just a feeling, and for all I know, it might be a memory from long ago, and they have left now, but it's a bit weird.

Something in his manner jarred with Molly, but her brain was buzzing with the alcohol, and her happiness that he wasn't married, so she chose to ignore it. "Well," she said, and pushed her plate away, "Leave it alone, and it will come to you. I think sometime soon everything will return, including your name, though I'm quite used to John now. It would be a shame if it were Alfonse, or Horace, or something. I might have to keep calling you John if I don't like your real name." She raised a hand to cover her mouth and giggled uncontrollably, and he laughed back.

"Maybe I'll keep it, just for you, even if I do remember. Especially, if it's something like Hubert or worse; Alliaceous." That set them both off again. Eventually, he stopped and looked serious. "Hmm, our glasses are empty, and you said you'd stop at two, but I reckon there's about half a glass each left in the bottle; it would be a shame to waste it." He picked up the offending bottle and held it up to her with a questioning look.

"Why, John, I do believe you're trying to get me drunk." She grinned and held out the empty glass. "It's a celebration," she said by way of explanation, and he somberly nodded his agreement.

He emptied the bottle, peering exaggeratedly to get it as close to an equal share as he could. "How about," he said quietly, "I stack the dishes in the sink, and we have that game of cards?"

"Deal," she replied, then realized what she'd said and burst into laughter bordering on hysteria. "See what I did there, the joke I made?" she mumbled. When she slowed down, he suddenly laughed too, which only set her off again. When they stopped, their gazes locked, and she yearned to kiss him. But, the last vestiges of her earlier promise lingered. Instead, she pushed herself to her feet and weaved her way across the room to the study to find the cribbage board and pegs.

When she returned, the table was clear, and John sat shuffling the cards and smiling. "Why John, you look almost professional, I could be in trouble here, I think." She sat down opposite him, "What shall we play for?"

"Hmm, well, I don't have any money, so it will have to be something else. How about the best of three games, the winner gets to kiss the loser, five times."

She laughed, "I get it, so even if you lose, you win?"

"Yep, sounds good to me."

They cut for deal, which John won. He rapidly dealt six cards each, and the game began. Molly and her father had whiled away many an hour playing cribbage from ten years old, but within two hands, realized John must have done the same as they seemed evenly matched. They leapfrogged each other's score by using the box, and they raced around the board until, with dismay, Molly saw that John would be cribbing just at the right time. With it being his first to score on her deal, he only required eight points in his hand, less if he wrote any before his turn to lay down. She put her cards down, counting up to thirty-one with all the skill she could muster and noted with glee that John looked concerned. When they reached the laydown, John had only written one point, while Molly had made five, which meant he required seven to win. She held her breath as she knew it would be tight.

"Fifteen for two, and a pair makes four, but…. a run makes seven, Molly." He grinned and fanned his cards out. "First blood to me, and one step closer to five kisses."

"Beginners luck, no more," she said, taking another sip of wine, and then gathering the cards in to deal. "There will be no kisses for you tonight, John." She boxed the deck, split, and shuffled, but a card flicked out and spiraled through the air. "That's embarrassing," she murmured and wondered if the wine was making her fumble. *Surely not*, she thought.

They began the game with Molly streaking ahead to an early lead with twenty points in her hand and twelve in the box, while John only had nine. "I can see you're out for blood this game," he said good-naturedly with a smile as he scooped in the cards to shuffle.

"It's early doors yet," she replied with a smile. Early doors was one of her father's sayings, a typically British expression, and she giggled when John looked at her questioningly. "It means there's a long way to go," she explained.

But she continued her winning run, and by the time she pegged into the last hole, John was only just over halfway. "Wow," he said, "You didn't just win, you annihilated me. I'm almost scared to play the deciding game."

"And let that be a lesson to you, never underestimate a McLaren." She looked down, and her wine glass was empty, *where did that go?* She wondered.

John was dealing, and as she watched the cards spin across the table toward her, she wondered if perhaps she had had a bit too much to drink. *I'm fine,* she assured herself, *I'm lovely.*

"Oh, I wouldn't dare upset a McLaren, don't you worry about that." He placed the deck down between them and picked up his cards.

He's grinning like a Cheshire Cat, so he must have a good hand, Molly thought. She drew her cards to her and groaned her dismay; she didn't have a single point. *It's all right, play smart, there's plenty of time.* She put her cards into the box and cut the cards for John to turn the top one over. When he did, she groaned again; it was the Jack of Spades, which not only did not help her hand whatsoever but immediately gifted John two points. *It's going to be one of those games,* she worried.

And it was. Despite Molly's best efforts, she never got closer than ten points. On the final hand, John romped home with sixteen points and sat back smugly. "You see, Molly, there are two types of people in the world; those who say they can and those who do. I think you owe me five kisses."

"Damn you, Honest John, damn you," she replied in her best Hollywood voice. "But first, you have to make a cup of tea; dem's da rules." She waggled a finger in his direction, then got to her feet unsteadily and walked to the couch and sat down heavily, to await the kissing debt repayment ceremony. Why is the room tilting this way and that? She wondered.

****

The next thing Molly was aware of was it was dark, and she didn't know where she was. Her head ached, and when she tried to move, pain shot down her body, emanating from her temples. Molly tried to think back, groggily, and figure out what had happened. She had been sitting on the couch, waiting for John to make the tea, and then it dawned on her*; she was lying in her bed.* Molly froze in abject terror. Had John undressed her, worse, had he interfered with her? She must have passed out from the wine, and he had… what, done what with her, other than put her to bed?

Outside the lighthouse, the storm raged, and a flash of lightning lit up her bedroom. She was under the bedclothes, alone, and just for a moment, she didn't know how she felt about that. Surely if John had done something untoward, he would still be with her, wouldn't he? She slipped her right hand under the bedspread and sheet and touched her chest before venturing further south. She breathed a sigh of relief; she was fully clothed, then as an afterthought, slid it under the waistband of her trousers. Again, she felt relief; she still had her underwear on, so her maidenhood was intact.

Her next emotion was a feeling of embarrassment. She had got drunk, for the first, and undoubtedly last, time in her life. Molly had passed out from drinking too much. Her mouth felt like the inside of a birdcage, her head ached, and she was ashamed. She burst into tears; worried John wouldn't like her anymore, how could she show her face to him in the morning?

Crying made her headache worse; the throbbing was horrendous. She sat up and swung her legs over the side of the bed and waited for the rotating darkness to slow down. When the next flash came, she saw John had left a glass of water on the bedside cabinet, and on the floor was her father's medical bag. Molly smiled; he must have known she would wake and need water and something for the pain. She felt ashamed, once again, she had misjudged him.

Molly fumbled in the dark with her top bedside drawer, the one which contained her underwear, and reached inside for the small battery torch she kept there for emergencies. Usually, when she went to bed, Molly took a Tilley lamp with her and turned it down to the lowest setting. That was because she didn't like the thought of waking up in pitch blackness, as she had. Batteries were at a premium, so she didn't want to use it often, while kerosene was plentiful. But, she reminded herself, John was not to know of her dislike of waking in the dark.

She slid the switch upward, and the pencil beam shot out across the room and hit the closed door. Again, she smiled; John had closed it thoughtfully so any noise he made wouldn't wake her. Gratefully, Molly picked up the glass and swallowed three mouthfuls, saving the rest to take the headache powder she would shake in when she found it. It felt good for her lips and mouth to be moist again, and she wondered what the attraction for people was to get drunk, she wouldn't be doing it again any time soon, that was for sure.

Molly delved into her father's bag, using the torch to show the many compartments, and she foraged until the found the elastic band which held several of the paper sachets containing the powders. Her trembling fingers took one out, opened its end, and tipped the contents into her glass, which she then twirled around and around until the Aspirin powder dissolved. In one motion, Molly drank the water and shook her head, trying hard not to gag and vomit. She hated the bitter taste of the powder, and would gladly have not had it, but her headache was dreadful, so it was the lesser of two evils.

Once she set the glass back down, Molly realized she needed to use the bathroom, which under normal circumstances she would have done before bed. Molly had no memory beyond sitting on the couch, waiting for her cup of tea, but she knew she hadn't peed. Molly stood up and blinked several times to ward off the pain, and when it eased, Molly used the light from the torch to show the way across her room. It was as dark on the other side of her door as inside the bedroom; John hadn't left a lamp glowing as she usually did, but she could hardly be angry with him; she was the one at fault.

After using the toilet, she made her way to the kitchen and lit the lamp, turned off the torch and used the light to get another glass from the cupboard and get a drink of water, she needed lots to fend off the dehydration she felt, knowing it would ease the headache, eventually. Molly leaned with her back against the sink and looked around the living area as she sipped her water. The place always looked spooky when illuminated by the single flickering glow from a Tilley Lamp, and tonight was no exception.

Molly put the glass down, beginning to feel just a little better. She wondered how John fared, whether he was suffering from the wine as she was, *probably not, he's used to drinking, being a man.* The headache retreated to a fuzzy numbness inside her forehead, and Molly felt like she had drunk enough water. "Back to bed," she mumbled and picked up the lamp.

Halfway to her room, Molly decided to look in on John if his door was open; just to satisfy herself, he was all right. *After all*, she reasoned, *he made sure I got to bed, the least I can do is look in on him.* Molly held the lamp up to shoulder height so she could read the clock on the wall and saw it was one-twenty. John was sure to be asleep, and she idly wondered if he slept clothed or naked, which brought a glow to her skin. As she approached, she noted the door was ajar but not enough to see into the room, so she gently pushed against it.

A rain squall chose that moment to hit the window in his room, which made her jump, though the wind was nowhere near as severe as previous storms. Molly almost dropped the lamp in surprise; his bedclothes were rumpled, but he wasn't there; John was gone.

Chapter 11

What is Truth?

Stupidly, for a moment, Molly stood and stared, dumbfounded. She wondered if he had been in bed with her when she awoke all along, perhaps under the quilt. Her panicked brain thought back to when she woke up and looked around. Yes, it had been dark, and no, Molly decided he hadn't been there; she would have screamed if he had been. She knew he wasn't in the bathroom or toilet; she had used both, so sitting on the couch, maybe? Molly hurried back to the living area, but he wasn't there; she was alone in the lighthouse. Perhaps he was in the radio room or possibly the watch room, not that she could imagine why he would be in either unless he couldn't sleep.

As Molly suspected, her father's study was empty. "John, are you up there?" she called up the stairway and was shocked at how nervous her voice sounded. The silence was the only reply, so Molly climbed the stairs. He wasn't there, either in the room or out on the balcony, and her heart sank as she realized with a dawning sense of horror, *he must have stolen the boat to make a dash for the mainland. That's why he got me drunk so he could run for it. Hang on, Molly, that's not true; you suggested the wine, not him, hold your horse's girl, and don't get your knickers in a knot*. But it was useless, once the seed was sown that John had run off, she was powerless to use logic and convince herself she was wrong.

Why, why, why would you do that, John? You'll never find the gap in the reef in the darkness and storm. Even if it's not as bad as last night's effort, its bad enough, you bloody idiot. Frantically she stepped into the room proper and let her eyesight track with the intense beam of light radiating out across the ocean, looking for the dingy, or wreckage which she was sure she would find scattered on the rocks from his failed attempt.

There was nothing she could see close in, so for the next circuit, she searched further out, keeping pace with the lamp as it turned. With each successive rotation after the second sweep, she used the Weiss glasses to explore, until she was sure the boat had not put to sea. Only then did she look downward to look over the island, and there, she saw him. He was walking back up the path toward the light, some three hundred yards away. His head bowed against the wind and with his hands thrust deep in his pockets. Molly didn't know whether to laugh or cry, be angry or happy, but she turned around and headed back down below to greet him when he arrived.

"Where the bloody hell have you been?" she asked and was shocked how harsh her voice sounded as the front door opened. She had taken up station on the fourth stair, with the lamp on the third, her arms folded across her chest as her foot tapped a frantic rhythm.

"Oh, hi, Molly, how are you feeling now?" He asked with a grin as he struggled to remove her father's oilskin cape.

She couldn't stop the rising tide that was her temper, and though she didn't know if it was through fear or worry, she realized she was damn mad with him. "Never mind how am I feeling, though, if you must know, I've been scared half to death with worry," she replied as her own personal Mount Vesuvius erupted in a torrent.

"I'm sorry," he responded as he hung up the dripping jacket, "I thought you were out for the count when I carried you to bed; you looked so peaceful. I couldn't sleep, as more and more memories came flooding back, so I went for a walk to the jetty because like you said earlier, being there might help regain more memories. You were right. Molly, it's all coming back to me now. Still only bits and pieces, but lots more details are filtering through the gloom. I thought if I went back down to the jetty, it might help me remember why I was being chased. I didn't mean to make you worry; I thought you'd be asleep; you were actually snoring when I left." He grinned, but Molly ignored that.

"And did it?" She felt her anger melting with the shame of realizing once again she had misjudged him.

He crossed the distance between them, stepped up the stairs, and put one foot either side of the lamp and hugged her tightly. "I am sorry if I frightened you, I didn't mean to, and no, still nothing about being shot at. Ouch, I've got to move, the lamp is burning my legs," he yelped, as he comically stepped back down."

That broke the ice between them, and she couldn't help but laugh. "I'm sorry if I sounded like a nagging wife, I feared that you had taken the boat and would die trying to get through the gap in the reef in this weather."

He stared back dumbly as if she had said the most stupid thing ever, and she blushed at her daft insecurities; firstly, for thinking it, then secondly admitting it. "Seriously? You thought I'd steal from the woman who saved my life and that I am falling in love with and be so desperate to get away from her I'd put to sea in a storm in a twelve-foot dingy?"

Her embarrassment level increased, and she was sure her skin glowed as brightly as the light above their heads. "I didn't stop to think, I saw you were gone, and just panicked. I didn't work anything out logically; I reacted. I went up to the watch room and searched for you. I've never felt so bloody frightened in my life, but not frightened for me, for you."

"You went into my bedroom to wake me up in the middle of the night? Why did you do that, Molly, did you want to get into bed with me for cuddles?"

"I, err, umm, no, of course I didn't want to get in bed with you. Just what do you think I am?" She was floundering. She had started out being angry but now felt more embarrassed than at any time in her life as she felt her very soul was being laid bare.

He smirked. *He is actually smirking at my discomfort,* Molly noticed. "What do I think you are?" he asked softly. "I think you are one of the most beautiful women in the world, especially when you're angry with me."

She wanted to kiss him, worse she wanted him to ravish her, yet her words told a different story. "You're so full of yourself, aren't you? I suppose you think if you shower me with enough flattery, especially after scaring me half to death, I will fall into your arms and let you have your way with me."

"Well, I hoped you might." He grinned, then feigned a duck as if she was going to slap him. "How about a cup of tea while we discuss your surrender, and I can tell you more of my memories; or would you rather wait until morning?"

Molly hesitated; she wanted to know what he had remembered, but it was the middle of the night, and if she was totally honest, she was embarrassed at the allusion of her wanting to climb into bed with him. "I think its way past my bedtime and yours too, and no; that doesn't mean we go to bed together." She picked up the lamp, turned on her heel, and started back up the stairs before he could give a smart-aleck answer.

****

The alarm clock woke her from a beautiful dream. She knew it was wonderful because she had a smile on her face and felt a sense of wonder in her tummy. But the content of the fantasy she had experienced disappeared behind fluffy white clouds the moment she woke, so she was only left with a feeling of happiness. Molly yawned, reached out and switched the ringing noise off, and sat up, so she didn't fall back to sleep. *God, I'm so tired. I'm unused to drinking wine and being up in the wee hours of the morning,* she thought.

Her mouth felt furry, and her lips were dry, so she picked up the replenished glass of water from the bedside cabinet and drank it all then wiped her mouth with the back of her hand. Better, she decided. I need a nice hot shower that will fix me up, and then what about breakfast? She shuddered at the thought of food and worked hard not to vomit. "Willpower, Molly, my girl, willpower," she uttered quietly.

Molly flung the bedclothes back and got out of bed, determined to wake up, and force her body to ignore the dehydration and hangover. Within a couple of minutes, she took out fresh underwear and clothes to wear for the day. Then she was ready to go to the bathroom. Molly chose beige corduroy trousers, a white shirt, and a matching polo-necked jumper to go over the top. She glanced out of the tiny window her room was blessed with and was pleased to see blue sky. At last decent weather, yippee, she grinned.

There was no sign of John as she crossed the living quarters. Her first job was to stoke the firebox and top up with fresh wood so she could put the kettle on the back of the stove. While the thought of eating made her shudder, a cup of tea would be very welcome when she came out of the bathroom. Next, Molly dropped her clothes on top of the wicker basket inside the door, and then climbed the stairs to the watch room. She doused the flames and turned the turntable off to stop the turning, then grabbed the glasses for a cursory glance around, looking for shipwrecks.

Molly was amazed at how much the seas had dropped during the night. Sure, it was far from calm, but largish waves had replaced the mountainous swells. Great herring weather, she thought with a grin. She nodded, pleased that the image of fresh fish hadn't made her want to throw up, and then stepped out on the balcony for her search of the reef. The only thing of note was way out on the horizon, where she saw a fishing boat cutting its way through the waves as plumes of spray were thrust out from its bow. It wasn't the *Morning Dawn*, it was nowhere near the reef, and it was heading away from Forbes, so nothing for Molly to be concerned with. *Shower time, come on Molly and shake a leg.*

Molly was careful to lock the bathroom door before turning the water on and undressing. She had an image flit across her mind of John opening the door to join her under the cascading hot water, and she leaned back to double-check the lock. As the water warmed up, Molly looked at her body in the large mirror with a critical eye that wasn't quite as criticizing as it usually was. *Not a bad body, Molly, my girl,* she thought, *shame about the red hair top and bottom, and the freckles.* In a second of naughtiness, Molly held her breasts, which overfilled her palms, and imagined they were John's. Part of her wanted to unlock the door, just in case he did wander in by mistake, and she admonished herself, but she grinned too.

Molly lathered up and washed her hair. The steaming water felt wonderful, and she dreamily realized she could stay there all day, quite easily. But Molly had jobs to do and responsibilities to attend to. John's dressings needed to be changed, she had to radio Rachel, and she desperately wanted to catch fish for her dinner because it had been days since she had fresh herring to eat. Reluctantly, Molly turned the water off, grabbed the towel, and dried herself. She stood naked as she brushed her teeth and hair, then dressed before taking a fresh towel from the shelf. Molly tied it around her head, turban-like, to help dry her long-wet tresses. When finished, she glanced at her reflection in the mirror, and for the first time in what felt like forever, Molly thought she looked lovely, well, she would if she didn't have the towel-turban to spoil the look. *Molly, you've dressed up for John, you sneaky cow*, she thought, but then immediately replied, *I have not, don't be stupid. You're not fooling anyone; you know that, don't you?*

The internal argument could have gone on for hours, but Molly dragged her gaze away from the mirror, picked up her dirty clothes, and tucked them in the basket. That was another job that awaited her, she realized; washing, now the weather would allow the things to dry. *Well, that's for later, it's a cup of tea time now.*

When Molly opened the door, and turned to go to the kitchen, her senses were assailed by the pleasant smell of cooking toast. John was in the kitchen, and he turned to greet her. "Good morning beautiful, sit you down it's my turn to look after you. The tea is brewing in the pot, the toast is nearly ready, and the poached eggs will be one minute. I hope that's all right with you?"

"Why, John, umm, yes that would be wonderful, thank you." Feeling dazed, she walked to the table, which he had already set. *Boy,* she thought, *I could get used to having a man cooking meals for me.* She sat at her usual place as he poured the tea.

"Gotta say, Molly, you look very fetching in a turban," he said, smiling as he placed her cup in front of her.

She blushed; embarrassed he had caught her like that. "I didn't think you would be up this early after your morning stroll. I planned to dry it while preparing your breakfast."

"I was too excited to sleep once I heard your alarm go off. So, while you were up dousing the light, I fetched the eggs, but I hid when you came back down because I wanted to surprise you. You've done so much for me; this is the least I can do to say thank you."

"Well, John," she said as she sipped from her cup, "Don't let me stop you from cooking a meal for me any time; I think I mentioned it's not my strong suit."

"That's just it; I've remembered it is mine. When I left school, I got an apprenticeship as a baker/chef. But, after my third year, the bakery that sponsored me changed owners; they sold out to some city slickers who wanted to retire down south, and sadly for me, they had a son. Unfortunately, also for me, he was a third-year apprentice, what are the odds? So, I got canned. I couldn't get a job to continue it at any of the bakeries or restaurants locally, so I became a deckhand on a tuna boat." As he spoke, he was buttering the toast, and Molly realized, much to her surprise, she was hungry after all.

"I'm sorry it didn't work out for you, John."

He turned and waved a butter knife at her. "It's not John, sorry it's Hank, Hank Drage."

"Hank?" She couldn't help herself; Molly burst out laughing. Of all the names she thought would suit him that was one she would never have guessed.

"Don't blame me; blame my parents, Susan and Lawrence Drage. I'm an only child." He removed the eggs from the heat and began using a slotted scoop to take each one out and drain it off before easing it onto the toast. My father owns a mechanical repair business in Margaret River, and his passion is speedway cars, and it's mine too; I race my very own car, and he works in the pits for me." He beamed his best smile, and then turned back to his task.

Just for a moment, Molly felt so sad she thought

she might cry. With the return of his memory, he would leave her, and she would probably never see him again.

Molly, my girl, get a grip. She forced herself to think. *He has a life, a family, perhaps a girlfriend, and guess what? That life won't include you, get over yourself.* She bowed her head so he wouldn't see how sad she felt, but it was as if he could read her mind.

John placed her plate in front of her and sat beside her with his breakfast. "I know what you're thinking," he said without looking at her, "and I promise you it's not true, I do not have a girlfriend." He grinned at her. "It's true, I swear. I live alone, I work on the tuna boat, and on weekends, I race my car with my dad working the pits for me, and Molly? I'm quick, I should switch from country racing to the big time, and one day I will when I get enough money behind me." He cut a corner off his toast, then dug his knife into the oozing egg and wiped the yolk on it. He popped it into his mouth and said, "mmm, it's good; try it."

Caught up in his enthusiasm, she tried some and smiled. It was just simple poached eggs on toast *but, how come everything tastes better when someone else cooks it for you?* She wondered.

****

"Is there anything interesting going on in the outside world, Rachel, over?" Molly asked during the ten o'clock radio check-in. John was doing the breakfast dishes in the kitchen.

"Well, funny, you should say that, but there is news just in from your home country. Boy, if you think you just lived through a bad storm, spare a thought for the poor people of Lynmouth. They suffered nine inches of rain in less than twenty-four hours, which caused a severe flood to race down the River Lyn. Apparently, thirty-four people died, four hundred and twenty are homeless from over one hundred buildings that have been destroyed. Over."

"Goodness, that's horrible. You don't expect that sort of weather in the UK; it's a temperate climate. I mean, the weather is bloody awful, not at all like here, but it's averagely bad, dreary I'd call it, if you know what I mean, over."

"Don't know, never been, my family hail from Canada. One other piece of news I can pass on, Molly, is regarding the bank robbery. The police found the getaway car, and they're keeping pretty tight-lipped about why, but they've shifted the search for the driver to Busselton, Margaret River, and the Dunsborough area, over."

"That's interesting, any idea at all why, over?" Molly's breath caught in her throat, and she suddenly felt cold inside. If the robbers had a local connection, could her visitor be it? Did that not explain in some regards, who had been chasing and shooting at him.

"Well, the brother of a friend of my neighbor, Phyllis, is a cop, and he says it's because they got a good fingerprint of the driver, from the car. So not only do they know who he is, but where he lives. If that's the case, it should be only a matter of time till there's a capture. It looks like while the criminals are from the Eastern States, the driver could be a local boy, over."

"Good, I hope they lock them up and throw away the key. Well, I've got lots to do today, after three days stuck inside, Rachel, so I better go. I will check in at four. Over and out."

She debated whether to mention the local hunt to

John; she couldn't get used to calling him Hank. Was the driver of the getaway car him? Rather than risk unsettling John, she decided to keep it quiet for the time being. Molly remembered how upset he was when he overheard about the robbery before; she thought it best to say nothing until she was sure or John remembered for himself. His memory was coming back quickly now, so she thought it best to see if he recalled that was what he had done and if it had been the two robbers who had shot at him. She feared if she told him, it could plant a false memory, if such a thing was possible.

****

Molly spent the next two hours doing her chores. She got the washing going, including all of John's clothes. She still had trouble thinking of him as Hank; somehow, it seemed discordant; he would always be John to her. He had volunteered to clean out the chicken coup and check out the vegetable patch because he said they were overdue for their fishing competition.

She hummed a song, feeling pretty good about everything, and especially him, except for the niggling doubt that he could have been a participant in a bank robbery. But, the John she knew didn't seem capable of that, so she wanted to give him the benefit of the doubt. For the first time, Molly wondered if they had some kind of future. Sure, he hadn't got all his memory back, but different things from his past were coming thick and fast, and she agreed with him, that if he had a serious girlfriend, he would have remembered something about her by now. So, when the *Morning Dawn* next called, they would take John away, but in her heart, she now believed it would not be the end, well, perhaps hoped would be a better word. She was sure Derek would understand her dilemma, and not report in that he had been staying on the island, so Mr. Harpington never needed to know.

When the washing was going, the kitchen was tidy, and the beds made, she went up to the watch room and grabbed the Weiss glasses to have a scan around. The weather was fining up; the waves were dropping, and the wind seemed breezy at worst, and non-existent at best. She hoped she wouldn't see any boats drifting in her direction, but there in the far distance was a white speck. Molly focused by turning the dial above her nose, and the object became just a little clearer. It looked like a powerboat; quite a large one. Molly could see a white hull with a red upper structure. It wasn't drifting; she could make out a bow wave flinging spray either side of its powerful bow. Her best guess was maybe a fishing boat and therefore nothing for her to worry about, she decided.

Later they walked hand in hand along the path toward the jetty kidding each other who would be crowned Herring King or Queen. As they mounted the last rise before the bay with the dock, the sunlit glinted off the windscreen of a boat that was around a mile away. They stopped to watch it as it cruised along the outer reef. Suddenly Hank squeezed her arm. "Molly, I've got an awful feeling about that boat."

She glanced up at him as he shielded his eyes from the glare of the sun. "Why? It's probably just some fishermen. I saw it from the watch room earlier, heading for us."

He looked thoughtful and kept hold of her arm, not letting her walk farther. "Molly, since coming here, have you seen many boats that size, this far out, cruising the outside of the reef?"

"Well, no, now you come to mention it, there is the odd boat comes to the reef to fish, but not that many. But then again, it's not like I've been watching out for fishermen either." For some reason she couldn't explain, his nervousness was contagious.

"On the boat, one of my jobs is a spotter for the schools of tuna. The reason for that is my eyes are pretty good. That boat isn't fishing; they don't have any rods in the holders, so they are not trolling. I think they are looking for a gap to come inside, and that bothers me, though I have no idea why. I have a sense of foreboding."

Suddenly, there was a flash from the boat, and Hank yanked her arm downward, so they both fell to a crouching position. "They've got binoculars, and they are looking this way, damn I hope they didn't see us."

"Why, John? What's wrong with them looking at the island and the lighthouse, and why are we hiding from them?"

"Shit, shit, shit, shit; the bloody life raft. If they see it hung up on those rocks, they will know I put to shore here on Forbes."

"No, they won't. They will see a deflated orange boat washed up on the reef along with all the other flotsam and jetsam from the storm. I still don't understand why you are so scared?"

He bit his lip; his eyes were darting between her and back out to the boat. "What if it's the men who shot at me?"

She jerked her head back in shock and immediately wondered what he wasn't telling her. "Why do you think it might be? What are you hiding from me,

Hank?"

"I don't know; it's just a terrible feeling I can't explain, but we're in danger; I just know it."

He looked frightened, but Molly also thought he was lying, and she was stung by his dishonesty. She stood up, and he yanked her arm back down, but she wrenched it free. "Now you listen to me whatever your name is. If we are in danger, I deserve to know why. I saved your life, how dare you put mine in danger without at least telling me what the hell is going on. Now, you've got ten seconds to tell me the truth, or I start waving to get their attention."

He let out a long, drawn-out sigh, while at the same time, had a look on his face of a frightened animal. "Molly, please, trust me. I remember some things, but not everything, okay? What I do remember is that two men were trying to kill me because I can identify them, though, for the life of me, I cannot remember what for. They wanted to stop me from going to the police. They imprisoned me in my own home, I have a vague recollection of overhearing them planning to murder me, and when I tried to get away through a window, they heard a noise I made and chased me. It was dark, the storm was coming, but I made it to the marina. One of them had a gun, and he shot at me as I was dropping the ropes to my boat. I remember falling, banging my head, and feeling dazed, but I was able to steer the boat away from the mooring with me ducking down as he was still shooting. I can still hear the sound of bullets thudding into the sides of the boat and splinters flying up in the air. Next thing I knew, I drove into the rock wall, but I was able to keep it from running completely aground and escape out into the ocean, though I know I put a hole in the hull. The sea was rough, getting rougher by the minute and what with the knock to my head, the pitching sea, and it being so dark, I remember feeling terrified. That's the last thing I recall until I woke up here. I must have realized I was sinking and launched the dinghy. My guess is, the two men waited out the storm in my house, and then got hold of a boat," he pointed, "that boat, and they've come looking to make sure I died at sea. If they find me, they will make sure I do. You have to help me, please."

Molly stared at his face, trying to decide if he was completely honest with her or only partially. Sadly, she realized something was tugging at her, trying to tell her he wasn't telling the whole truth. She had an idea; "Let's go back, and radio in. We can get Marine and Harbors to send the police boat out."

He shook his head. "No, Molly, that won't work. Firstly, I don't know what I can identify them for without my full memory, so the cops are not likely to believe me. That will also get you into trouble for having me here, and I don't want that. Secondly, no matter how bad my gut feeling is about that boat, it is possible, as you say, they are harmless. We should go back to the light, and watch them, see if they find the way through the reef. If they start fishing or head back out to sea, then we know I worried about nothing. It's important, though; that they don't see me if they have binoculars trained on the island, in case I am right. We will get a better view of what they are doing from the watch room."

She hesitated for a moment, to think about his logic and saw he was right. If she radioed in and the boat was harmless, there would be hell to pay. She could get kicked off the island, and her father could lose his job. She tried to study John's face; she had to know if he was lying to her when he said he didn't understand what he could identify them for, or that he had wanted to report them to the police. Wasn't that just a bit too convenient? Hadn't she had the feeling all along he was hiding some part of the truth from her? Her emotions for him had possibly blinded her judgment, yet, he seemed so kind and genuine. She didn't know. But then, there was the report of the local connection to the bank robbers; could that be it? "All right, John, you make good sense, let's go and keep an eye on them, and decide from there. Meanwhile, try to remember why the men were shooting at you."

"Keep low until we are back below the level of the rise, just in case," he replied, with a severe and no-nonsense kind of voice, then turned and still holding her arm, led her away.

On the way back, as they walked half crouched, she worried if he had been sincere. The more she thought about it, the more she feared he hadn't. *Am I in danger because I saved his life?* That was the thought that rocketed to and fro in her mind like a pinball bouncing off the rubbers.

A hundred yards away from the lighthouse, suddenly, the certainty hit her like a sledgehammer to the solar plexus. She stopped suddenly, almost pulling Hank off his feet. He was the driver for the bank robbers. *Oh my God, that makes sense. Rachel said the police had shifted attention from Perth to down south for someone, probably the driver, because the robbers are from the Eastern States. No wonder he doesn't want me to radio in; he's one of them! He's been telling me what a good speedway driver he is, it was he who drove the getaway car. For some reason they had a falling out, he tried to get away, and they shot him.*

"What's wrong, Molly, why have you stopped?"

She calmly put her bucket down and turned toward the ocean where the boat was searching for a way to the island, which she was convinced it was. They were in a dip, so Molly hoped they could not be seen by them, even if they had binoculars as powerful as the Zeiss ones on the hook in the watch room. Molly sat down on a convenient protruding rock with a flat surface. "I'm not doing this anymore, John, or Hank, whatever your bloody name is. My grandfather had a saying about our family that you should pay heed to: 'Don't mess with a McLaren,' except his language was a bit more colorful, coming from the Glasgow shipbuilding yards as he did."

"I, I, I don't know what you mean."

"Yes, you do. You're lying to me. If you want any help from me at all, I want the truth, warts and all. You're one of the bank robbers who shot that security guard, aren't you?"

He looked as if he had been slapped, and Molly realized he could not be that good an actor. He, too, sat on a rock on the opposite side of the path. John put his head in his hands and wailed softly.

Molly waited patiently, knowing finally, he was going to tell her who he was and why he was on the run.

Eventually, he sighed. "I didn't know for a fact; I hope you believe that. I wasn't lying to you, Molly; I just wasn't sure how much truth there was in the vague memories that came back. But now I know; I remember everything." He sighed again and kept his head down. Molly realized he didn't want to look her in the eye; he was too ashamed.

She decided to prompt him to talk to her. "How did you get involved with these people; they're murderers?"

From behind his hands, he shook his head and began. "It was about a month ago, I was racing at The Busselton Speedway Classic, and I won. Dad and I were celebrating at one of the local pubs when these two guys asked if we wanted a drink, and that they had watched me race. It was a good night, and they kept buying the beers while complimenting me on my driving skills." He paused, "I was just plain dumb, soaking up all the BS they were selling, and thinking I was king of the mountain. They played me like a fiddle, Molly, they led me to believe they were businessmen looking to invest in sponsorship to get me to the big time. They offered me up to fifty thousand dollars, which would not only get me to the majors here, but it would be enough for a stake in the US, and my dream charter boat. They left it at that but wanted to meet again to discuss the details and get me to sign a contract. I realize now what they wanted was a meeting without my father being there. He tried to tell me he thought it was all too good to be true and to be wary, but of course, I knew best.

"It was two weeks before I heard from them again, and by then, I was more than a bit frantic; I thought it was all over, and they had found another driver. Naturally, I was devastated. I'd even looked into travel costs, buying a car in Florida, and sourcing a pit crew." He sighed again. "Out of the blue, they were at the pub where I usually go there after work on the tuna boat. They wanted to see where I lived, and so I invited them home. Once there, they showed me a briefcase with lots of cash in it and said if I wanted it, I had to do a job for them first to earn it. I should have said no, but…. well, they were pretty persuasive, and the money blinded me. They got me to agree to the job and total secrecy before they told me what it was, and once I'd done that, it was too late to back out. They had guns and made me realize that once I knew who and what they were, I was trapped, and they would kill me to keep me quiet. They moved into the house with me, and I was never alone after that."

"When did they tell you, they were bank robbers?" Molly asked, so deeply fascinated by his story, she forgot she was angry with him.

"They brought suitcases in from the car and took out two sawn-off shotguns which they put on the table. At first, the threat was implied by the guns being there; join them or be shot. We had just finished the fish and chips which we bought after the pub. As soon as I saw their weapons, I knew I was in trouble. They said I had missed the chance to say no; that I had gone past the point of being able to refuse. Molly, I was horrified, but when then they outlined the plan, and they had done this sort of robbery many times before and no one had ever got hurt. They said they had inside information about a big payroll, and they would be in and out in two minutes. The more they banged on about it, the easier it seemed, and the lure of the money and my chance to go for the big-time race circuit seduced me. There was no way out; after that, they didn't leave me alone. They wanted someone with local road knowledge, who could drive fast in case something went wrong and they had to make a quick getaway. They also wanted someone who lived in the country out of Perth, so they had somewhere to use as a hideout until the coast was clear, and they could get away, back to Melbourne. They made me phone my boss on the tuna boat and tell him I had to take a couple of weeks off after my long-lost brother and friend turned up for a visit, which was their cover. They made it all sound so easy, and I could follow my dream for two minutes of work and put up with them at my house for a few days. I was just plain dumb, Molly, but I'm not a bad person."

She stared at his sad face and saw he was full of regret. But someone had been shot during the robbery and was expected to die. Possibly the guard was already dead and John was a part of that. He couldn't run away from the feeling of guilt he must be suffering from the return of his memory.

"Rachel told me this morning," she said softly, "The police have shifted their search down south, they must know who you are."

He nodded, "I must have left a fingerprint in the car. I thought I'd wiped everywhere, but obviously, I didn't. Once I heard the gunshots from inside the bank, I was in a state of panic and shock. I realized everything had gone wrong, but it was too late. When I was eighteen, I was involved in a fight at the pub," he shrugged, emphatically, "It was just one of those things, no one was hurt, but we all had our fingerprints taken. It never went to trial, I think the cops just wanted to scare us, and it worked on me, so they've had them on file since then." He looked directly into her eyes. "The thing is Molly; I decided to turn myself and them in because I couldn't live with the guilt. I'm not a bad person, I swear. That was why Nick and Barry wanted to stop me; they could see that once I'd heard they shot someone and I thought he had died, I wanted out. They said I had lost my nerve, my bottle they called it, and I agreed I had. They told me to go to bed and think about it overnight. Then I overheard them talking, they were going to kill me and bury my body in my back yard, then they would make their getaway in my car. They intended to drive to Adelaide, and then fly back to Melbourne from there. That's when I knew I had to make a run for it, out the back window. So, I opened it, but they heard me and came charging in to stop me. I barely got out in time, but just as I got outside, they clambered after me and chased me. You know the rest."

Molly wanted to believe him, and she thought he was finally sincere. She wondered how hard it must have been for him to lose his memory and not be one hundred percent sure which ones that came back were real and which were imagined. "So, let's go and radio in and get help."

"My only reason for not wanting to do that was to protect you, Molly. I think you're the most amazing person I've ever met, and it simply would not be fair if because of me, you got kicked off the island, and your father lost his job. I was going to steal the boat after you were asleep tonight, not to run away, but to hand myself in to the police. I wanted to leave you out of it, so I was going to leave you a note to advise you to report the boat broke free of its tether during the last storm."

Her heart melted further, like a glacier crashing into the ocean. She also felt horrible because she had believed he had intended to steal the boat for nefarious reasons, rather than to protect her and her father. "John," she said softly, but with mettle in her voice, "If you knew my father, you'd know he would rather lose his job than refuse to help someone in need or run away from a fight."

He smiled crookedly. "Like father like daughter, hey?"

"You better believe it. Don't mess with a McLaren, remember?"

"Well, let's go and radio in, send the police to save you, and arrest me." He stood and looked out to sea, then promptly dropped back down again. "Damn, we're too late. The boat is coming through the gap now. While we've been talking, they found the way through; I seem to remember one of them talking about growing up on a boat. There's no time left, Molly; we're on our own. Do you have any weapons in the lighthouse?"

Molly ignored him while her mind raced, bugger, bugger, bugger. Where can I hide him? She wondered. Molly realized with a dawning horror that, in the lighthouse, there was nowhere to hide.

Molly stood up slowly and peered over the rise. The sleek, somehow menacing-looking powerboat was inching through the final turn of the passage; one man stood on the bow using his arms to show someone in the wheelhouse which way to steer to avoid the reef. They would be inside within minutes.

"Right," she said, as she bobbed back down. "The radio isn't going to help us now the nearest help would be an hour away at best, possibly longer. If they are looking for you, we need to get you out of sight."

"It's them, I'm positive; I recognize the one on the

bow, that's Barry; the one who tried to shoot me. Molly, you go back to the lighthouse and radio for help and then hide. I will go down to the jetty and meet them. I don't want you hurt, and if I hand myself in, they won't look any further."

Molly felt her skin turn ice-cold, she would be damned if she was going to slink away and let him go to certain death, just who did he think she was? "Now you listen to me, Hank, that's not going to happen, so forget it. You're not going to be like a lamb going to the slaughterhouse, and besides, if you give yourself up, they will probably come to find me to finish the job anyway, so it's not going to happen. No, there has to be another way; let me think."

There's nowhere to hide in the lighthouse, and we can't get to the boat because they will be going to the jetty themselves, plus there is just the one way through the reef. Think, Molly, think. She snapped her fingers, "I've got it. You go to the cave and hide there, it's virtually invisible, and they will never find you there. I will go and talk to them and tell them the raft just washed up on the reef, and I haven't seen anyone for two weeks. Don't argue with me, don't be chivalrous, that would be stupid, this is the only plan that makes sense."

She could see the indecision in his eyes, and she loved him for it; he didn't want to see her hurt. But, she thought he could also understand her idea was the only one that might mean they both survived. "Go, keep low, make sure they don't see you, and don't leave the cave until dark," she urged. "Then, if their boat is still at the jetty, take the dingy and get help. If I can convince them you're not here, I will come and get you once they leave, now go before it's too late."

He shook his head decisively. "I can't leave you alone to face two murderers while I go and hide. These men are here to kill me. What sort of a man would I be if I slunk off and cowered in a cave, leaving you to face my enemies for me?"

She smiled and suddenly saw that for him, it must be Hobson's choice; which meant no choice at all. Hide and let her possibly get hurt; or worse allow himself to be killed in the name of honor. He would know then she could get killed afterward anyway, they would realize the lighthouse had to have a keeper. She flung her arms around him and hugged him, knowing that no matter how stupid he had been, he was a good man; one her father would approve of.

Molly moved her head back and looked him in the eyes, then softly kissed his mouth, lovingly and sweetly. "John, I'm sorry, but you will always be John to me," she whispered when she pulled away again. "I understand how you feel, and bless you for wanting to save me, but my plan is the only way we might both survive, surely you can see that?"

His shoulders dropped, and she pressed home her advantage. "John, they don't know you are here; they are searching in case you are. Unfortunately, they've seen the raft, but it's deflated and wrecked on the rocks so again they can't know it's from your boat, or that you are here on Forbes. We've just had three days of unrelenting storms. I am the keeper of the light, and I never realized until recently how important a job that is. It is my responsibility to go and meet them as keeper, and if I don't, and you go, they must know someone will be here who has seen them, and they will hunt me down regardless. The only hope for us both to survive is if you go and hide in the cave, and I convince them you were never here. Now go, so I can go to the jetty and meet them, trust me, John; it is the only way."

Molly didn't wait for a reply, or further argument, she turned and began walking back down the path toward the cove, praying John would see sense and go to the cave, but she did not look back to confirm. She thrust her hands in her jacket pockets and hurried her steps; she had to get there before they fully docked in the hope she could stop the boat from tying up.

She spared a thought for her father, lying in his hospital bed. Molly wondered if, in the same circumstances, if he would have done the same? She suspected he would have radioed in at the first opportunity he had a survivor, and she knew at that moment, that was her biggest mistake. She sighed and thought through what the sequence of events might have been if she had reported she had an injured man shipwrecked. The storm was too severe for them to have sent a helicopter or boat immediately. They could have tried yesterday, she supposed, when the seas had dropped, and the wind had eased. Molly grinned in the realization that if they had evacuated John the day before; she would probably still be going to face the two men now, not knowing they were bank robbers. She also saw that they wouldn't have known he had been found, so either way, she would be walking to meet them; at least this was on her terms, not theirs. She shrugged and remembered the words from a song that had been one of her father's favorites; *Que Sera, Sera,* which translated meant: *whatever will be, will be*.

Molly, my girl, she thought grimly, *this could be*

the last day of your life, have you wasted it? Molly took a few moments to consider that; had she? No, she didn't think she had. Molly had devoted herself to helping others in a nursing career. She thought she had been a dutiful daughter and hadn't done anything wrong that she could remember. True, she didn't want her life to end, but if that's what some higher power had decreed, at least she could try to save John or Hank; she still couldn't get used to Hank. Molly grinned at the dual use of names she had for him.

Regrets Molly? Yeah, I suppose I have a few. I didn't get to finish Moby Dick*; did Ahab get his whale?* She would probably never know; maybe she could ask St Peter at the gates if he had read it.

Molly rounded the curve in the path where the jetty came into view, and there, thirty yards away, was the boat heading for it. She quickened her pace to get there before they docked. Molly waved her arms in the air to get the attention of the skipper. "Ahoy," she called. "Ahoy, you can't berth here, it's a restricted area."

The boat throttled back as a man appeared around the side of the cabin, obviously intent on jumping ashore from the bow. He had a coiled rope in his hand and waved at her with the other. The side window slid open, and a second man leaned out. "Hello," he called.

They both looked to Molly to be in their mid-thirties, with short but untidy hair, one brown the other fairer though not quite blond. They wore suits and ties, which, Molly thought, seemed unusual for bank robbers hell-bent on taking revenge on the high seas. She almost giggled at her wit, but then reminded herself these men were at Forbes to murder John and possibly her.

The boat motor idled, but the wind was pushing it closer. Molly tried again to dissuade them from coming ashore, she cupped her hands around her mouth and called, "This is Forbes Light. It is operated by the Department of Marine and Harbors and is restricted access; you must not come ashore without written permission."

The man inside the cabin thrust his arm out with what looked like a wallet opened. She couldn't see what it said at that distance, but it looked official. "We're from the police, searching for a dangerous escapee; we need to talk to you. Can we have permission to tie up?"

Suddenly, Molly realized she faced a dilemma, and it shocked her to the core. Was what John told her the truth; was his name Hank or what? What if everything he told her was a pack of lies and these two men were the police, and they were hunting him? John had been overly interested in the boat from the moment she had mentioned it. Possibly, he had been waiting for the seas to calm right down before he made a run for it. Is he a dangerous criminal? She wondered.

A hundred thoughts tumbled through her mind, each vying for supremacy, some doubting, some believing, and some were telling her she was paranoid. She did, after all, only have John's word that he was an unwilling participant in what was a violent crime. The men on the boat did, she had to admit, look like plainclothes detectives. From what she could see, they wore inexpensive cheap fitting suits, and they certainly didn't look like bank robbers, not she had the faintest idea what they would look like, but still, it was unnerving.

Then another thought struck her. *If these are*

genuinely cops who are searching for John, should I tell them he is hiding in the cave? And then hot on the heels of that came another; equally unnerving. *What if I tell them where he is, and John was telling the truth, and they are murdering robbers? They will kill us both. Oh, my God. But then, if I don't tell them, and he is on the run, I could go to prison for helping a criminal escape from custody. Either way, I'm damned if I do and damned if I don't.*

She saw a future mapped out ahead of her behind bars all because she had saved a man in a life raft, and that wasn't fair. *Now I think about his memory loss; I doubted that from the start, didn't I? It seemed like every time I confronted him about it, he remembered a bit more, but if I hadn't prodded him, would he have talked about his past?* She recalled getting information from him had been like pulling teeth, but did that mean he was lying? What did she know about amnesia anyway? It was all just so confusing.

"Do we have permission to tie up so we can speak with you?" The man yelled from the cabin, and with a jump, she ceased her thoughtful debate. Molly noticed how close they were to berthing. She waved a beckoning hand in agreement, *what else can I do?* She wondered. *If they are lying, they will come ashore anyway, and if they are honest, I'm only getting myself in deeper by trying to avoid it.* She walked to the forward bollard and held out her arms to catch the rope from the man standing on the bow.

"You must not stay for long," she called back as she decided to lie to gain time. She needed to determine if they were telling the truth or not. "I radioed in when you were coming through the reef, and I'm to report back in shortly to tell them what it is you want. This is a government lighthouse, and no unauthorized persons are allowed on Forbes Rock."

"Half an hour, no more, I promise." He smiled and stuck his head back inside to steer to the boat in for docking. *He's got a friendly smile if he's a bank robber;* she mused and was surprised how calm she felt.

She caught the rope and coiled it around the post, then walked to the stern end to wait and tie that end off too. The skipper turned off the engine, and the usual sounds of lapping waves and the wheeling gulls of the island descended again.

This is it; show time. Molly steeled herself, still not knowing whether to continue to hide John or give him up. Molly waited at the side of the cockpit for the men. The man from the bow clambered around the outside of the cabin and passed her the rear rope. Molly noticed he was wheezing noisily from the exertion. She idly wondered if he suffered from asthma or emphysema. The man who had been inside was now approaching her through the rear door.

"Hello, miss," the sandy-haired man said as he stepped outside. The jetty was the same height as the gunnels, so she stood above them. "Didn't expect to see a young woman running the lighthouse all by herself."

"Who says I'm by myself? My father is the keeper of the light; I'm just helping. What's your business here?" *Let him make of that what he likes,* she thought and felt better for making them believe there was a man on the island too.

He nodded, with a slight smirk on his face, as if he could see through her deception. "I'm Detective Bannister, and this is Detective Cook. I'm not sure how much you've heard of the news being out here, but there was a nasty bank robbery in Perth a few days ago where a guard was shot. We have reason to believe one of the perpetrators is from Augusta. We know he tried to escape by putting to see in his boat, just before the storm, and there is a major search to find him because he is known to be dangerous. One man was shot and killed during the robbery, and we believe this man will stop at nothing to evade capture."

So, the guard died; that made Molly realize no matter what his role was, John was, in part responsible. Molly didn't like the man who had called himself Detective Bannister. She didn't know why, but she didn't. It wasn't that he sounded insincere. If she had to take a stab at knowing why she disliked him, it would be the smirk when he so obviously disbelieved her statement that she wasn't alone. Her hackles bristled. "It's not Timbuktu, you know, it's only nineteen miles off the coast, and we have a radio. Yes, we do get the news out here; it's a lighthouse, not a penal colony."

He held up his hands in defense. "Sorry, no disrespect intended; you keepers do a great job in keeping seamen off the reefs."

"Hmm," she mumbled and liked that she had him on the back foot and decided to press home her advantage. She wasn't going to let them intimidate her. "Since when do the police not use a police boat or charter a local who knows the waters? You've been up and down the reef for ages looking for a way in, and you should know Forbes Reef is a dangerous place to be if you don't know what you're doing." Molly saw his face turn a light shade of pink and took more satisfaction at his discomfort.

"The launch is based at Busselton and is scouring the waters north of here. Other boats are searching in different directions out of Augusta. Before I joined the force, I had my skippers' ticket, so we hired this tub so we could come and see if he made it this far. The storm has caused a lot of damage to boats and buildings in town, which made it impossible to get a local skipper." He shrugged his shoulders. "So, we're it. We saw the life raft beached on the rocks and came in to see if he made it to the island and is hiding out."

Sounds plausible, she thought, worryingly. But then an idea struck her that made her realize maybe it wasn't entirely believable, and for one very good reason. "I don't understand. Sorry if I'm just a dumb female, but if this man is so dangerous, why haven't Marine and Harbors radioed me to be on the lookout for his boat. And another thing, why didn't my boss let me know you were coming here? I'd have thought you being police officers; you would know you need permission to berth at a government installation." She jerked her head back toward the lighthouse, and she wanted once more to imply she was not alone on the island. "From up in the watch room, we have a perfect three-hundred-and-sixty-degree view of the waters around Forbes Reef. Why haven't we been asked to look out for him? No one said a word when I reported the washing up of a deflated life raft two days ago. They just told me there were all sorts of small boats and debris coming ashore from the storm and not to worry about it." She amazed herself with how easily she lied, and Molly felt she was on a roll with her act of being an officious lighthouse keeper's daughter.

"Look, miss…"

"McLaren," she interrupted.

"Miss McLaren, thank you." There was now a steel edge to his voice, and Molly feared she had possibly gone too far. "We have a job to do, which is to check to make sure this man hasn't come ashore and put your life in danger. I can't say why you've not been notified, possibly no one thought to, but if my bosses didn't tell your bosses that's no reason for us not to come and check up on your safety, is it?"

Molly gave him her brightest, most condescending smile. "Thank you for doing so, but you've done your job. As you can see, I'm fine. Thanks for calling."

"Just what exactly is your problem, girlie?" the other man spoke for the first time, and Molly realized she could be in trouble. His tone of voice left little doubt he wasn't a police officer. Molly thought he sounded far too uncultured and uncouth. She realized John was probably telling the truth, probably.

I'm in trouble! She thought, trying hard not to let panic set in. Molly turned her gaze to him, still determined to stand up for herself. "I'm not your girlie, and I will thank you to be civil. I represent the West Australian Department of Marine and Harbors, and you have moored in a restricted area. I've thanked you for checking on my wellbeing, but you've had a wasted trip. The seas have been the worst I've ever seen, and no one could have survived if they were out in it. If the dingy was from his boat, it washed up two days ago during the worst storm I've ever seen, and I have reported it. There is no way even a fully inflated raft would have been able to come through the gap in the reef, let alone one that had a hole in it. Hell, look how long it took you two in good weather. Whoever this man is, he didn't make it to Forbes, so I suspect his boat sank, the raft broke free, and he has drowned. If he's a murderer, all I can say is good riddance."

Blondie, as Molly thought of him, exchanged glances with the dark-haired man, then looked back at her. "Well, that all sounds reasonable, so I tell you what we'll do. We'll check on your father, and have a quick look around the lighthouse, to make sure Hank Drage isn't up there now holding a knife to his throat to make sure you get rid of us. You could even be thinking you can save him by doing what he wants. That could explain your unwelcoming attitude. So how about you lead the way, then it will be the sooner we can leave you in peace once we know all is well."

With a sinking heart, Molly saw she had outsmarted herself. By telling them her father was with her had put her behind the eight-ball. Suddenly she saw that if they were genuine, the things they said made sense. They would need to check she wasn't under duress. Yet, if they were criminals, they would know there was another witness who could identify them, so either way, she was sunk. She had an idea that would help her discover if these men were from the police or not, and at the same time, Molly saw that she should stop being so hard-nosed with them and try to calm the situation down. She smiled and hoped it didn't look too false.

"Listen, guys, I don't mean to come across as some stuck-up cow, and I do appreciate you risked coming through the reef to make sure we were safe. If you want the truth, we'd normally enjoy the company because we don't get visitors, and it does get a bit boring." She shrugged and broadened her smile even further. "But the thing is, we have stringent rules, and I can't let you come ashore, let alone up to the lighthouse, we could lose our jobs. I promise you there is no one up there, with or without a knife. Let me offer a solution which should show you I'm genuine and offer a compromise."

"What's that, girlie?" The man who acted the deckhand asked gruffly.

"You've got a radio on board?" She nodded her head toward their boat. "I can give you the frequency for you to call my boss and request permission to search the lighthouse because you fear for my father's safety. And if I hear he gives it to you, I will make you both a nice cup of tea while we're up there, and you can check the place out to your heart's content." *Now yer bastard, squirm your way out of that one,* she thought in her father's voice.

"Good idea," the one who called himself Bannister said and nodded eagerly, "But I've got a better one; how about you come onboard and radio them yourself, then they'll hear your voice?" He stared back, with an insolent looking air, and Molly thought he was daring her back. He even held out his arm to take her hand so he could help her step down onto the deck.

Her bravado had snookered her and *damn the man*; she still didn't know if he was telling the truth or not. *Molly, my girl, you better do as he says, sounds like maybe they could be the good guys, and John is the killer.* She still couldn't bring herself to think of him as Hank, even if he were a criminal on the run. He would always be John to her.

Molly shrugged and took his hand. "Yes, let's get this done, you're right, it *is* a better idea."

Inside the cabin, there was a smell of cigarette

smoke, which almost made her gag. As she walked to the radio through the haze, Molly wondered if that could be a clue. Surely, wouldn't a police officer respect a boat he had hired enough not to smoke inside it? The seesawing indecision was driving her insane and giving her a headache. *Let's get this done;* Molly decided as she turned the dial for the Marine and Harbors call-up channel. She then picked up the microphone and pressed the transmit button on the side. "Whiskey delta Oscar one zero, this is Forbes Light, are you receiving, over?" She smiled at the two men who now stood between her and the exit, which worried her.

"Whiskey delta Oscar one zero, this is Forbes Light, are you receiving, over?" She said again after waiting. Static was the only reply, and it was a further two minutes later when she tried a third time. Disgustedly, she hung the microphone back on its hook. "Either there's a problem with your radio, or it's not a strong enough signal to reach Fremantle."

"Maybe as we are on this side of the island, the cliffs are blocking the signal from here," Bannister suggested, and Molly didn't know enough to dispute him. She had to make a decision, whether to trust them or not, and she didn't think she had any other alternative but to do so. She'd tried her best to use her guile to test them, and she had nothing but John's word, and vague suspicions they were anything but honest.

"Okay, gentlemen, I've tried my best to check your credentials from here. I must ask you to wait while I go back and radio from the lighthouse." She looked from one to the other.

Bannister shook his head slowly. "Nope," he said softly. "I can't let you do that."

Moly felt as if an icy wind had blown into the cabin, and she felt chilled to the bone. *Is he threatening me?* Molly wondered. She wanted to scream, fight, run, or do anything, but they blocked the exit.

He interrupted her rapidly panicking thoughts. "Calm down, Miss McLaren, look, why not let us come and check the place out, make sure your father is safe and Drage isn't up there threatening him. If it's all clear, we will get out of here and take the ruined life raft with us for testing. You can get on with your lives, and we will get back to the search for wreckage. You must see that if he is up there, we can't let you go back to danger."

"But he's not, I assure you."

"Miss McLaren, you must see this from our perspective. If he was there, and your father was in danger, you would say that he wasn't to save him, wouldn't you? Any daughter would. If we left without checking, and you were both murdered by him, well, it wouldn't look too good for us, would it?"

She had to agree; he made sense. "It would look even worse for us being dead. Yes, I see what you mean, but when I said he isn't there, I didn't mean this Drage character, I meant my father. I wasn't entirely honest with you; he is on the mainland in the hospital. I am here helping, that much was true, but only while he is incapacitated; he has a broken leg. I'm here alone, and that's why I'm so cautious."

He grinned, and Cook laughed, while Molly squirmed with discomfort. She suddenly saw she could be in grave danger from the two men who possibly were not the police. If they were genuine, Molly had lied to them and hid an escaped bank robber. But if they were not cops, she had admitted to being on the island alone, and they might do anything to her, and no one would hear her scream.

Chapter 12

Whitecaps Washing Ashore

"Well, well, it seems like we could have a party then, girlie," Cook murmured with an evil-looking grin on his face.

His partner shook his head. "Settle down, Barry; we've got a job to do." He turned his gaze to Molly. "Now you're in a truth-telling mood, where is he? Are you hiding him at the lighthouse, and that's why you didn't want us to go there?"

In that instant, because he had used a Christian name, she knew they weren't cops. John had said their names were Nick and Barry, but he never mentioned their surnames. If they were police, there would be no way John could have made up such a story and fluked their first names. The question she had to answer was if she told them where he was, would that save her? Probably not. The thought was abhorrent anyway, and she realized, with a sinking heart, nothing was going to save her from them other than her guile.

Before she could answer, the radio crackled to life. "Forbes Light this is *Morning Dawn*, are you receiving Molly, over?"

Maybe, just maybe, there is a chance now. She breathed an internal sigh of relief. Molly snatched up the transmitter and pressed the talk button before either man could stop her. "*Morning Dawn*, this is Molly receiving loud and clear. I'm on a boat called...." Molly rapidly looked around for a boat name and spotted it on a brass plaque. "*Tandanna.* It's been hired by two policemen who have landed here on Forbes in the hunt for an escaped bank robber named Hank Drage. I was trying to raise Marine and Harbors from their boat to get permission for them to come ashore and search, over."

"Best you be good and not say anything silly to bring them here, girlie,"

From somewhere, Barry Cook had produced a pistol. It was an ugly-looking revolver, and it was pointing at her chest.

Molly had no doubt he would kill her; his eyes were dead; totally emotionless. She remembered one of her father's more colorful expressions; "Like piss holes in the snow." he'd said once when describing a drug addict's eyes he had treated in the hospital. She'd never really known what he'd meant before, but she did now.

"Molly, is everything all right there? You sound a bit strange. You said the boat was *Tandanna*, that's Rick Charles's boat; I wasn't aware he was hiring it out. We're a couple of hours away, but we can swing by and help out if they need it. I know the Drage boy, he had a reputation for fighting when he was a youth, and I heard he's half a decent speedway driver now he's grown up. There are cops all over Augusta asking questions, so that explains it if he was driving the getaway car. How do they think he got to Forbes, over?

Before Molly could answer, she heard a loud double click as Cook pulled the hammer back on the gun. She had no doubt they were going to kill her, but maybe if she could gain some time, a miracle might happen. She took a deep, steadying breath, then pushed down the talk button. “Yeah, I’m fine, thanks, Derek. I’m just not used to visitors here; I haven’t seen a soul here since you dropped me off on my first day and took Dad to the hospital. I’ve tried to tell them he’s not here, but they want to search the island for my safety. At the height of the storm, a couple of days ago, a deflated life raft washed up on the rocks. These officers think it’s from his boat and that he made it this far after it sank, over.”

There was a silence for a while, during which time she stared at the man holding the gun. Eventually, she heard Derek’s voice again. “Sorry, Molly, I had a job to do; I wasn’t ignoring you. Well, young Hank was working on George McClure’s tuna boat, so he’s probably a reasonable seaman, but that storm was a shocker. Can’t see him surviving the rough seas and guiding a life raft through the reef. Hell, I’ve gone through there a hundred times but wouldn’t have risked it in that weather. Tell them they’re dreaming. If he went out in his little boat, he’s drowned by now, over.”

“See? I told you so, even they don’t think anyone could have survived that storm,” she said and thought how whiney she must sound to them. Then Molly realized anyone would seem that way with a gun pointing at them.

“Tell him we’re going to do a quick look around in case the body washed up onshore. The sooner you get rid of him, and we have a look around, the sooner you can be rid of us,” Bannister snarled.

She pushed the talk button again. “Derek, I think they realize that. They say they want a quick look around to see if his body washed up, then check the lighthouse to make sure I'm not hiding him under the bed, over."

"Young Mikey wants to be the only man hiding under your bed, Molly. We'll be there in a bit under two hours, tell them to hang on, and we will give them a hand and do a sweep of the reef and island. No one knows Forbes better than me, over."

She looked at Bannister for direction, but he just shook his head, and she understood it was to tell Derek not to come. Molly's heart sank further. "He says no, Derek. They don't need any help. And, you can tell Mikey he's welcome to hide under my bed any time, over." She hoped she had dropped enough hints to let him know she was in danger, but his reply when it came told her he hadn't.

"No worries. We better get back to pulling our pots then, Molly. See you when we make the next supply run, over and out."

"Bye, Derek. Over and out."

Molly hung up the microphone again and tried not to cry. She would be damned if she showed these bastards how scared she was. If only she could buy some time, though time for what purpose was beyond her. At least John was safe in the cave, and that thought lifted her spirits a little. "What now?" she asked the men.

"Party time," Cook replied with an evil-looking grin on his face, which didn't travel up to his eyes.

"Don't mind Barry, that's his sense of humor. We are going to do exactly what you told your friend we're going to do. A quick circuit of the island to see if there is any sign he came ashore, then check out the lighthouse, and, if you've been honest, we'll be on our way."

Molly didn't say anything, just stared at the gun until with a shrug of his shoulders he slipped the pistol back into his jacket pocket. He patted the weapon through the tweed material and said, "Don't try anything cute, girlie."

She decided to play dumb and not let on to them that she knew they weren't cops. "What do you mean by that? What kind of police officers are you that you feel you have to wave a gun around?"

"Tired ones who have been on the go since very early this morning," Bannister said. "We want to get back to the mainland, so can we go and get this over with, please, Miss McLaren? Show us where the raft originally came ashore."

Abruptly she moved toward them, and they parted to let her through the door. They climbed out of the boat, and Molly took off across the rocks with the two men close behind. She hurried her pace, surefootedly like a mountain goat on her usual trail, knowing it would take them to the spot she wanted, which was short of the cave. From there, Molly intended to take them to the lighthouse via the cliffs on a trek that would be above where she hoped John was hiding.

Molly had no idea what they were going to do with her once they discovered she was alone, but she feared the worst. One thing she did know was if they thought she suspected they were the robbers; they would silence her to stop her from identifying them if the real police came calling. That was why she kept up the charade; it was her only hope.

Bannister kept up with her, but with great delight,

she heard Cook gasping and panting in what seemed like no time at all. After hearing him wheeze on the boat, she planned to try to bring on an asthma attack when told she would be guiding them on the hike, to separate them. Cook was stumbling quite a lot; his breathing more ragged with every step he took. Molly could hear him in distress. When he fell after a rock slid under his foot, Bannister grabbed her arm to stop her walking onward.

"For God's sake, Barry, give me the sodding gun; you go back to the boat and wait for me there."

"If you'd…bloody slow down…I could keep up. You know…I've got asthma…and I left my inhaler…back at the house," he responded, panting and gasping as he reached into his pocket for the pistol.

Molly's heart soared just a little; her plan had worked; it looked as if she would have one minder and not two; *surely*, she thought, that helps my cause.

"You don't look well, Detective. I'd have a sit down if I were you, looking very green around the gills." She tried to keep the glee out of her voice.

He scowled, passed over the pistol, and sat slowly on a table-sized boulder at a convenient height. His face looked flushed, and he was sweating profusely.

Molly wondered if he was close to a heart attack but then thought she couldn't possibly be that lucky. He mopped the sweat from his forehead, and she tried to admonish herself for her cold-heartedness but failed. "Take your jacket off and undo your tie a bit," she offered, but he just waved for them to go on and leave him alone.

"When you've got your breath back, go to the boat and wait for me there. Once I've checked Drage is not on the island, we'll be on our way," Bannister said then nodded toward her. He grabbed Molly's arm, turned away from his partner in crime, and they set off across the rocks once more.

Around five minutes later, Molly stopped and pointed to a spot where the waves broke on the shore a hundred yards away. "It was around there I first saw the deflated life raft wash ashore. Then when the wind and tide turned, it was dragged back out to sea and ended up where it is now, hung up on the reef."

They were only around two hundred yards from the cave, and fifty above it. Molly wanted to keep Bannister away from the shoreline, so he didn't see the opening.

He took three or four deep breaths and looked up and down this stretch of coast. "So, you came down here during the height of the storm when you saw it was already deflated?"

"No, don't be ridiculous. I was ordered not to leave the lighthouse during the storm, so I wasn't injured like my father was. I watched it through some very powerful binoculars from the watch room. It was not much more than a big bright orange rag in the water, being picked up by the waves, and tossed around in the surf. It had next to no air left in it, which I could see, and there was no way anyone was inside it. Stuff comes ashore here all the time. It washed up right there," she pointed with her finger again.

He didn't answer right away, as if he were weighing up whether she was telling the truth or not. His glance shifted from her face to the ocean, and she stayed silent, hoping he wouldn't go anywhere near the cave. He pointed off to his left. "Augusta's that way, right?"

She nodded. "A bit over twenty miles."

"Nothing between there and here, I mean no other reef systems?"

"No, nothing significant that I'm aware of."

"I wonder how the raft got here, and yet there's no wreckage from the boat."

What's he getting at? She wondered. "Well, I'm no expert, obviously, but I suppose if it took a big wave, and let me tell you the waves were huge, maybe it took on too much water, and it sank rather than break up. The wind and current would have driven the raft this way."

He nodded thoughtfully, still gazing out to sea. Molly thought about making a run for it, but her problem was where would she run to? When he spoke, she realized he was undoubtedly the brains of the crew. "I would agree with you, Miss McLaren, that is the likely scenario. But that's where your version then starts to fall apart. As the boat would have been sinking, Drage would have inflated the raft and got inside it, that's your interpretation. Yes, that would explain the lack of wreckage. Then, as you say, the wind would have driven the life raft in this direction."

"Riiiiiight," she said, dragging out the world to show her confusion when, in reality, her heart was sinking with his logic.

"You say there is nothing between where that would have happened and here, and when you noticed it, it was already deflated and washed up on the rocks. So, the question is, what made it lose its air?" He turned his steely gaze to her. "I think you're lying to me. The raft washed up here yes, but it was fully inflated when it did, else it wouldn't have arrived in the first place. After Drage got out, the boat rubbed against these very rocks, which holed the hull, and that's what caused it to deflate."

Chapter 13

The Gig is Up

"Cut the rope, drop the pot, we're getting out of here right now!" Derek shouted out of the side window of the cabin on the *Morning Dawn.*

Mikey looked up with a questioning look. He was using the winch, which was twirling the rope from a cray pot, traveling up from the depths.

He held his arms open to ask why, but the look on Derek's face made him realize his best course of action was to do what he was told immediately. His skipper would never cut the rope on a valuable pot without good reason, especially as it could be full of crays.

Mikey slid the razor-sharp bait knife out of the sheath at his hip, pressed the deck button with his foot to stop the motor, and with a single swipe, sheared the rope. He almost lost his footing as Derek gunned the diesel engine, but he recovered and staggered toward the wheelhouse.

"Molly's in trouble at Forbes," he shouted at Mikey to be heard over the roar of the straining Cummins motor. "She said there are two men there who are cops, but some things she said don't make sense, and I think she was trying to give me a message. I don't think they are police; she says they chartered *Tandanna*, and that sounds like crap; Rick Charles would never let the cops take his old tub. I've got a feeling that if anything, they're the bank robbers from Perth, and she's in danger."

Derek shrugged as he turned the wheel, "Maybe I'm wrong about that, but we're going to go and check. A young girl like her, alone on an island with two strange men; her father would flay me alive if we didn't go and help, and something happened to her."

He'd told Molly they were nearly two hours away, but that was a lie to make the murderers think they had more time, believing they were listening. The *Morning Dawn* was much nearer than that, and he hoped they were close enough to be able to help.

Derek had been an infantryman during the war and was wounded at El Alamein. He'd almost lost his arm having been shot in the shoulder by a German sniper and had received an honorable discharge. Derek had brought his service Lee Enfield rifle back to Australia with him as a souvenir like a lot of soldiers did.

Derek nodded toward the bench seat, and Mikey knew what his boss wanted. Mikey knelt and slid open the drawer that held the medical kit, safety flares, and tool kit. He took a terry-toweling bundle out and untied the string around it, then unrolled the thick material to show the gleaming weapon inside. Once a week, one of them would clean and oil it and occasionally use it when the boat was bothered by large white pointer sharks.

Mikey opened a small wooden box inside the drawer, which contained the .308 caliber bullets and calmly loaded the weapon's magazine. He liked Molly a lot, and if she were in danger, he would fight to the death to save her.

****

"I'm telling you," she said emphatically, "The bloody boat washed up there, and it was practically in rags. Check the lighthouse by all means, but you won't find anyone there."

He smiled and slowly put his hand in the jacket pocket that held the pistol. Molly felt her breath catch in her throat. "I think you're a smart woman, so probably you're telling the truth now; he isn't in the lighthouse." He took the gun out and pointed at her. "So, if he isn't in the lighthouse, where is he hiding, Miss McLaren?"

She flicked her eyes up toward the top of the cliff, where the gorse bushes were, then dragged her gaze back to the dock area. He'd seen it and fallen for her deception. Molly could tell by the grin that lit up his face he thought he had tricked her when it was she who had tricked him.

Molly had no real plan in mind, other than to get the killer away from the cave where John was hiding. After that? Heaven only knew. *One step at a time, Molly*, she told herself.

"What's up there?" He jerked his head in the direction of the cliffs.

"Nothing, other than some bushes," she replied, deliberately quickly. "Just what sort of policeman are you, and why are you threatening me with a gun?"

"One who doesn't trust you. You do realize that harboring a dangerous criminal is against the law, and I believe you are hiding one now. So, let's take a walk up to where you don't want me to go." He waved the gun, gesturing her to lead the way.

"You're wasting your time," she murmured, but

turned on her heel and started across the rocks, angling away from the cave. Molly tucked her hands in her pockets and gave a slight grin as she bent her head down to watch her footing, with Bannister four paces behind. *I got you, you bastard. At least John will be safe, even if I'm not.*

Her mind raced for an idea as she attacked the incline; any plan that would get her out of the mess she was in would be good. Once again, the idea of running for it crossed her mind. She pictured it happening; wait till Bannister was halfway up the slope and out of breath and run like the wind. She should be quicker than him by rights. Although he didn't look like he was unfit, she was younger. So, okay, I get free, but then what? The lighthouse, that's what. The thought hit her like a stone hitting water and sinking. *There is nowhere to hide in the damn lighthouse!*

If she did hide, the men would know she couldn't get off the island, so they would search until they found her; they couldn't afford to leave her alive. So, if they looked hard enough, the men would not only find her but probably John in the cave too, then everything she had done would be for nothing. Molly hoped John could be relied on to tell the police what his part had been in the bank robbery if he survived. Even though he would possibly go to jail, once the men had left and he could take the boat, she wanted to believe he would do the right thing. *Wouldn't he?* She sighed. She thought he would, but of course, there were no guarantees. Maybe he would take the boat and run, leaving her dead body on Forbes. But, with the police knowing his name, just how far could he run? No, she thought she knew him well enough to know he wouldn't do that, he would face the music and avenge her, knowing she had sacrificed herself so he could live.

No matter what you do, Molly, my girl, you are probably not going to survive, she realized. *Whether they get John or not, they cannot possibly leave you to be a witness. So, you may as well try to do something first and go down fighting,* but what?

She reached the part of the slope that became steeper. It was where she almost had to crawl up using her hands for purchase. It wasn't dangerous, but it required concentration and both of her hands for purchase.

Molly had an idea. Just above where she was now, about three quarters to the top, was a small plateau. It dawned on her when she reached there, Bannister, below her would have both hands on the rock face, ergo, he would have the gun in his pocket.

Okay, he won't be able to shoot me immediately, so what, throw rocks? Hang on a minute, maybe that's not such a bad idea, drop a big boulder on his head. The thought shocked her, could she really do that? Could she knowingly hurt the man, even possibly kill him? Her adult life had been about saving lives, not causing pain, could she drop a rock on a man's head? *Best not to think about it; get to the top, look for a boulder, pick it up, turn and drop it.*

Molly pressed on, deliberately ignoring her half-baked plan, watching where she placed her feet, and listening to the man behind her. It didn't sound as if she was getting any further ahead of him than he would allow, though she didn't want to stop and turn around to find out for sure. Should she, or shouldn't she?

Molly still hadn't decided if she could drop a rock

crashing down on the man's head when she had a blinding flash of inspiration. There was a weapon of sorts in the watch room. Could she get to it? Then another thought, if she could, could she use it? *Oh my God, if I used it, would it kill him, can I murder him, even if it is in self-defense?*

What was it her father told her about the gun? She remembered back to when she had holidayed on the island, and she had to have the obligatory safety induction. What to do in certain circumstances, some of which were stupid, as her father went to great pains to explain by ridiculing the government that issued them. For example, there was the escape boat that was too small to be of any practical use. But there was the ruling that it had to be there in the event of an evacuation. Surrounded by the reef and dangerous currents, if the weather was so bad they had to evacuate, how on earth could they make it through the gap in that little thing with a tiny outboard motor? The very idea beggared belief.

Next, he spoke of what to do if he were injured and disabled, and the radio failed. Molly stared back as if he were speaking a foreign language. He told her if such a thing happened, she would have to fire the Very pistol.

Molly had no idea what a Very pistol was. Her father told her it was in a locked box on the wall of the watch room. The key was kept in his study drawer for safekeeping, which he showed her. He removed it; then, he climbed the stairs with her trailing behind him.

"Molly, pay attention now," he began in his most serious voice, the one he used when he was about to impart vast knowledge or wisdom.

"Aye aye, sir." She gave a mock naval salute,

which always elicited a grin from him; it was one of *their things*. Sometimes he would respond by calling her Seaman Molly, but that day he didn't smile, so she knew he was deadly serious.

He slid the key into the lock on the front of the highly polished wooden box, which measured about eighteen inches square and about six inches deep. The door dropped down to hang on its hinges to display an ugly-looking gun with a ridiculously oversized barrel. It was held on by quick release clips to the back wall. Below that was a small rack containing five tubular cartridges about four inches long and around an inch in diameter. Despite Molly's dislike of any firearms, she found herself morbidly interested. He pulled the gun clear of its retainers and then slid one of the tubes out of the rack.

"Molly, I cannot even imagine a scenario where you would have to fire this, but as you will be here a few days, I must show you how to, just in case, do you understand?"

"Yes, Dad." Molly didn't feel like kidding around anymore. She was repulsed yet attracted to the gun at the same time.

He smiled faintly. "That's my girl. Now, any weapon can be dangerous, and you must pay this as much respect as you would any other pistol. Who knows, one of these may one day save your life. The first rule is not to load it inside the building. If you don't load it in here, you can't fire it accidentally, can you? Because, if you were to, you could burn the place to the ground. Each of these," he held up the cartridge, "is full of incandescent phosphorous. In other words, it's a flare gun. You fire it up into the sky, and it will burn very brightly and come down slowly. Even in broad daylight, it will be seen for many miles around and is the recognized signal at sea to show you are in distress. It is a centerfire projectile that will climb around two to three hundred feet in the air. If fired accidentally inside the lighthouse, it could cause irreparable damage. So, Molly, what's the first rule of a Very gun?"

"Don't load it inside."

"That's my girl." He smiled, then led the way to the door onto the balcony. He opened it and held it for her to step through, which she did into the noonday sunshine. Gulls weaved and cawed as they sailed through the gusty breeze, while Molly leaned against the steel railing as her father closed the door behind him.

"Now," he began, speaking a little louder to be heard over the wind and screeching birds. "Watch carefully." He put the cartridge between his teeth so that both of his hands were free then wrapped his left hand around the ridiculously thick barrel, while his right held the handle. With his thumb, he slid back a small catch and made a downward movement. The gun came apart on a hinge to expose the inside of the tube-like barrel. He handed her the pistol, and she took it gingerly as he removed the flare from his mouth. "Molly, my girl, no need to be frightened of it, practice opening and closing it a few times, get a feel for it.

She did as he instructed, surprised it wasn't as heavy as she imagined it would be. The handle fitted snugly in her hand, and within five times of opening and closing the weapon, she felt confident. Molly wasn't sure what she should think about that. Guns were dangerous, hurtful things, and she was a nurse, dedicated to helping and curing the ill and wounded.

Molly hadn't tended a patient with a bullet wound but, of course, had studied the effects of them during her training.

"Good girl Molly, you've got the hang of it. Now put the cartridge in." He held it out to her, and without question, she took it and slid it home effortlessly. Without being told, she then closed the pistol.

"Now's the time to be careful, girl," her father said grimly. "If we accidentally fire this off, every boat within twenty miles will come running, so whatever you do, don't pull the trigger."

She nodded, understanding the seriousness of the situation, though Molly wanted to giggle as she imagined a hundred fishing boats heading to Forbes because she accidentally fired a Very gun.

"Molly, this is a single-action pistol, do you know what that means?" She shook her head to show that she didn't. "Okay, so you have to pull the hammer back manually till it clicks into place. Once it does hold the gun high above your head, so you don't get any stray sparks fly into your eyes and pull the trigger."

She nodded her understanding, and before he could stop her, she pulled back the hammer and thrust her hand up above her head.

"Jesus, Molly stop, don't you dare pull that trigger," he yelled.

She grinned. "Gotcha," she said impishly, and lowered her arm. As if by instinct, she held the hammer with her thumb, pulled the trigger to release it, and gently lowered it back. Then she snapped open the gun and caught the cartridge as it spat out of the barrel.

"Just call me Annie Oakley." She handed the weapon back to her father, feeling very proud.

****

Molly wasn't sure what damage, if any, a Very gun cartridge fired into a human being would have, but she thought it was worth a try if she could get to it. She knew from her studies that phosphorous caused severe burns and was incredibly flammable. That was why it was so efficient inside incendiary bombs during the war. The small plateau was coming up, and she hurried her pace to try to put a few extra steps between her and Bannister. The smaller rocks slid under her feet as she climbed, and she bent forward to use her hands for additional purchase, not caring if she showered the man below her.

As she stepped onto the rocky platform, three-quarters of the way up the slope, her eyes scanned for a suitable rock. *There,* she thought and took the two steps to pick one up that took both her hands to hold. Trembling with fear and excitement, she turned back to the slope with the boulder held at chest height.

At the last second, he must have had a premonition because he looked up sharply and saw the inevitable. Molly let go, aiming at his head. He tried to twist away, and he almost made it.

The rock collided with him on his right shoulder with a dull thud. He screamed and lost his grip and clattered down the hill. Molly didn't wait to see if he survived, though she suspected he would. She had gained the precious minutes she needed and set off back up the slope as quickly as she could. She took an angled course, which would take her the quickest way to the lighthouse, and the weapon she thought that could just save her life.

At the crest, she bent forward, intent on watching her footing and started to run, skirting the gorse bushes on her left. Suddenly, a shape reared up from a gap in the hedge. Molly almost fainted in shock as a large piece of wood swung at her head. She ducked, yelling in fright and, as she did, noticed her father's trousers. In a daze, she wondered how he could be there, with his broken leg before it registered it was John.

"Hell, I'm sorry, Molly. I thought you were one of them," he said, dropping his club and grabbed her arm.

"What the hell are you doing here?" she screamed, half in shock and half in anger.

"I thought they might have seen the cave before they rounded the cape to the lagoon, so I thought I'd hide up here among the bushes. When I heard you coming, I thought it was one of them, and I could take one out with this driftwood branch I found." He gave his lopsided grin. "Thank God I didn't hit you."

"Yes, John, thank God you didn't." She was still wildly angry with him, but somehow glad to see him too. "We need to go; he is behind me and pissed off because I threw a rock at him. We must get to the light and radio for help. Run like the wind, go."

Chapter 14

Don't Mess With a McLaren

The lighthouse was in sight when Molly heard the first crack from behind them and realized Bannister had fired his pistol at them. She daren't stop to see how far away he was, and she had no idea how close the bullet had come to hitting either of them. "Run, John, run. He's shooting at us; we must make it to the light."

The next shot came as they reached the door, which Molly fell against, exhausted, her heart racing from exertion and fear. She heard the gunshot and six feet away, at head height, a piece of stone broke free where the bullet hit it. Molly hurriedly turned the handle and stumbled inside with John on her heels. She flung the draw bolt across, and with a sinking heart noted that it didn't look too sturdy, but hopefully, it would hold long enough for them to get upstairs to the gun.

With her heart ready to burst from exertion, she attacked the spiral staircase taking two steps at a time.

They entered the living quarters, and between rasping, labored breaths, said, "Get on the radio, start pedaling, and build up the charge, I have to find a key."

Find was the operative word because she couldn't remember which drawer it was kept in. Frantically she opened one after the other, almost tipping the contents on the floor. It took precious minutes to find the key, by which time Molly was a nervous wreck. She held it aloft, thanking God, and was further relieved when John said, "Molly, we've got enough power to radio for help, do want me to make the call?"

She shook her head, no. "I think we'd be better if I do. I'm the keeper of the light; they will recognize me and respond quicker, knowing it's not a practical joke." She snatched up the microphone just as the first loud crash sound came from the front door, only one level below. "Mayday, Mayday, Mayday, this is Forbes Light. I cannot transmit for long. There are two dangerous armed men on the island trying to kill me; please help."

She dropped it with a loud clunk, but it was drowned out by the sound of the second crash. But this time, the door below banged open and hit the wall. "Go, go, go up to the watch room now," she urged John

"You go first."

Molly didn't have time to argue over what she thought of as his bullshit chivalry, and she dashed for the doorway. She turned right and fled up the stairs. Molly heard John's footsteps behind her, and the clatter of Bannister's below them.

A shot rang out, and a bullet whined off the wall beside them, the sound deafening in the confined stone building. Then came another bang, and John screamed. Molly turned; he was still on his feet, but his arm hung at an unnatural angle, and blood was streaming from a wound. She took three steps down and put her arm around him. "Run, John, come on, we have to climb, now."

"Yes, John, run and hide," Bannister shouted, and

laughed uproariously, which made him cough violently. Molly realized he too wasn't used to running as far and as fast as he had. She was glad it gave them a few more seconds. "But where are you going to run to, John?" Bannister shouted when he got his breath back. "There isn't anywhere to hide, and I'm coming to get you both."

Undeterred, Molly slipped her body under John's good arm and clung to him, urging him to climb on. They had only ten more steps to go. Fortunately, there were no more gunshots, and they fell into the watch room together. Molly swung the door shut and with dismay, saw there was no lock on it. *Well why would there be, you idiot*? She scolded herself.

Molly glanced at John, his face was ashen gray, and he looked like he was about to faint. His arm was drenched in bright red dripping blood. *Oh Lord, please help me,* she thought, and slapped his face, hard.

"John, wake up, I need you to hold that door, if you don't, we both die. Now do it." She pushed him, and he nodded, a look of hazy determination on his face.

She saw him rest his unwounded shoulder against the edge of the door and grip the handle, wincing in obvious agony.

With trembling fingers, she tried to push the key into the slot, but it didn't want to go, and she almost dropped it with frustration. She heard her father's voice in her ear, trying to calm her. *"Slow down, Molly, my girl, more haste, less speed. You've got the key upside down."*

There came a knock on the door, and a gleeful voice came from the outside. "Little pigs, little pigs, let me in, or I will blow your house down."

Finally, the key went all the way into the lock of the gun cabinet, and she twisted it. The door clanged down, and there was the Very pistol. It gleamed in its ugliness, but Molly had never seen a more beautiful sight. She snatched it with one hand and broke the barrel apart as her father had shown her just as Bannister screamed and lunged at the door. It lurched open six inches, but John's resolve held firm, and he slammed it shut again. Molly could tell it had taken a lot out of him; John looked like he could fall at any moment. She doubted he could withstand another attempt.

Molly grabbed a cartridge and slid it home in the chamber, closed the gun, and took three steps, so she was in the line of sight of the door. She took a deep breath, cocked the hammer, and took aim at where she imagined the man's stomach would be when he came crashing through the door. Molly elected to aim there as she thought the shell might bounce off his ribs if she tried to hit him too high. *Yes*, she reasoned it might crack a bone, but he was armed, and she needed to stop him from killing them. "Let the door go, John," she said quietly but with a determination in her voice that shocked even her."

John looked up and saw the gun in her hand, and like a startled rabbit, he lunged and stepped to the side of the doorframe. He cowered with his undamaged arm over his head. Molly only had eyes for the oak door, noticed with her peripheral vision; John was sliding down the wall. The blood left a bright red streak all the way down until he hit the floor in a sitting position.

When you see him, gently squeeze the trigger, Molly, my girl, don't jerk it. You can do this, her father's voice echoed in her mind. "Yeah, yeah, yeah, Dad, I got this," she said out loud. John was oblivious; he had passed into unconsciousness.

The door crashed open and swung till it hit the wall with a resounding slam. Bannister stood there and took two steps inside. Molly was glad to see his gun was in the belt of his trousers and not in his hand. She was also happy to see the rock she had dropped on him had done some severe damage to his shoulder as it seemed to be hanging from its socket. That explained why he had put the gun away while he wrestled with the door; he could only use his left hand.

"Make no mistake," she said with ice-cold certainty in her voice, "if you move, I will shoot you."

He laughed loudly. "You're kidding. You're going to shoot me, with that blunderbuss?" He laughed again, even louder, and then suddenly stopped. His eyes narrowed, and with his left hand, he reached for the pistol in his belt.

Time itself seemed to Molly to bend and slow down. She pulled the trigger and felt the gun jerk in her hand. There wasn't a bang sound which she thought she would hear; it was more of a whoosh. The projectile shot from the barrel, and she could almost see it as it crossed the eight feet between them. All the while, she thought, *please don't miss, please don't miss, please don't miss him.*

Bannister's face registered shock and looked as if a mule kicked him. He screamed in pain and staggered back through the doorway to the balustrade, which stopped him with a thud. He looked at her with pure hatred and began to raise his pistol to shoot her. Then the flare ignited, and the front of his torso was engulfed in flames. Molly shielded her eyes, but too late, she was blinded by the intense brightness, and Bannister's screams became louder. The gun toppled from his hand and clattered its way down the steel staircase, spinning and rolling all the way to the bottom, the noise echoing off the stone walls. Bannister gave one last scream and tipped backward over the railing. He resembled a free-falling fireball and landed with a dull clumping noise on the wooden floor below.

Molly couldn't stop herself; she turned her head to the side, retched in horror, and then vomited over the floor. She fell to her knees, weak from the adrenaline, tired from her run, and sick to her stomach at shooting a human being.

Molly dropped the gun as her thoughts solidified, and the smell of burning flesh and wood rose up from below. She remembered her father's words of warning that she should never load, let alone fire the Very pistol inside the building because it would burn the place to the ground. It dawned on her that she and John were above the flames, and the phosphorous would stick like glue as it burned and spread. The floors were wooden and very old wood at that. She realized in saving John and herself, she had doomed the lighthouse she was supposed to protect from destruction. They needed to get moving and fast before they became trapped in the conflagration below and burned to death.

She crossed to John, who was unconscious. Quickly she inspected his arm. It looked terrible; the bullet appeared to have smashed the bone halfway between shoulder and elbow. He was in shock and was losing a lot of blood. "God, you helped me before, please help me again, I have to get him onto his feet."

She slapped his face and watched as his head rocked to the side. She hit him again and again until he stirred groggily. "John, wake up, we have to move. I'm going to remove your belt, don't think you got lucky, I need it for a tourniquet for your arm." He gave the ghost of a grin at her humor, but then his eyes fluttered again. She knew she had to keep him awake. "For God's sake, Hank, wake up and help me, or we will both burn to death!" she screamed in anger at frustration.

She undid his belt buckle and as roughly as she could, yanked it through the loops of his pants. His body jerked in time, causing him to groan in pain as it jarred his broken arm. Molly knew she had no time for pleasantries. She was damned if she was going to leave him to save herself after all she'd been through, and she had no desire to die in flames either.

"I'm sorry, John, this is going to hurt, but I have to stem your blood loss." She lifted his arm and passed the belt around it above the wound, then threaded the end through the buckle. She cinched it tight, and John screamed. *At least he's awake now;* she thought as she passed it around his arm again in hopes it wouldn't slip.

"Open your mouth." He did, and she thrust the belt between his teeth. "Clamp your teeth down on that John, and don't let go, it will hold for now while we get out of here. Now move, up on your feet."

"I'm not sure I want to marry you anymore; you're so bossy," he mumbled, but he did help her get him to stand.

"I told you once before, don't mess with a McLaren." She slid under his arm once more and led him out of the watch room.

The smell was overpowering, and the smoke stung her eyes. Being a lighthouse, there was nowhere for the smoke to escape as none of the windows opened. There was only the balcony door in the watch room, which was kept closed, and the entry door down below. Soon she knew they would not be able to see, let alone breathe.

They were six steps down the staircase when Molly realized she hadn't picked up the Very gun. She had been concentrating on saving John, and it dawned on her there was still one more man on the island. They were far from out of danger. He would have heard the shooting and was probably on his way to the lighthouse while they were fumbling around in the acrid smoke. *Oh my God, will this nightmare ever end?* She wondered.

Molly decided she didn't have enough time to go back for it or worry about what might happen. She had far more pressing matters at hand.

They made it somehow to the next landing into the living quarters, where the body lay burning on the carpeted wooden floor. Molly turned and saw the corpse where it had fallen; it looked like a burning inferno. But strangely, she noticed the flames had not spread throughout the rest of the area as she thought it would.

Possibly that was because Bannister had landed on his back. Maybe, she thought, I can still save the building if I move quickly.

"John, hold the handrail and keep going, the smoke is thinner here, so get outside. I need to try to stop the fire." She twisted her body out from under his arm and placed his hand on the steel railing. "Go, I'm right behind you."

Molly took a deep breath and dashed through the smoke in the direction of the kitchenette where the brass fire extinguisher sat hanging from a bracket on the wall. Molly had full training in firefighting as part of her nursing in the first few weeks of joining the hospital. Every nurse had to be familiar with dealing with fire and evacuating patients. Feeling her way, she was almost out of breath when she found the sink. By touch alone, she found the tea towel hanging where it was supposed to be with her right hand while her left turned the tap on full. She doused the cloth in cold water and squeezed the worst of it out then held it over her mouth as she breathed.

Better, but not perfect. Molly tied it around her face and over her nose, then stepped her body to the right. The brass canister was cold to the touch as she jerked it from the hook. It was a lot heavier than she remembered, or perhaps it was just that she was more tired than she had been during her younger training days. Molly knew she could manage it, so long as the smoke didn't overcome her first.

Molly turned her back to the sink and tried to recall the layout of the room, so she didn't fall over anything getting back to the blaze. She couldn't see a thing; the smoke was too thick and getting thicker by the minute. Molly could feel where the blaze was by the radiant heat of the flames, and the smell. Molly headed in that direction, hoping the fire would light the way when she got closer.

The smell was putrid, and it was all Molly could do not to vomit again. Holding the extinguisher in both hands, so it hung between her legs, she waddled back the way she'd come, the brass container hitting her thighs with every pace she took.

Molly had smelled some bad things in her time; a gangrened wound was the worst she could recall; other than some patient bowel movements, she would rather not remember. But the odor from the burning body was unlike anything she had smelled before. The wet tea towel helped, but not as much as she'd hoped, and Molly tried to breathe only through her mouth rather than her nose.

Molly made it to the corpse without falling over any furniture, and to her dismay, saw the fire had spread in the short time she'd been in the kitchen. Like ripples on the beach, they spread outward from its near molten center, searching for more fuel. Except these ripples, she thought, were flames licking across the carpet, not the ocean surface.

Molly stood the extinguisher on the floor as close as she dared, because the heat was so intense. She released the safety clip, which was a pin on a string through the trigger assembly. It was a pump type, and Molly hastily started pumping to build up sufficient pressure. Once she felt the plunger stiffen signifying the liquid within had climbed to capacity, Molly grabbed the end of the hose, aimed it at the carpet, and pulled the trigger.

White, creamy consistency foam squirted out, and she moved the stream over the burning wooden floor, drenching the flames and dousing them by robbing them of oxygen. By moving the extinguisher around, Molly was able to halt the spread, though the smoke got progressively worse. Suddenly, Molly couldn't breathe as there seemed to be no oxygen available. She dropped the hose and dashed to the stairs to find fresh air.

Molly took six steps downward and dropped to sit and recover. The heat above was drawing air from the open outside door below. Molly was grateful for the chance to clear her lungs. The cool breeze blew on her face as she gulped it down as her vision swum, and she fought to stay awake.

She felt dizzy with vertigo and realized it wasn't only the smoke that had got to her, but the burning phosphorous fumes, which she recalled from her nurse training, could be dangerous. Slowly, the fresh air cleansed her lungs, and she felt ready to continue.

Molly turned around and crawled back, so her head just rose above floor level. She saw she had been successful in halting the spread of the fire, but the body still roared. What did she know about phosphorous? She searched her memory from her father's talks of his time in the war.

He had said it was used in all sorts of artillery shells and bombs because it created a chemical fire and smoke. He once related a story of a ship he saw struck by incendiary bombs dropped from a Luftwaffe Stuka. The freighter had burned to the waterline and sank with shocking loss of life. He'd said it was impossible to douse the fire all the time it had fuel to burn. With the temperature so high, everything became fuel. The extinguisher she'd left behind would probably have only one third left in its cylinder, she estimated. She knew all she could do was use that on the surrounding carpet and floorboards to try to contain the blaze from spreading further. She could do no more than that.

The decision made, Molly leaped to her feet after taking three huge breaths and ran back to the fire.

She pumped quickly and re-coated the smoldering floor around the burning body until the extinguisher spluttered and died. Then Molly turned tail and headed back to the stairs, gratefully gulping down the smoke-free air again. As she descended, she heard the unmistakable sound of a gunshot from inside the building below. That was followed by a double boom, fired very close together from a different sounding gun from outside. Barry Cook had arrived.

Chapter 15

Don't Mess with a McLaren (2)

"John," she screamed and ran down the staircase as quickly as she could, her breath ragged and wheezing. Hank Drage lay face down on the concrete floor near the open door. She crept down the last few steps and with her foot, kicked the door closed. The broken handle and latch fell off as it slammed against the jamb and clattered onto the ground. She knelt by John's side and turned him over. Bannister's pistol fell from his hand, and she gasped at the sight of the gaping open wound in his chest, which had pumped what blood he had left out over the floor. He was dead. Molly had seen enough death in her time to know it when she saw it; she didn't need to take his pulse to confirm it.

For a moment, she felt sadness like she had never experienced since the day her father told her of her mother's death. In a way, she had loved John, though she hadn't allowed herself to think like that about him; she had anyway. He had tried his best to stop the robber from entering the building and given his life to save hers. All she wanted to do was lay down and cry.

But that feeling of tired depression was soon overtaken by anger. White-hot, seething rage coursed through Molly's body. Her life had been turned upside down, and the lighthouse nearly destroyed. She had been shot at and had been forced to take a human life. Now another killer was outside who had murdered John, the man who had started it all. *The bastard, the absolute bloody bastard. I will be damned if I will lie down quietly and let this man shoot me like a dog.*

"Hey, girlie," Molly heard called from outside.

It sounded to her as if he was near the lean-to with the chickens. Molly picked up the gun and then stood and rested her back against the stone wall. She took long slow breaths and tried to slow her pounding heart. Her survival depended on staying calm; Molly knew that was her only chance. She was up against a man who was much more conversant with murder than she would ever be.

"I know you can hear me, girlie; it was you who shut the door after I shot your boyfriend. I've got some news I know you're dying to hear. Get it, dying to hear?" He laughed as if he'd just made the funniest joke in the world.

Well, Bucko, you won't find me so easy to kill, she thought as she brought the pistol up and examined it. She didn't know the first thing about guns, but she supposed it was just like the Very gun; pull the hammer back, aim and pull the trigger. "I'm listening," she shouted. "Go ahead and enthrall me." Molly was surprised how calm she was, while inside, she was a seething melting pot of undiluted rage and fear. Molly thought she sounded normal at worst, and extremely brave at best.

"I loaded the gun, girlie. Nick didn't carry any spare shells because I forgot to give him some when he took it from me. I've counted five shots fired from it, so you only have one left. But the good news is I've got lots in my pocket if you can take them from me. I've got a shotgun too, though, which is going to make a huge mess of you, quite soon, just like it did your boyfriend."

One bullet? Bloody hell, she thought, despite her bravado. "How's your chest now, dickhead?" she shouted back, determined to stay resolute. "Do you feel all right after your long walk up the hill to get here? You still sound wheezy. I've got some news for you too; do you want to hear it?"

"Go on; I'm listening."

Ahaa, you don't sound so sure now, do you? Didn't expect me to stand up to you, did you? "Well," she began, "I could say I only need one bullet for the likes of you, but as it happens, I have lots more. What can you smell, dickhead, does it smell like burning bank robber to you?"

"You better stop calling me that, girlie, I'm warning you."

She laughed, loud enough so he could hear; she wanted him to know she wasn't frightened, not anymore. "Oh, I'm so scared, dickhead. I'm only going to give you one warning, just like I gave your mate, I hope you listen better than he did. Your warning is this: Don't mess with a McLaren. I shot your friend dead with a phosphorous shell from a Very gun, which is standard equipment on a lighthouse. I've got lots of spare cartridges for it too, just for you, dickhead. Can you smell what that one shell did to him? Oh, I think he's going to burn for days yet. You see, that's the thing about phosphorous, you can't put it out, no matter how much water you tip on it until it runs out of fuel. For fuel, it's using his body. Now, if you're quick, you can decide not to mess with me and scurry on back to the boat and try to get it out of the reef system around Forbes. That will be no mean feat by yourself, but do you know what, dickhead?"

"What?"

"You'll have much better odds out there on the reef than you will if you stay here and face me. If you don't leave right now, you never will trust me on that. Soon, I will start firing shells in your general direction, and dickhead? I only have to get close, within say six feet, and you will get showered with burning chemical phosphorous that you can't extinguish. Then you can join your mate, in hell. Your call, but make it soon or I start shooting at the lean-to. The only reason I haven't already is I'd like to save the chickens."

That's it; I'm done in. If he calls my bluff, I've got one bullet, and I'd have to make it count. She pulled the hammer of the gun back until it clicked into place and stepped across the doorway to stand on the opening side. Slowly, she pulled the door open just a crack so she could look through the gap, but it wasn't wide enough. She could only see across the path and the rocks which disappeared into the distance. The lean-to was to the right, and to see that, she would need to open the door wider and just about step through. That must be what John did, and that's what got him shot dead when he came face to face with Cook.

"You talk a good talk, girlie, but I don't believe you. There's no point my leaving you alive to describe me to the cops; either way, I'm done for. So, you shoot, girlie, go on I dare you, remember your chickens though, they will die a horrible death too."

Molly couldn't bring herself to answer; she had

gambled and lost. She couldn't get back to the flare gun, and even if she could, she doubted she would be able to find it in the thick, dense smoke that would be up there. Sooner or later, Cook would make a move, and she had to face him with one bullet in the gun in her hand.

"I take my hat off to you, girlie; you got more spunk than I gave you credit for, but what we got here is what we call a Mexican Stand-off. Ain't it fun? You know, as soon as you open that door, you're dead, most likely before you can shoot at me with whatever contraption you used on Nick. So, I tell you what; let's make it interesting. I'm going to count to ten, and then I'm coming in there; it's party time. Let's you and me have some fun. One."

Molly's fear ate away at her; *he was coming in?* She hadn't expected that. She looked around frantically, knowing what she would find, nowhere to hide. Her heart pounded, her head ached, but she had to think.

"Two."

There, under the stairs, one of her father's cray pots with a coil of orange rope sitting on top. He must have brought it in before the storm that saw him break his leg. Maybe she could hide behind it and gain enough time to shoot Cook when he walked through the door. But it seemed impossibly small and would not protect her at all against a shotgun.

"Three. I don't hear that smart mouth of yours now, girlie."

What if I hide there and he sees me, and then I miss him with my one and only shot, what then? Molly wondered, barely holding on to her sanity. *Then, Molly, my girl, you die. We don't want that do we? So, think,* echoed the soothing voice of her father.

Yeah, Dad, I get it, don't state the obvious, help me. How can I improve the odds, where can I hide?

"Four."

You know where to hide, Molly; the cave.

How can I get to the bloody cave, Dad, without running right into the arms of a madman with a shotgun?

Use the rope and climb down from the watch room balcony while he is coming up the stairs. He will be going slowly because of the smoke. He knows you are armed so he won't rush. You have enough time if you move now.

"Five. You know girlie, I owe you payback for Nick. I might play with you for a while before I kill you, how does that sound?"

Molly held on to the hammer of the gun, pulled the trigger, and gently let it come to rest against the only bullet in the chamber. She didn't want the gun going off accidentally and shooting herself in the leg, so she crammed it into her trouser front pocket. Then she moved to the cray pot and snatched up the rope, turned, and started to run back up the stairs. But a loose coil caught on the end of the handrail and brought her up short. Her body suddenly yanked backward, and she nearly fell over.

"Six."

Remember what I said before, Molly; more haste, less speed.

Yeah, right, Dad, jeez, you're a nag. She unhooked the rope and took the steel stairs two at a time and headed back up the steel steps into the dark smoke-filled upper area.

"Seven."

The smoke was worse than before when she reached the landing, and still, flames belched from the body. Molly made the mistake of taking a look as she gulped down another breath before plunging into the dense, acrid mire and wished she hadn't. The middle of Bannister's body was gone. All that remained was the chest upward, and hips and legs down. She choked the bile that threatened to vomit from her stomach and plunged into the abyss of darkness, feeling her way by the handrail.

Molly knew she couldn't inhale; the fire had stolen most if not all the oxygen, and she was almost ready to pass out when she reached the open door of the watch room, just as she heard the front door below being kicked open and the roar of two gunshots inside the entrance.

Fear and adrenaline forced her on; at least she could see from the daylight flooding in through the windows. Frantically she crossed the room, skirting the tub of mercury which contained the light, and opened the balcony door. A gale-force burst of welcome, clean, sweet tasting air rushed in.

Oh, sweet Jesus, she repeatedly thought as she poked her head through the gap and gulped in the life-giving air into her tired and over-used lungs.

"What's this, girlie, a nice game of hide and go seek?" her hunter's voice echoed up from the depths below. "We've got plenty of time, but I'm coming for you."

Oh God, oh Jesus, oh God, oh Jesus, her panicking brain pleaded. The calming voice of her father filtered through. *Don't lose your marbles, Molly; you've got this covered. You know the layout inside the lighthouse, he doesn't. He's got the smoke to contend with, and he knows you've got a gun. Calm down, don't make a noise when you close the door, and it will take him ages to get here and see that you've gone.*

Tears sprung from her eyes and ran down her soot-covered cheeks. *I love you so much, Dad, I don't think I ever told you enough, but I do. I'd be lost without you. Even when you're not here, you're still with me.* She stepped through the door, into the sunshine, not caring, or even noticing it was cold after the blazing heat from the fire inside. As calmly as quietly as she could, she closed the door behind her.

Molly felt tired; all she wanted more than anything was to lie down for a while and close her eyes. *"If you do that, you'll never be able to open them again, Molly."*

Yeah, Dad, I get it, there's no rest for the wicked.

Molly took one end of the rope and tied a makeshift knot around the upright stanchion of the railing that ran around the balcony. She almost grinned when she realized she had used the same knot as she would on a stitch across a wound. Molly hoped it would hold her weight when she climbed down. Once tied, Molly pulled and jerked on the rope, satisfied it would hold, and then threw the coil over the side.

She leaned over and looked down, and her fear returned all over again. She'd never been a lover of heights, and the ground looked impossibly far away. *Climb down or get shot—it's an easy choice, really,* she told herself.

Before she could lose her resolve, holding onto the top rail with a white-knuckled grip, she raised her left leg and swung it over, and then followed by her right. Suddenly, she was standing outside the railing. *Oh my God, now what do I do?*

Her father's voice came to her again in his ever-calming way. *"If you were a Navy girl, you'd have done this exercise many times, Molly. Hold the rope and feed it through your hands one over the other. Lean back, out from the wall, and step down in time with your hands, like you're walking down a ladder. It's easy, I promise. Breathe slowly, and you got this kid, you can do it. Now go."*

She did as he'd instructed her, slowly, trying not to panic. The outside stone surface of the wall was rough, which helped. She also realized the lighthouse was narrower at the top than the base, so it wasn't quite a vertical drop, which helped. Slowly she descended, trying her best not to worry about where Cook was in his search for her.

Halfway down, Molly realized her mistake. She had not looked where to drop the rope, and she was about to draw level with the first-floor window. If the man inside saw her, or her shadow changed the light coming through it, which it would as she passed over it, the game would be up. Once again her father's voice filtered through her panic filled mind. *"Too late now, Molly, no use crying over spilled milk, go as quickly as you can, and when you hit the ground, run like the hounds of hell are chasing you."*

Oh, God, how could I have been so stupid? She worried, as fresh tears of fear, frustration, and anger flooded her eyes. Her father's voice in her head made sense, though; she couldn't do anything about it now. She had to trust her good luck would hold.

Her hands were starting to hurt and tire. She felt moisture, but whether it was blood or sweat, she had no idea and was too scared to find out. It hurt enough to be blood, but she daren't look for fear that if she was bleeding, it might cause her to lose her nerve.

As quickly as possible, she straddled the small window and crab-walked down over it. Suddenly, she lost grip a few minutes later and slid down. Molly tried to hold on, but it was useless. Before she could stop herself, she knew she was falling. Molly gave out a muted yelp and pushing out with her feet, jumped from the wall, hoping she would land on her feet.

She hit the ground and felt her right ankle wobble and twist over. She heard a cracking sound like a rifle shot and feared the worst. She instinctively rolled to her left-hand side to minimize any damage to her foot, hoping it wasn't broken.

Without stopping to see and hoping it was only sprained, she leaped to her feet. Pain lanced up from her wounded ankle, but Molly started running, half expecting a gunshot from the balcony to hit her at any moment. She felt shooting pains radiating up from her injured foot but knew she couldn't stop. She was down on the ground, that was all that mattered, and if Cook hadn't heard her fall, or seen her descend through the window, she thought she could make it to the cave.

"Now go Molly, don't stop, don't look back, just get to the cave," her father urged.

Please, Lord, let my luck hold, let me make it to safety, I can rest then.

She didn't look back; she needed all her concentration as she ran from rock to rock. Her ankle hurt like blazes, and she was limping horribly, but she had to concentrate on not falling, or breaking her leg in a crevice.

The further she traveled, the slower her pace, due to the pain growing in intensity. She realized by trying to sprint, her weight was coming down too hard on her injured ankle. Molly tried taking off from it and landing on her good foot, but she found using it as her fulcrum hurt just as badly. She had no alternative; she had to walk, not run, and risk Cook might see her.

She reached for her pocket that held the gun only to find it empty; she must have dropped it somewhere, probably when she fell off the side of the building. Molly groaned and looked skyward, *Really, Lord, you call this helping me? First, my ankle, now the gun, do you want me to get killed? How about if you give him some bad luck for a change?*

Molly risked a glance over her shoulder and couldn't see him, but that wasn't much comfort. She had covered only around two hundred yards and had a long way to go. If he had made it to the watch room, he would see her quickly enough then go back down the stairs to hunt her, knowing the direction she had gone in.

Her spirits sank lower and matched her exhaustion; she was almost ready to give up. Without the gun, Molly had no chance if he followed her to her secret cave, but she could do no more than hope. She hobbled on, wiping her tears, and smearing the soot on her face; she had never felt so alone or scared in her life.

Chapter 16

The Haunted Cave

Molly felt a little better after she crossed the ridge on the rocks that led down to the shoreline. She knew she couldn't be seen from the land once she dipped below that. That was cold comfort if Cook was in the watch room or on the balcony, using the Weiss glasses to track her. For all she knew, he could be watching where she was going. She was so tired she no longer cared. Her only focus was on getting to the cave and lying down to get the weight off her foot.

Her mouth and throat were so dry. Molly passed some time by distracting herself by trying to work out how long it had been since she last had a drink. Several hours, she knew which was unusual for her, being a huge fan of her cups of tea. What she wouldn't give for a cup right then, anything to wash the taste of smoke from her mouth and lungs. But that would have to wait. *First, you survive, and then you drink,* she told herself, mimicking her father. That would be her reward for living through the nightmare.

At least she still had the tea towel, now strung around her neck, which she could rinse in cold seawater and wrap it around her swollen ankle, which might ease some of the pain.

Pain. Searing white-hot pain, the likes of which she

had never experienced in her life, throbbed and radiated up from her foot in time with her ragged heartbeats. Molly thought of her father's medical bag back at the Light. It contained all sorts of helpful things, such as compression bandages and painkilling drugs. *Yes, Molly, and there's also cool water, endless cups of tea, a hot shower, and a comfortable bed, so why not go back there instead of the cave?*

She shook herself; she was being silly and remembered again her mantra, *first you survive, and then you drink. Of course,* she told herself, as she gingerly crossed a large gap to the next house-sized boulder, the operative word in all this was *if* she survived. It seemed to her that her only chance was when Cook realized she had shinnied down the rope, he'd think she was heading for the boat and go that way to get to her before she put to sea. So, she mused, knowing she was trying to distract herself from the agony, if he did that, what would Cook do when he got there and found she hadn't? Would he run, or would he search the island all over again, determined to kill her? She had to hope he would run.

She crushed the next thought as soon as it surfaced. *What if Cook watched me from the balcony heading toward the cave, and not the boat?* Molly didn't have to think too hard about what the outcome of that would be. *There would be another dead body left there to haunt, but this one would be murdered, not shipwrecked.*

Finally, Molly reached the water's edge, where small waves gently lapping on the rocks. She untied the towel from her neck and squatted, wincing with pain. Molly dipped it in the cold water of the Southern Ocean and loved the feel of it. With the cloth still dripping from her hand, she turned and shuffled to the small opening, bent almost double, and shuffled inside to what she hoped would be her haven of safety.

With a loud gasp and groan of agony, she sat on her favorite rock and stretched her legs out. Molly peeled back her trouser leg and was dismayed at what she saw. Her ankle had swollen to an impossible size, and it took all her effort to use her uninjured foot to kick off the shoe, which felt as if it had been welded in place. Once off, her ankle throbbed in gratitude. *If that's not broken, it's an A grade, first magnitude, sprain Molly, my girl,* she told herself. She didn't believe it was broken, surely she could not have walked on it if it was? *What is it with us McLarens and damaging our legs or feet on this God-forsaken island?*

She used the wet towel to wash her face, enjoying the cold on her skin, and being able to remove the caked-on grime off from fighting the fire. That thought made her stop. Molly hoped upon hope she had been able to save the lighthouse. *Oh my God, if I get out of this, will I be in trouble with Mr. Harpington, or even worse, the police for firing a flare gun inside the lighthouse? First, you survive, then you drink tea—and then you can worry about the aftermath.*

That was all well and good, but she realized she was in trouble anyway. She had harbored a man on the run from the police. He had participated in a serious robbery where a security guard had been shot dead. There had to be repercussions, and Molly doubted they would be good ones.

Yeah, but I didn't know about that until today, and then I sent off a damn Mayday call shortly after finding it out. But then she saw the error in her logic. That's semantics, and you know it. You should have reported him when the raft washed up, you knew that, but you chose to disregard it, and look at what's happened.

She sighed and bent forward at the waist and carefully wrapped the cold, wet towel around her aching and throbbing ankle. Best you don't walk on that for a while, and that thought made her grin. Like what else was she going to do? Molly knew she couldn't stay there forever.

The Mayday, you dummy, help will come sooner or later. She hoped it was sooner. She leaned back against the cold stone wall of her prison, and before she knew it, she was asleep.

****

Molly woke suddenly. She felt cold, and her mouth was drier than she could ever have imagined possible. Molly tried to make saliva and swallow, but nothing would come for a long time. Her face burned as if had been sunburned, and she looked at her arms, which were a bright red color.

The sun was closer to the horizon, so she knew she had been out for more than a few minutes, but why had she woken up? Then Molly heard a noise. It sounded like a boot scraping on a rock, and her skin crawled as she realized she was no longer alone. Then came another scraping sound; Cook was coming closer.

Molly wanted to scream in fear and frustration. God damn it; it wasn't fair. She had survived all that she had only to be murdered in a cave? No way, no way would she go down without a fight. She looked around frantically and spotted a decent size rock. She stood and nearly fell over with shooting pain from her ankle. Undeterred, she bit her lip and hobbled over so she could pick it up in both hands.

As quietly as she could, Molly half shuffled, half hopped over to the side of the opening. She raised the rock above her head, her arms trembling with the weight, and pressed her back against the cold wall of the cave. The moment Cook stuck his head through the opening, Molly intended to bring the rock down on it. One of them would die; she was determined of that.

She slowed her breathing, trying to stay silent so as not to give her position away, there was still a chance Cook would look in, not see her and continue on his search, but she had to be ready, just in case.

Then, she heard another noise from outside, much closer now, and then she saw a shadow outside as Cook bent to look inside.

"Molly, are you in there? It's Derek; you're safe now."

Luckily, she dropped the rock, she held above her head, before she fainted.

Epilogue

Thanks to Molly's efforts when she used the extinguisher to halt the spread of flames across the floor to fight the fire, Forbes Light did not burn to the ground. Mikey and Derek had gone to the lighthouse first to search for Molly and between them doused the last of the flames from the remains of the smoldering body and surrounding floor. There was very little left of Nick Bannister by then.

Derek recognized the body of Hank Drage and realized from Molly's mayday, there was still one bank robber at large. When they could not find Molly, they went to the cave, hoping to find her there.

Mikey volunteered to stay the night to tend the light and had received instructions from a frantic Mr. Harpington by radio. That permitted Derek to leave and take Molly to the hospital and they carried her back to the boat using the stretcher they had used for her father. As a safeguard, Derek disabled the escape boat and *Tandanna* because they could not find Barry Cook and wanted to stop him from leaving the island.

They propped the balcony and front doors open at the lighthouse to help the smoke clear, but it was still far too acrid for Mikey to sleep inside. Instead, he spent the night under the lean-to, alongside the chickens, in a sleeping bag they kept on the boat. Mikey held the Lee

Enfield to his chest all night, just in case, and later told Derek that he hadn't slept a wink, hoping Cook would appear. Had he done so; Mikey would not have hesitated to open fire. He was in a seething rage for putting Molly through the hell he had. As soon as she recovered, Mikey had made up his mind to ask if she would consider a date, as Derek had urged him to do since he first saw the effect she had on him at their first meeting.

Derek wasn't happy leaving Mikey behind, but knew he had to get Molly away, even he could see her ankle was a mess and he worried any undue delay could be catastrophic. The light had to stay operational and Cook had vanished. He couldn't see any other alternative but to leave him behind.

Derek pushed the boat to its limits to get to Augusta while Molly drifted in and out of consciousness. She had earlier guided him how to give her a morphine injection which made the pain bearable for the sea journey.

Though not broken, doctors couldn't believe she had been able to walk on it at all, and that doing so had made a severe sprain, so much worse with the extensive soft tissue damage she had suffered.

Before she let them do any work on her foot, which resembled a football in size when they wheeled her into the Busselton Hospital, she told them they had to take her to her father, and she would not take no for an answer.

She screamed at first sight of him, then hugged him desperately. Malcolm reached for her while still in traction in his bed, and she couldn't rise from her wheelchair, but they managed. Molly cried unstoppable tears while he stroked her back and listened to her incredible tale.

Malcolm couldn't understand why she continually thanked him for being there in her head, helping and guiding her, in her darkest hours on the island, as he always had throughout her life. Molly was distraught, and he tried to explain he hadn't been with her, anything she had done she managed alone. Her bravery was her doing, not his, but she would have none of it. So far as she was concerned, he had helped her every step of the way.

Eventually, Molly permitted the nurse to take her away, but she wanted one more thing before she let them x-ray her foot. That was a cup of tea. She told the matron; she had survived, and she damn well deserved her cup of tea.

****

The *Morning Dawn* arrived back at Forbes just as the sun rose the next morning. On board was an experienced keeper named Benjamin Florence who had arrived from Esperance at short notice at the request of the Department of Marine and Harbors. He was accompanied by Mr. Harpington and Detective Inspector Reginald London, who was to head the investigation into what had happened on the island.

There were also twenty constables on board, charged with completing a thorough, inch-by-inch, search of the island for Barry Cook. Each police officer was armed and had orders to shoot him on sight if he did not immediately surrender, but by nightfall, they were forced to admit he was not on Forbes.

****

The weather was beautiful with clear skies and

calm seas when Molly returned for the first time to Forbes Rock on Derek's boat to visit her father seven weeks after she had left on a stretcher. He had resumed his duties eight days before. Molly's foot had recovered, though she still walked with a slight limp and she smiled as she thought they could compare limps as he too favored his right leg.

The lighthouse had been redecorated and refurbished after the smoke and fire damage. It also received an overdue upgrade with the installation of a generator, which provided electric lights and a radio that didn't require treadle power.

It was a special visit for Molly and a surprise for her father who didn't know she was coming. She wanted to show him in person the letter she had received the day before which offered her a scholarship position at the Royal Perth Hospital Medical School to begin her training as a doctor. She wanted to see the look on his face when she showed him because she lived to see him smile and missed him more than ever after her experience with the three bank robbers.

When Malcolm learned the full details of what Molly had endured because she had agreed to mind the light to protect his job, he very nearly gave up the job. He told her repeatedly if he could have gone back in time, he'd have done anything to avoid her living through the hell she had on his behalf. But Molly shrugged it off; she had survived, it was enough, and she urged him to stay and finish his book.

Two weeks before her trip back to Forbes, Molly was summoned to police headquarters by Inspector London. Mrs. Frost granted permission for her to leave the hospital halfway through her shift and Molly feared the worst. She thought it meant that with the completion of the investigation, she would be arrested for harboring a fugitive.

On arrival, she was led into a large room filled with people. A very confused and subdued Molly was directed to a small stage where she was presented with a Commonwealth Medal for bravery by the Governor. To her delight her father was there on crutches and she saw he was clapping more loudly than anyone else, as tears poured from his eyes with pride. Mr. Harpington stood beside him also clapping; he had arranged transport, as a surprise for her, as it was Malcolm's first day out of the Busselton Hospital.

The manager from the William Street Commonwealth Bank was there, and he presented her with a passbook for an account in her name which contained twenty thousand dollars. That was the reward for the capture of the robbers and recovery of the stolen money which the police discovered in a haversack on *Tandanna*.

The celebration went into the night with her father and nursing friends. Even Mrs. Frost attended to give her congratulations and to Molly's delight, Derek and Mikey arrived at seven after they finished the day's fishing and made the long drive to Perth.

****

Mikey stood up on the bow, as Derek slowed the boat, for the first turn into the passage through the reef called purgatory. Molly was alone in the stern, enjoying the cooling breeze on her face; winter had made way for spring in all its glory. The island looked as wonderful as any she had ever seen, and she realized she had missed the rugged beauty of Forbes Reef.

Molly smiled at the sight of the freshly painted lighthouse and wondered if they had repaired the bullet hole made during the wild chase. She felt a warm glow course through her body as she leaned against the port side gunwale and realized she felt as if she were coming home.

Molly had arrived by bus in Busselton the previous evening and enjoyed a lovely dinner at the Lobster Tail Restaurant with Mikey that night. It was their third date. She even let him kiss her when he walked her back to her motel room after the meal, knowing her father approved of him as a suitor. She'd changed her mind quite a bit about Mikey since her ordeal; he had definite possibilities she realized, and he was a fantastic kisser.

Barry Cook had never been apprehended. He wasn't on the island when they searched, and the police assumed when Cook saw the *Morning Dawn* approach he stowed away on it when the men left to investigate the smoke billowing out of the lighthouse. The other possibility, they thought, was that he tried to swim to safety, and had drowned, or perhaps been killed by a shark. Sometimes, Molly almost believed that was the case; at least, she fervently hoped it was.

The boat slowed further, as it took a starboard turn. Molly gazed forward, intent on seeing the island she had come to love as if it was for the first time. She made a mental note to retrieve the copy of the book *Moby Dick*, which she had begun but never finished. That was assuming it hadn't gone up in flames. Molly still needed to find out if Captain Ahab got his whale, and what became of Ishmael.

Behind her, silently, the lid of the giant fiberglass

crayfish tank lifted and swung all the way open. A man covered from head to foot in black soot stepped out. He held a shotgun and trained it on Molly's back. His lips parted in a snarl, and he spoke in a smoke damaged voice, making her jump in shock. "Hey girlie, did you think I'd forget all about you?"

Molly turned to see Barry Cook.

He pulled the trigger, and just as the shot sounded, Molly woke up from the perpetual recurring nightmare she had most nights of the week. She was in her own bed in the nurse's quarters at the hospital.

She got up to get a drink of water, or maybe she thought, a cup of tea. There would be no more sleep for her that night, and she did love her tea.

Authors Note

As always, dear reader, in writing about an area of the state in which I love, and live, I have taken certain liberties. While the 'line' of turbulence where two oceans meet at Augusta is a fact, and there is a wonderful very old lighthouse there, Forbes Reef does not exist. If it did, I'd like to visit it, but sadly I can only do that in my imagination. I hope I did Forbes justice for you.

In deciding when to set Molly's tale, I chose an era after the war, and before modernization occurred in lighthouses around our massive country, and so 1952 felt right to me. I think of it as a romantic era and admire what a lonely life lighthouse keepers led. I have the utmost respect for them and the dedication they showed to keeping boats from harm in dangerous waters. These days of course we have satellite navigation, radar, and other electronic aids, but in 1952 seamen had to rely on lighthouses far more than today.

It was an interesting era for me to write about romance too, and I so hope I got Molly's thoughts and feelings true to the less promiscuous times than we have today.

I'm quite sure if any lighthouse keepers read this who worked in the fifties, they could criticize some technicalities I may not have got right. I did as much research as possible and I promise you this story is as authentic as I could make it with the information I could find.

The lighthouse at Augusta is open to tourists and they have guided tours. It is the tallest on mainland Australia and was built in 1895. I thoroughly recommend visiting it if you're 'down' this way.

A word from the author…

I was born in the UK, what seems like an epoch ago, and moved to Australia at age 16. I was a long-haired rock guitarist and poet/songwriter, before real life got in the way, and I gave it all up for love.

I've always felt I had tales to tell and won short story competitions and published poetry in my wilder, younger days. More recently I've written and published ten novels. While they have all been police procedural thrillers, mainly focusing on serial killers, they all have a love theme running through them.

I believe love and family are everything. Anything else you gain in life is a bonus.

I live in Perth, in Western Australia, and am fiercely patriotic and parochial. My wife is amazing in that she not only puts up with living with a writer, but encourages it. I've been blessed with five children, and I adore them all.

http://stephen-b-king.com

Thank you for purchasing
this publication of The Wild Rose Press, Inc.

For questions or more information
contact us at
info@thewildrosepress.com.

The Wild Rose Press, Inc.
www.thewildrosepress.com